REMEMBRANCE DAY

a novel by:
Brad Thomas Batten

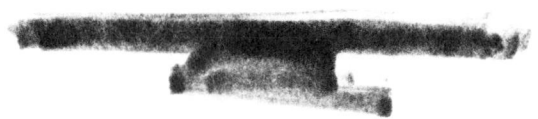

FriesenPress

Suite 300 – 852 Fort Street
Victoria, BC, Canada V8W 1H8
www.friesenpress.com

Copyright © 2014 by Brad Thomas Batten
First Edition — 2014

All rights reserved.
No part of this publication may be reproduced in any form, or by any means, electronic or mechanical, including photocopying, recording, or any information browsing, storage, or retrieval system, without permission in writing from the publisher.

ISBN
978-1-4602-4587-3 (Hardcover)
978-1-4602-4588-0 (Paperback)
978-1-4602-4589-7 (eBook)

1. Fiction, Literary

Distributed to the trade by The Ingram Book Company

For the boys of childhood,
friends of inspiration to this day:
Pete, Chris, Jock, Graeme.

The wind, the wind is
blowing,
through the graves the wind
is blowing,
freedom soon will come...

Men will come from the shadows...

Leonard Cohen

SAVAGE, Jonathan Francis. Quietly at home, on August 26th, 1975, in his 77th year. Pre-deceased by Giselle (nee Gauthier). Father and father-in-law of Zachary and Elizabeth (nee Littlewood). Grandfather of Zachary Jr. and Jonathan Francis. A soldier of the Great War. Private family service.

I REMEMBER THE MORNING WHEN I first approached Vimy Ridge, walking barefoot across the landscape of my grandfather's war. There was a mist winding above the tree line, and a lone raven, its wings singeing sky. The wind crackled out of the southwest and the fields were slick as I stepped along, the lower pale mists soaking against my skin. I found a trench in a clearing and wriggled down inside, brushing my hand along the pasted rock walls, the uneven girders, the withered black moss, the water-stained footholds that hadn't been used in years. The hollowness inside was cold and unexpired, the sun having never warmed the ground where I stood.

Only a curve of moon showed through the mist that morning in August of '95. A soldier's old moon, like the eye of my grandfather's ghost. I imagined the life there through his moon's eye, picking out artifacts of loss—pocket watches, signet rings, bent crucifixes—wedged into the chalk earth. A piece of embroidered sleeve still supple with the lavender scent of a loved one's wrist. The hurried testimonials that had been penned on unbleached parchment and placed in military envelopes (unsealed, not yet censored), then pinned into sandbags black as burnt flesh, on a night prior to battle. All this beneath a moon conceived for last letters home.

Vimy Ridge is an earth careful to wake, its history a long vein. The many fronts of war that have moved in and back, staining soil, staining memory. During the Great War, the front cut the ridge in two, leaving a lateral scar. German troops were on one flattened edge, the French and British and Canadian corps on another. Men were separated by barbed wire and blood-soaked craters, liquid mud, while hurling grenades and insults across spare spaces ten, twenty meters apart. World War II brought the Nazis and their intimate means of public executions, lining up resistance fighters in nearby fields and introducing those captured to a single, bright bullet to the head or throat. If only for the point, good old war's sake.

I roamed the ridge for three days and nights, every road an exhausted empire. I listened for the dead, those young men who had been cut down too early and removed from a life of stars and rivers. I sensed their spirits breaking the bitter seam between the graves and my feet. I passed beneath the quiet shadow of the great, sorrowing Vimy monument, beneath its twin pylons and the closed wing of a carved mother figure. I read the names of the vanquished that were etched into her limestone walls, I ran a finger over curved letters, feeling nothing but stone. My grandfather's name was not there, but it should have been, I thought, after all the blood he had left, the arrested grief.

I roamed, having left Toronto a week or so earlier with an old map of the Vimy sector and a ghost or two up my sleeve. A third I did not know. I roamed, having left my brother, Zee, in Paris two days earlier. We had argued, we had spoken final truths. I roamed like the rich young man in the Bible, a prisoner of possessions. My feelings were like fireflies whose glimmer had been dimmed by great winds. Each evening I found somewhere quiet on the ridge and sat and pondered, with only an orange slice upon my tongue for relief. At times, I took out my notebook and pen and I wrote a few things down about the weathers, the mists, our family. About an earth that had been stripped, and about men.

Because it was there, in April of 1917, an Easter Monday, that the four divisions of the Canadian corps readied themselves along the ridge for the big push that would alter the path of the Great War. Men (hell, they were just boys) crammed themselves into trenches and subway tunnels thin as vines carved beneath the earth. They huddled in that damp underworld, sweating and shivering, smoking and praying, drinking their rum in place of the wine meant for Christ. Then, at 5:30 a.m., the unparalleled barrage commenced. The whole of the ridge became engulfed in machine gun fire and the thunderous drone of constant bombing. Such urgency of sound that soldiers senses were shattered. A quarter of a million shells were launched, wiping out the earth and ridge. Forests forced into lean extinction. Drums of oil were launched at German strongholds, burning lives on impact. Underground mines suddenly exploded, volcanic in intent. Fire twisted from the earth that was more luminous than the sun, which refused to show its face. Waves of soldiers like lava reversed itself, spilling upwards against an alien current of war that had been holding them back for months, for years. The French failed to take the ridge; the British also failed. Victory there was a stranger, pushed back by the permanence of bad weather, by superior enemy weaponry, and by the long, steady slope of the ridge. Now, it was young Canada's turn. Send in those boys not yet drained by battle or lamentation, not yet hardened to death as the ultimate, the final, glaring end. There was still something privileged there, heroic about that mud and time.

My grandfather, my namesake (Jonathan Francis Savage), was one such young man. A nineteen year old with a belief in adventure, his time of heroics. I have an old photograph of him. It was taken on the gray morning of the battle. He's covered in mud. His uniform and face are indivisible from the torn earth. There is no trace of smile or guile in his expression. He looks bent, as if clothed in an ill fitted sorrow that he's been forced to adorn well before the physical years of his body were able to apprehend his place in the world. As if there, turning in the mud and dark cold of war, is the thought that his heroics are suddenly expendable, unutterable, but confined to the faded epicenter of a photograph. As if he's had the adventure all inside out, as if the photograph somehow betrays his intentions and only its silence conveys a truth, saying, 'You will fade, you will diminish, you will no longer be.'

He will survive the ridge and photograph, but not without a measure of chill and permanent wounding. He will never speak openly about the war, its assault within himself. The climate of shelling and nerve gases and barbed wire. He will die, at the age of seventy-seven, in the attic of our Moore Park home, on the edge of a Toronto ravine. The man missing an ear, half a face. A disavowed hermit spending his last years in that attic room, the curtains pulled tight. When we find him in the room amongst the twisting sheets and darkness (actually I find him, stumble upon him, shiver in that terrible presence), my own father will take my small hand and place it on my grandfather's shrunken chest. The thin, pale skin will still be warm. I will try to pull away but my father will press down on the back of my hand and keep my palm in place until the eerie warmth on my grandfather's chest disappears. There will be the new terror of not knowing what to feel, and the hours, like forever, entering me. I will sense the blood my grandfather has fought and exchanged his future for quicken against my palm, carving life lines. My mouth will become dry, beyond thirst. I am eight years old and feel a first terrifying truth still my heart: How life, like love, holds death close to the chest.

I tell you this, my son (sitting on this dock, legs dangling in the water, holding you in my arms on a Sunday morning), because so much of our story has been withheld, not told. As if the history of us (my father, my mother, my brother, my grandfather's pale ghost) had been shamed into silence long before we ever dared enter the verbal world. As if we were nothing more than star dust, collapsing novas. I tell you this because you are the new born at the conclusion of this century and it is time I raise the voice that had been put under and stifled right back at this one hundred years inception. In the muds and whirling dark of my grandfather's war. I tell you this because everything is alive in me, everything is present. Even the past is rich, black loam. No matter the soreness of the memory or the snake of fear that brushes alongside our travels.

This much I must bequeath, a kiss for your soul.

1

THERE ARE TIMES WHEN HISTORY works in collusion with the everyday in life and remaps the world we think we know. Silences undo and the mystery within things is aroused. I first sensed this that summer in a bright slick of blood along my cheekbone, a shaving cut I couldn't stop from bleeding. I had been drinking the night before, alone in the back yard. In the shaving mirror, I saw my father's face, tightening, and behind his tired disorder there was my grandfather's spent expression. Both men were then down on all fours, ripping at the earth with their fists like claws. I closed my eyes and was there, crawling and digging, swearing at a moon that hung like an iron ball over their warring worlds. I opened my eyes, my hands shaking, my face sweating, the blood on my cheek gone black. I pressed a wet wash cloth against the cut and stepped into the living room, opened the door onto the back yard and lay on the floor. First light swerved into the basement, splashing pink and yellow over the green canoe that was up on a couple of saw horses against the west wall. Naked, the day's heat pressed across my brow, the humidity already heavy in the room, as if tropical, pushing in from disparate directions. It was too hot to weep. The hour was touched by silence and my body felt like a rock I wanted to skip toward any basin of water that might take me in. There was a permanent snarl of smog over the city and I was tired of the violence it takes to become a man.

I was a brittle drunk. Groggy after a few sips of wine or beer. I was the guy at the party who would fall asleep in various acrobatic positions; slung across the back of a sofa, legs high wiring a wall, or lying flat out beneath a glass coffee table, as if in an aquarium, sleeping with the fish. Friends could shuffle me from room to room, prop me in closets, on beds, arms crossed, like a corpse. Or dress me up like a scarecrow and plant me on a front lawn. There were times when I'd mumble when drunk, and pass out. I'd recite strange bits of verse, parables, sometimes speaking without moving my lips. I was forever slipping into ancestral dramas, old world plots. Then there were the three or four nights a year when I'd rise, entranced, leave the party and make a trek through the neighbourhood, a drunken two step, always finding my way to my place of work, Mt. Pleasant Cemetery. Because on some level of soul, that's what my life had become, a freaky transference with the dead. For too long, I had pushed back the myths of my heart and those in my family (the dead and the alive), who rocked my soul with their blackened comedy. Wherever I pushed, my memory screamed. Each rush of alcohol obscuring and diminishing me, washing away and inviting more and more of me to slide with it. Until that summer, in '95. I was twenty-eight and a new sense of wind and water insisted I listen.

It was the morning of the summer solstice and I was at work, digging a grave. A small child's grave. I was a few meters into the shocked earth, sweat dripping from my brow and upper lip, hair drenched. The back hoe had broken down and I was left with my hands and a spade. I had been working at the cemetery (in-between carpentry and landscaping jobs) on and off over the years, ever since my high school career ended and I was thrust like chaff into the work force and my time with the dead. They never asked much of me and I never asked much of them. I was used to the work, digging graves, filling them in, cutting grass, raking leaves, watering plots, tending weeds and flowers and bramble. Winter brought other moods of earth to enter, the heavy frosts, the tearless depths. But that year, that summer, because of the heat waves, and with only traces of rain to measure, the grasses weren't growing, the flowers were straining and there just wasn't much for me to do. That's how the foreman put it.

He approached from the distance, his forest green truck slowly making its way around a corner. The sky tinged yellow. The truck pulled up to the section where I was digging, no sound of braking. The foreman (old Gord) opened the cab door and climbed out. He moved across the grounds, peering from gravestone to gravestone, and nodded, as if the dead were nothing more than his mossy neighbours. Standing before me, all chest and shoulders and a neck slightly bent from years of nodding to his graves, he scanned my morning dig, then tilted back his green cap, opening his weathered face.

"Sorry, son. Have to let you go. It's tough times and tougher times ahead and hot as hell, and the city says we can't use any more water. We're verging on a drought as it is, son. But look, 'cause I like you and 'cause you're loyal as a pup, I've worked out a few weeks wages for you. Come autumn we'll need you right back, to rake up the leaves. For now, I say get out there and enjoy your summer. Jesus, you haven't had time off in years. Years, I say."

Old Gord turned on the grave, sunk, then stepped back up, shaking his boot. He moved back across the section (the clean General leaving his troops) to his green truck. The world in change for a lack of water.

I stood with the spade in my callused hands and my feet those few metres into the earth. Shaken, perspiring, at a loss. All I could do was finish digging the child's grave and honour my obedience to the dead. I did not know what the universe had in mind, because there, across the section, was a familiar plot and a gravestone, its shaded epitaph staring out at me. *'For wherever your treasure is, there will your heart be too.'* A beautiful, frightening font.

It was my grandfather's gravestone. Our family plot.

They're all there now, sinking. I imagine my mother (the last to join them) shifting in her yellow bones, busy with vacuum and duster, wiping away all traces of earth and weeds from her skin and prayers. At times slipping a mickey from her blue apron pocket and taking an eternal sip. My father is next to her, his hair combed back, every strand accounted for. He wears his prized three piece banker's suit, light gray with faint black and white stripes. Just a shadow of his pencil-thin moustache undergoing a process of decay, which, to my father, is too slow. Next to him is his father, my grandfather, his body wrapped in his greatcoat, a leftover from the Great War. In death, he is at odds with himself and the earth. He pulls at roots and worms, rubbing skins between his fingers, concocting a strange ink potion. He scribbles against the dirt walls of the grave, using a long, inward turning fingernail to spread his sour ink. Words collide, tell of exile, and lash out at God with a slanderous tongue. You see, I am not the first in our family to try to write out our pains and angers and wrestle with the idea of redemption through the telling of a story.

There are places of earth that pull us in and grind us down, if only to prepare our faith and sorrow for a second birth. Ethereal births, psychological births. Births that hinge not only on water and spirit, but on those shadows whose power is wrapped in warm peat, stoked in the jaws of time. Flesh is brief. Standing in that child's unfinished grave, I knew that place, felt its prescient pulse as if the stars were there, pressing through the dirt.

Mt. Pleasant Cemetery. An unnerving silence. A sense that the longer we stay away from ourselves, the more elusive is the return.

I lived that summer (as I did for ten or so previous years and summers) in a basement apartment on Merton St., at the north end of the cemetery. The street was an east-west artery, designed with speed bumps to ease traffic and slow time. Trees (oak maple birch pine elm chestnut) lined the street, offering vertical contour and adequate shade. The homes were a mix of bungalows and town-homes and old renovated structures, modernized and well-kept. A few homes carried the burden of time and were once surrounded by fruit trees and farmers' fields and stories from an era of immigration and escape. There were two small parks along the south side of the block, between Bayview and Mt. Pleasant, the same stretch where I lived. The parks were like bookmarks nestled between the homes. One was called the Mission Ground; the second the Pottery Playground. Both parks offered a sense of reprieve. I could sit and read a book or close my eyes and listen for the arrival of birds, their migratory arc, and feel myself drifting in their summer song, until later (come autumn) when I might fade into red into yellow, leaves swirling at my feet, like radiant collectables for the winter.

Pottery Playground was a small child's paradise and included a shallow pool and great, over-arching shower heads shaped into a dinosaur head and paws that spouted cool water at the touch of a button. All summer long, in the heat, I could hear children's laughter. I forgot that just beyond the wooden fence at the back of the park was the cemetery. So many lives, all that energy, working through the earth, on two sides of a fence.

The Mission Ground had a different appeal, its story being one of loss. A dry and sparse and defunct land. There was no magic pool for dipping, no water running through a child's hands or hair. Only a lone park bench marked its earth, and a garbage bin and boulder, upon which there was a plaque and some chiseled words that detailed the park's lonely history. It's a place too of ghosts, where the Merton St. Gospel Mission once stood, between 1890 and 1970. A place noted for adopting war orphans, its doors open during the Great War and World War II. A small sanctuary in an unsure time.

A large gray stone wall pricked and worked by the weathers separated the Mission Ground from the cemetery and the dead on the other side of the wall. The same wall cut through the back yard behind my basement apartment, a few doors east of the park. The wall, the stone, felt ancient and honed by the dead. There were days and nights when I'd sit outside on the back patio and look at the wall and absorb its curves, its own implicit stare. I didn't necessarily feel impeded by this wall of stone, because I did work on the other side of it and passed through it on occasion, ghost-like in my own skin. And because I knew so many of the names belonging to the dead there. History has its ruins, its wailing walls, and Merton St. apparently had its own. Vines crept up from the ground and scaled the wall, reaching for the sky, like so many thin, tired hands closing and opening one last time to the vastness of the world above.

The basement apartment was contained ten feet beneath the earth, a dug out bound by a frost line. There were two windows onto the outside world; one facing south and the stone wall, the other facing east and a rose garden. If lucky, I might receive a glimmer of the sun rising, penetrating the day, then passing over like a whisper. Light at times would reach the back rooms, after having squeezed through a maze of trees and branches and leaves. A summer light opulent and long, lingering and still; a winter light that unclothed itself, huddled a moment, then bundled back up and left by the side door. A vagrant light.

Outside the east window, placed in the rose garden, was a small, bent blue and white statue of the Virgin Mary. How she landed there, by whose hand she was placed, neither my neighbours nor my landlord could tell me. Had a previous tenant or home owner installed her, or had she slipped the confines of the cemetery, broken off from a gravestone and jumped the wall, like a holy fugitive? I didn't know. She was chipped at the elbows and feet, yellowing and dampened by creeping moss and the moisture that would drip from the overhead gutters. I would see her there, permanent in her rose garden. Her angled back, her semi-reverent posture. At times, when sitting alone in the living room, the lights out, a candle or two lit, I'd swear I'd see her adjust her posture, sneeze or yawn, then peer back over her shoulder into the basement room. In winter, her over-the-shoulder glance was well defined, like dark storm clouds. There was such wind in her expression as to rip through me. As if I hadn't yet soul enough nor flesh enough to be marked a child of her God. Because I lived those years a quiet, underground life, where things (thoughts, feelings, emotions, dreams) were safely stored, I was quite certain that nothing revelatory in the world would reach me. More certain that it didn't matter that my self-imposed solitude (at the time, that summer, with your mother away) was really a desolate exercise in hiding out, in avoiding sky. And even (to a degree) avoiding my brother, Zee.

He was back. Your uncle. He had spun, as if counter clockwise, back into my life after an absence of a year and a half. All six feet of him, muscling in on me. The dark glimmer in his eye, the Gitane smoke ring round his head. Zee. Zachary Littlewood Savage. Zachary, after our father, Littlewood being our mother's maiden name. My blood and brother, four years my elder. The then thirty-two year old wearing a backwards baseball cap, t-shirt and army fatigues. The guy with the goatee. The guy who was always disappearing and reappearing and disappearing again, for months or years on end. Tree planting out west, driving cab in Montreal, tending bar in Halifax. He was an odd ball sailor, a wandering gypsy, a traveling photographer. He was also the guy who had written off the family years ago and dropped out, as if through crystal ball eyes he had very early in life peered into the cold fronts and wind storms of our ancestors, our parents, and so worked to erase himself from those connections, those conduits.

"What kind of man has a five year old climb a 32' ladder in a driving rain storm to clean the eaves and upper windows, and not have that child tie the bloody ladder off or even bother to hold the damned thing for him," Zee once said of our father.

About our mother, he rarely spoke.

Yes, Zee had returned, dragging with him the tick tock crash bang rattle of narrative that somehow (at one and the same time) linked us and crushed us. As if with every moment of memory and illumination between us, a dark, sticky fog stepped in behind, drunk, screeching to be heard, then stepped back out, casually, as if feigning sobriety, into the recesses of the night. Now he had returned with an air as if he had never been missing. Time relinquished in the seasoned crinkle of his smile. All he said was that for the past 365 or more days he had been off in a wilderness. He wouldn't say where but that it was wild. Wild for my brother is not in the trees. Wild is a four letter word. Zee said that he had been off working on his graffiti, getting it out and down. Zee always insisted there was only one way through the mess of a life (his life, my life, our ancestral life) and that was to spook it out of one's system and purge. A gob of red clay and a knife with which to give it shape might do the trick, work out the inner life, or perhaps a steady rant through a local priest's confessional slot might ease the tremors, still the past. But to be honest, at the time of Z's return, that kind of art and cleansing was at best a dead end, and at worst, a lie.

There he was, my brother, standing next to a maple tree and aiming his omnipresent camera at my quiet, perspiring face. I was standing on the edge of a sunken grave, the day of his return a few weeks before my being laid off. He took a snapshot and then another. All the slivers of our past about to emerge. The muted colours, the random stabs. What mattered to Zee was the here and the now, the ribbons and bows of whatever disease or disorder. He was the talk show host and you were this week's bony guest, put under the spot light of his interrogative banter.

"I see you're still the patron saint of the underworld, digging your graves."

"It's an alternative lifestyle, yes," I said, slipping into the role of guest.

"Still sharing your body with the adoring Rachel Raine?"

Approving nod.

"Plotting the names you two will give your children?"

Second nod.

"And how is our blessed girl?"

"Couldn't be better."

"I assume she's out and about, mopping up after other bodies and souls?"

"You assume correctly, yes."

"Whereabouts?"

"Zambia last month. Rwanda, this month. A four month contract with Doctors Without Borders, but there's talk of the contract being extended."

"Miss her?"

"Inside out, upside down."

"And you? How's your holy cup? Half full, half empty?"

"A little of both."

"Going to Mass?"

"Not that often, no."

"Interesting," Zee said, taking another snapshot of me as I adjusted myself against the grave. "Any temptations of the flesh to report? I mean, have you veered at all from your dear Rachel or are you resolute in your devotion to her?"

"Resolute, yes," I said, clear, a witness. "I've been here, working. I battled with a bout of pneumonia this winter and a series of fevers and sore throats. Otherwise, things have been just peachy."

"Sore throats, hmm," Zee nodded. "Thus the slight whisper."

"Thus."

"And your other colourful angels and demons, the crooks like the old man and dear old mum who burgled our souls?"

"What about them?"

"Don't be coy, mon frère, it's me, Brother Zee."

"I'm not sure I want to be psychoanalyzed just now."

"It'll help, Little Flower, in our catching up. You know I've always felt a certain moral obligation to remind you of where you come from, of certain wounds, each a tiny wisdom, so that you might begin the very important work of finally forgetting where it is you come from. You know I love you. You know that, don't you?"

"So you've said."

"Right then, trust me." Zee smiled and took another snapshot. "Now, where were we?"

"Wounds, each a tiny wisdom," I whispered, feeling the heat, the graves.

I'll tell you this, it's difficult to disengage (and perhaps to differentiate) yourself from someone you've been grafted to for most of your life. Even though we were brothers and have the blood and papers to prove it, Zee insisted early on that we mix our blood, just in case something at our births had not taken root. Just in case our parents had lied to us and pulled a fast one, as if we were not brothers in blood and mood at all but had been adopted. There was the age difference between my mother and father, fifteen years, to consider, and the separate beds, I remember. There was the fact that Zee and I looked nothing like the other, bore little resemblance in the eyes, the shape of our mouths, chins, noses, how we stood. Even our mannerisms seemed to indicate our having been raised in different rooms, at different ends of the house. I was five and Zee was eight or nine years old when he first took me down into the ravine (forbidden, out-of-bounds, do not enter) behind the house. He took out his pocket knife, slit both of our index fingers, then stuck them together until they became seared under one, dark scab. A tiny curve of scar remains, as small, as artful as your pale eyebrow. Zee then proclaimed life to be an experiment; live it and milk it, perish or die. The ravine became our laboratory, the vessel both sacred and profane. The hidden creek, the supple forest, the tree houses we built, forts shaped out of leaves and branches and stone. The battles involving other warrior-kids from around the block, shoot em' up bang bang games. Re-enactments of two world wars, Vietnam, all we had studied on TV or at the movies. Major operations, military campaigns against frogs, snakes, turtles, raccoons. Skinning things alive. Filling tin cans with firecrackers, lighting wicks, blowing up tree trunks. And the times we pretended to run away and make camp, like vagabonds, hobos, like kids of the Depression sitting round small campfires, singing good ole songs (Row row your boat, Puff the Magic Dragon), while drinking black tea disguised as whiskey, just like in the movies. There were nights under a dark canopy of leaves, stars poking through. I must admit, for a time there I felt protected, I felt innately small but wild, linked to things shining and moist and of the earth.

Then Zee required diversions, situations where life was charged and somewhat edged. As an early teen, he took on his stint as a neighbourhood cat burglar. He rummaged through Moore Park and checked out the humble wealth and attire of its older, distinguished gentlemen. Men like our father and grandfather. Zee would enter a home by a back window and later leave by the front door. His signature move, always taking with him an older man's hat and coat. The Hat and Coat thief. I'd watch him step out of a target-home, an old brown fedora or a golf cap on his head, a trench coat over his shoulders. *Back in a minute, honey.* At times, he'd tip a hat to a neighbour who happened to be standing in a driveway, watching.

Zee would actually exchange hats and coats with other homes. Leave one house, enter another, swap his haul. Men would wake in the morning and find a neighbour's hat and coat in their closet, then later, when leaving for work or a game of golf, spot their own hat and coat worn by a neighbour across the street. A befuddled glance between the two men, their surprise at the perfect fit, the impossibility of it.

Zee was daring, always cunning, right out of the womb. As a little boy, I was content in his shade and power. Content to accompany him on his sojourns involving girlfriends and first kisses, fleshy highs while coupling in the ravine, on a bed of pine boughs. Content to witness his many pursuits and addictions, seasoned nights when nursing first beers, first joints, timing highs, lows, the in-between. Anything to beat back and trample down the coming snows and frosts, the harsh silences that surrounded our home, school and church, our parent's refined sense of conversation, or a distinct lack thereof.

I became his watchdog, the detached eye, the younger brother put on guard. His look out for cops, parents, other teens. I'd whistle like a bird as a passerby approached my brother and his chosen girl in their bed of boughs. I'd toss pebbles at windows to warn him if someone was coming home as he was parading around their house in a borrowed hat and coat. I stepped easily into this role, this habit of watching out for him. If only because he demanded this of me, begged. If only because there was something in my nature already at home with a life of studying shadows, a ghost within shaping my skin and eye. It would take me years to break this shape and spell, this habit. Years, and some blood.

There is a time, I believe, when we must lose our lives to find our lives. Give up whatever concepts or precepts we have about ourselves. Call it the wilderness years. You can be happy as a red button and deep in love (as I was) and still it can happen. You can be visited by certain darkness at noon hour, in mid-sentence, while opening a door. A blade slips and the soul gushes, and we are thrown back against ourselves, flawed and artless. We begin the search for the right word or gesture that might grant us entry back within ourselves, no matter how fragile language might seem, how inadequate. And with nothing in the world to feed from but the frayed edges of memory.

Ravines. Graves.

The past blesses us at the precise moment we see that it is our future that most needs forgiving.

2

A PURPLE STREAK OF CLOUD over the far shore, a lone caravan carrying nomadic waters. This cloud has travelled hours to reach us. If we're patient, it will unlock its moisture, lend its rain, and our skin will come alive like the gold and red markings on a map. The blue curves of primary road that tend toward the heart.

Lake Baptiste. Here, I'll dip your little foot in the lake.

Your mother loves water. Our beautiful Rachel. Each morning she dives into the lake at a point where the water appears seamless. She stays under for a minute, swimming deeper, as if closer to the source of a dream. There are times when I lose sight of her and feel a rap of panic against my chest. Then I spot her refracted shape, like a silhouette, angling back toward the surface. The shape is thin, longer than she is, and has many folds of water and light that bend like a blue accordion. When she emerges (dark hair gleaming, the wet rattle of her many bracelets preceding her surfacing), she twists around in one fluid motion, exposing her belly and breasts to the sky. Nothing interrupts this action, this exchange of self. Even when the waters are rough, the current unrelenting, she is there, choosing the right wave to nuzzle beneath, rise upon and turn. She will float there and come to a still point. Her skin's dark hue and the lake water come together like a kiss. Sometimes, I admit, I'm jealous of these waters. How they flatter your mother's countenance and provide for her a unique current of intimacy.

I was in my thirteenth year when I first saw her. She had fifteen bracelets, thin silver bangles flashing along her thin arm. A bangle for each year, presented to her as a birthday gift in an unmarked red envelope, as if from a secret admirer. She always knew the admirer was her aunt and godmother, Mrs. Pinto. There were eighteen silver bracelets riding your mother's left arm when we arrived at our first serious kiss. Nineteen bracelets the day of our first, deliberate snowball fight. Twenty-one bracelets when we lay on a motel bed, in Montreal, overlooking another cut of water, and making love for a first, tentative time. There are spaces between each bracelet like the years Rachel and I were apart. Times when my silence occupied me, the ghosts weighing on me. Times when your mother was rediscovering her own roots, in Europe, in India, in Fiji. Times when she was studying medicine. You see, we have always been a constant in one another's lives, regardless of the climate and her travels, or my own fears and weathers. And our letters (there were letters, love notes, blue ink on birch bark samples) have always served the goodness of our intentions, the various promises we might include in a word and exchange across the continents.

The afternoon we married, I gave your mother a ring to go with a thirty-second bracelet. A silver wedding band to reveal myself as her true secret admirer. It was the first time in my life that I made a unique gift of myself, freed myself. In the same way heat frees itself through our bodies, when after a swim, Rachel steps from the lake and lies against me, naked and dripping, sweet with water and sun. Such miracles of energy. Because, you see, for years I had been pulled by stone cut silences and not by the life force of water, nor the heat of seed. I did not step easily through the world. As if always behind a cloud of myself, a tempest mood.

There is quiet over the lake. Waves roll as an afterthought. Rachel is up the hill, behind the house. She's tending to the gardens, stringing up tomatoes and bean poles. Her hands, her slender fingers, I'll tell you, look good in dirt. She moves between her love of gardening and her medical practice with great care. When I listen to her digging and tilling and watering the earth, I sense a place in my heart like an empty page I've held onto for years but have not yet coloured or written upon.

Last night we received a short series of storm clouds. They passed quickly, leaving in their trail close to two centimetres of rain. A good soaking. The loons called through the night. Sometimes I sleep through their concert, their wild tremolo. At other times, I wake startled, gripping myself at the knees. It is a cry that had me up the other night, at 3 a.m., checking you in your sleep. My cheek next to your small dark mouth and nose, reassured by your breath and the sweetness of you. Moonlight filled your room, a splash of its arc across the walls that are painted in your mother's favourite colour: robin's egg shell blue. It's the colour I now call upon to guide us through this narrative, a painted stone I skip through time.

3

ZEE HAD BEEN MISSING FOR a few years prior to his return. The last time I saw him, two things happened, which according to my brother were important but the order of which didn't matter. This being that the Toronto baseball team won its second World Series in as many years, and that our mother died.

Zee always told me, never answer a door if someone is knocking at 8 a.m. It was sure to be the police, he said, delivering a court summons or just plain bad news. One morning, I was too exhausted to think of his advice and pulled myself out of bed at the sound of a knock, only to find a young police officer at the door. I tightened, then opened the door. The officer (clean cut, hands folded) asked me if I was Jonathan Francis Savage, son to Elizabeth Savage, who lived on St. Clair Ave East, at number 171, apartment 301. I nodded.

"I'm afraid there has been an accident at that address," the young officer said.

"Accident?"

"Your mother has had a fall. A bad fall, I'm sorry to say, sir."

"Is she okay?"

"I'm afraid she's no longer alive, sir," the young officer said, looking me in the eye, then away.

"No longer alive?"

"That's correct, sir. No longer alive. I'm very sorry for your loss. Now if…"

I felt my glands fill with sweat, my lips tremble. There was a starkness within my emotions, like a desert, toward my mother in those days. She had become a woman who had chosen a latter life of estrangement, little more than bone. Since my father's death, she had receded further within a life of drink, living alone in a small one bedroom apartment, not far from the cemetery, and not far from the family home. I saw her once or twice a month, less and less, in the years after Father died. Sometimes I took her to Sunday Mass when she was feeling too frail to walk alone. The last time my mother and I spoke, she was drunk and quietly angry, ranting. I had come over to help her with some chores and her laundry and to take her out to lunch, but on the way out, she rolled over on her ankle, twisting it on a step. She fell into my arms, thin as a stick. She scowled at me. I was in her way, she said, always in her way. Like my father, like every man she had ever known. Useless, she said of the men in her life. This is language I was accustomed to. It permeated my mother's every breath, rode my skin like a blade. I lifted her in my arms and carried her back up the stairs and into her apartment. I wrapped ice in a cloth and eased it around the ankle that was then swollen and blue. She wanted a cigarette, she wanted a stiff drink. I suggested both might not be appropriate at that hour. She shot me another look. So I fixed her the drink, one last martini, I thought, after a lifetime of martinis. Within an hour, she was asleep, in her chair by the window overlooking St. Clair and her church up the block. Our Lady Of Perpetual Help. I sat with my mother for an hour, listening to her labour in her sleep. She began to snore, her mouth hung open. I removed the ice wrap from her ankle and the drink from her hand, and poured the remains down the kitchen sink.

"Mother," I said, "I'm leaving. I've got to go. Is there anything else you need?"

She groaned, then opened a single eye. She looked at me as if not recognizing my face and fell back to sleep. I stared at the wrinkles around her eyes and lips, searched a moment for an aspect to her character that had always been hidden from me, only to realize what I was looking for had been hidden from herself. A gone sun.

In the following weeks there were a series of phone calls from my mother, incoherent calls. Five or six a day, long into the night. Drunk. Most of the time I let the machine take them and I listened as she rambled, demanding that I come and see her, that she needed my help with this drama or that dilemma. She pulled her voice through lasting hurts, talked through silences that had forever haunted us. This was not her attempt at cleansing, nor a sharing in intimacy. This was blame. She went on about my father, the man who had everything but left her nothing, so little to live on. Oh, once he could provide, but in the end he had gone missing. Emotionally missing, psychologically missing. An absolute no man's man, she said, slurring her words. She went on about my brother, her first born, her hope, but what kind of son (please, Jonathan, tell me) walks out on his family, his home, his mother? She stammered into the machine. Can you believe it, Jonathan? My first born son, treating me like this, not talking to me, not coming to see me, for years and years and years. How long has it been? Jonathan, you won't do that to me, will you? You're not planning to disown me too, are you? Like your brother? Jonathan? Are you there? Pick up... There was a tone in my mother's voice, a viciousness that made me tired. When I heard it, I felt obliterated, the years slapping back.

She died after falling down the stairs on her way to the apartment laundry room, hitting her head hard on the floor and breaking her neck. It was hours before she was found, twisted like a small bird on the basement floor. When I identified her body, I spotted a gash along the side of her head, a deep bruise the colour of black tea. There she was, diminished, limp, lipstick smeared. She had pushed away life, she would push away death. The two did not dance. Her awkwardness in life worked against her, smothered her and those around her. I couldn't summon up a single tear for her. Not one, not there in front of the young officer.

Even today (the lake flowing, the wind down, the calm of your body in my arms) her voice sometimes shocks me, shakes me. It has its own hidden current, its own electrical switch. It can throw itself on at the strangest times, in weathers I'm just learning to accept.

That autumn day of my mother's death, I contacted Zee and told him the news. There was a silence from his end of the phone as if he were clearing a space in his mind and conjuring up the last image he had of our mother. The day he walked out, he turned his back and hopped a box car for Montreal, then a flight for the west coast. It was years ago. He was near sixteen and stoned, stubborn, and to me, radiant when he ran away. Then the silence on the phone shifted and he began to laugh over the receiver, an eery, inconsequential laugh. I moved the receiver away from my ear, only to hear Zee say,

"So, miracles do arrive in all manner and time."

We buried our mother, the two of us, and a parish priest from Our Lady of Perpetual Help. Gray sky, autumn leaves, black earth. Every ingredient my mother hated about the world and worked her life to stay away from. She was not fond of the education found in black soil or the dirt beneath the fingernails.

"I'm only here for you," Zee said at our mother's grave. "Not her. Best forget her, brother. She doesn't deserve your grief."

An awkward sadness overtook me anyway.

"Let's get drunk." This was my brother's heartfelt motto, an old family credo.

He pulled me from the cemetery the day of his return, taking me by the hand and leading me back to the basement apartment. *Ah, mon frère, good to see you.* The air was austere. Zee stepped through the side door and into the basement with a bow, like a country squire. He went straight for his packsack and pulled out a few beers. One for me, two for himself. A moment later, he began his perennial prowl of my space. His white glove inspection, all reminiscent of our mother and her need for constant order. Zee ran a stern finger over my books, CDs and videos. He overturned magazines and newspapers and spied on their creases.

"And what would you be listening to these days?" he asked, brushing the stereo with a pinky finger.

"Mr. Bach as interpreted by Yo Yo Ma. Vintage Cohen. Chet Baker. And of course, Ms. J. Mitchell."

"I see you're still working on the infamous canoe," Zee turned and grinned at me, running the same pinky along the canoe's rough edge.

"That would be correct, sir."

I had possessed the canoe (that very canoe over there, on the dock) for a few years. An old green cedar strip, an original Chestnut canoe your mother and I picked up at a neighbourhood garage sale. The canoe was in need of re-finishing, new stem bands and thwarts. Every now and then, I'd slip my hands into its shape, feel the warmth of its cedar, my nose beneath its buoyant layers. I was a novice then in the art of canoes (still am in many ways, though it's one of the things I do now, how I occupy my hands, re-storing old canoes, fashioning new ones), but just the odour of the cedar was enough to kindle in me images of tripping and losing myself to open waters and verdant forests whose thickness concealed the eyes of wild ones. Places, you see, I had only dreamed of, rarely been. Not until your mother and I unwrapped ourselves and decided, yes, let's scurry north, let's find some wilderness, let's... ah, but I'm getting ahead of my voice and the arc of my life's lullaby.

"It's as if you're planning a damned escape with that thing but won't make the necessary sacrifice," Zee said of the green canoe, working on his second beer.

"It's a process," I said. "When I do get the chance to work on it, I have to move it outside. That means always having to take the door off the hinges, just to squeeze it through."

"Forget the hinges," Zee smiled, pointing at me with his beer. "What I see is that you still don't have a paddle."

Zee settled into my basement world, his things strewn on the floor. Keepsakes, maps, a small collection of videos and CDs. Each morning he'd sit back on the couch, feet up on the coffee table, a nice Canadian beer in hand and one of a dozen cigarettes on the fly from finger to finger. He watched TV, *Charlie Rose, Oprah,* or *The Three Stooges.* He seemed so at home I wondered if it wasn't me who had returned after an absence of a year and a half. The Prodigal Son.

The day I lost my job, Zee took it as a sign, a message from what he called the gods of transformation and Saturn's swing.

"I told you," he said. "The world is getting harsh. Even the one business sure to never lose interest, death, is caught up in this wicked cycle of downsizing and globalization. Soon they'll tell us it's cheaper to have us boxed, shipped and buried in a Third World country, with a Third World priest."

Zee sat with the newspaper over his lap and veered each morning through the editorials and entertainment sections with surgical-like precision. He lamented that the Toronto baseball team was off to a terrible start and what had the new world order come to. He conversed between rings of cigarette smoke and passed off his own op-eds as if he were offering me a series of halos on a silver platter.

"Bloody climate change. Increased droughts and famines. All at the glorious cost of our First World grip on natural resources the world wide. I know you green types say we're running on empty and calling it full, but how else are we to control our blessed right to addictive behaviour if we don't take the world apart field by field, sea by sea?"

"Speaking of which," I said each morning, "Do you think you could smoke those things outside."

"I forgot," Zee winked. "Non-smokers can't be trusted. Always on the moral high ground, ready to legislate us off to our own smokers' colony. You'd vote for that, wouldn't you, Little Flower? Just to squeeze out a few extra licks from your beautiful lungs before we all go kaboom."

"The thought has occurred to me, yes."

Zee picked himself up from the couch with newspaper, beer and cigarettes in hand and moved each morning to the side door and positioned himself on the steps leading up to the back yard. A gust of heat breezing in, carrying the metallic odour of summer. Zee sat there, like a time bomb, the Virgin at his back, sore and blue in her rose garden.

"You've really got to get out of here, little man," Z said, sitting on the steps. "Travel or something, see the world, educate your soul. Good God, get laid once and for all by someone other than just your beloved Rachel. It's not normal to be that monogamous in this day and age. It's almost inhuman."

"I'm fine with it, thanks."

"Look at yourself. Always the crazy clown hair and the down cast eyes, and what's with your wardrobe?"

"It's my style."

Blue jeans. Black t-shirt. Running shoes.

"How long have I known you?" Zee said, chirping.

"Are you serious?"

"Come on, how long?"

"About 28 years, 14 days, 13 hours and 21 minutes," I said, checking my calendar watch.

"Are you sure?"

"To the minute."

"All I know, and I don't regard much of our childhood as anything like Hucklefuckleberry Finn's, but you seemed happier as a kid. Not so blue."

"Who didn't?"

"That's pretty naive, little man."

"Is there any way we might not get into this right now, please? Talk about the weather, the heat and smog or something."

"You had this aura," Zee pushed on.

"You're kidding me, right?"

"Always the clown altar boy with the block wide grin. That was you, little Francis. You had this crazy gift, a prat fall here and there over the altar while helping serve Mass. It wasn't just your abundance of left feet, your Charlie Chaplin twists and leaps. You didn't care what people thought about you. You made people laugh. That's why they came to Mass. Not for the bread and wine, and certainly not for the old priest's rambling homilies, but to witness you trip and stumble and pop back up and grin at yourself like some holy fool, some grinning child of God."

"Now you're really kidding, right?"

"Serious as delirious, mon frère."

"Because there's just one blip to your theory."

"Go on, divulge."

"I was an altar boy, yes. A minor holy stint, after you. But it was you, one fine season, you who were the grinning, stumbling one, the one who spilled the wine and tripped over your robe and embarrassed Mother and turned her church upside down."

"Well, yes, I'll admit that, but you know what I'm really getting at, little J, don't you? That you were mamma's little altar boy round the house, pleasing your way through existence, just to survive her drunken disorder."

"Who didn't in that house?"

"Me. I got away. You never really did. Psychologically, you still haven't. Sure, you checked into this basement and worked your years, but you fear the world, don't you? You fear what's round the corner and you just can't live like that."

"Just a phase."

"A phase, you say. A phase is a few weeks, a season or two. Perhaps the length of Mr. Picasso's blue period. Not the length of a decade. That's for world war vets, old souls like grandfather, guys who've really had their guts ripped out."

"Your holy point?"

"Even darling Jesus left his solitary hills and that Buddha dude left his wealth and holy tree behind. That's why you've got to travel. Best medicine for you. To be out in the world, lapping at its rims and rivers, filling your secret journals with other lovers and adventures. Out in the world, that's where you come up against your true self and experience life as death and death as life. It's an old, mystical teaching, little man, but a good one, a vital one. Humbling, I think. Because most of us won't grow much bigger than six feet and that's pretty small in a world of mountains and trees."

"You've got this down, I see."

"You're not convinced?"

"I'm tired and hot."

"Right. Next best medicine: a movie," Zee said, shifting his tone. "There's a new Bond flick and what's this, *Die Hard with a Vengeance*. So much juicy violence to choose."

"Not in the mood."

"Let the mood come to you," Zee said, fanning the air. "I'll bet they've got the air conditioning cranked up in the theaters, the cool darkness. That'll be good for you, little man. Some artificial air. My treat."

Zee would put his life down for the movies. Anything recorded on film. A rare influence he had ingested in the shadow of our father, in another basement room, a screening room bunker our father had constructed in our family home. There, as children, we'd watch silent films. Celluloid propaganda. Saturday afternoon's *The World at War*. WWI footage. WWII. The Atom bomb going off, mushrooming, sound blasting. We'd see men without their faces, shell shocked limbs, those left limping through the rest of their lives. Men like my father and my grandfather. Destruction came at us in black and white. The past, like my father's basement room, belonged to a time and place without the red and purple hues of the imagination. Death was without colour. This enabled men like Hitler to come along on his grainy reams of celluloid, march across the basement screen and occupy a great harvest table that had just been hand carved out of a forest he had ordered reduced to stumps and rubble. He'd sit in the middle of the conquered space and begin his victory feast, eating the produce of the vanquished. Later, we'd watch him laugh and stomp his big, fat boots all the way up the Champs-Elysees.

I remember Zee taking this world in. Like my father, he'd sit in absolute stillness before the basement screen, eyes wide, images flickering. *Battle of the Bulge. The Longest Day. The Great Escape.* Give my brother his saints. Give him John Wayne, Robert Mitchum, Steve McQueen. Give him his glorified Brits. Caine, Fox, Shaw. Zee knew their moves, how to pose. A world of gallant men, hard drinking men swooping in to open a door for the starlet, bowing and lighting their cigarettes. Casual courtesies now lost to the archives of film. A world of army fatigues and the quick transition into a tuxedo. Honouring his silver screen heroes, Zee would often (even to that day, that summer, in the heat) wear a tuxedo jacket over his wide selection of colourful t-shirts and a white silk scarf wound round his neck. He'd also add his own twist of fashion. Along with the Tux image, he'd wear cowboy boots, plus the ball cap, worn backwards, as was our generation's manner of revolutionary style.

We didn't go to the movies that afternoon. There was this.

"So, what brings you back?" I asked, soldier to soldier, changing my tact.

"Stuff," Zee put it. "Good old fashioned stuff."

He lit a cigarette, handling a fourth beer. A snake of smoke in the air, stretching back through the open door.

"Could you be a little more specific, sir."

"Nope."

"Pretty please."

"Just here, mon frère, for you."

"That's very kind of you, sir."

Stuff could mean anything to Zee. It could mean a month's worth of laundry. Another woman. An irate husband on his trail. Stuff could mean he was back if only to take up a collection, turn round and hit the road again. It could mean the persistent boredom and insomnia that seemed to get in the way of my brother's personal sun had caught up with him once again. Zee's other personal thesis (a life outside of the movies) was that life at its core was dull and ineffectual. It's an age old hypothesis, nothing new, I admit. An existential quirk that every generation must work out at its café table tops and cultural labs. Zee spent a great deal of time attempting to sell me on his capital D, capital B theories about Dullness and Boredom. He'd point to rush hour traffic and shopping malls and church pews as places where the demons Dullness and Boredom would sink their teeth and stance and begin their relentless quest for the human soul, our souls.

"What is the conquering of physical space and the industrialization of the planet but the absence of spiritual space within ourselves," Zee once put it, vaingloriously drunk at a café table, one lone night years ago.

I was never hemmed in by the same boredom as Zee had felt cramped by, victim to. Like anyone of our century, I've opened and closed to the passions. I was taught as a child not to trust in my senses, my body. It took your mother and a little love at initial sight to yank me out of that sham, our first touch, our first kiss. In my childhood home, there in Moore Park, under the yoke of my mother's teachings, it was important to remain quiet. There were *hideously* crooked demons battling to get into our home, she assured us. Creatures who would slide into our beds at night and smother us. Little did she know the poor demon was already in the house. There were those age old Sunday sermons, always being told—by my mother, by the priests—that Jesus died for us. Died again and again, over and over, every Sunday, for us, for me, for Zee. Died, my mother believed, because we (the two of us, Zee and I) were born sinners, hardly worthy of cup and bread. There are fallen angels still falling and collecting souls for their war against your flesh, my mother warned. They will enter you through your eyes, slip into the back of your mind like a thief. No graceful breeze could wipe them out. If we were sinners, my brother and I, what was the use of pursuing a life of goodness, of passion.

As a child, there were moments in dreams where I'd find myself crawling near a fire that was raging orange upon a funeral pyre. I'd press my ear closer to listen for word from the flames, but as soon as I'd do so, an unseen force would extinguish the flames, yet not before I'd spot another shape on the pyre. The gleam of it. A shape strangely familiar and resembling my own body, burning away, until all that remained was the ash through which a whole new being had to emerge. I didn't know that then and now can only guess at the process of this phenomenon. Regeneration comes slowly. There isn't a religious thought or an artistic impulse that doesn't first arrive to us through the soil at our feet or the nutrients that rub off on us after something we eat. It takes many skins and fires to reach this insight, many shed lives before we can look to the passions again and not fear. The passions use many devices to teach us. Foods. Weathers. Holy tools.

I sensed this (strangely enough, out of the wild of wind) when Zee stood up from the back steps, stubbed his cigarette out against the brick wall, flicked the stub over his shoulder, then stepped back into the basement, dropping the newspaper on the floor while going for the fridge and finding himself a few more beers. He filtered back into the living room (handing me a beer), and sat himself on the floor, his back against the couch. It was ten a.m. He opened a beer, took a long, patient sip, an eye on me. He crossed his legs, sinking into the carpet, while in the shadow of the green canoe. He finished off the first beer and opened a second. Then, reaching for his packsack and the TV remote, he pulled a video from his belongings and placed the cassette in the machine (on a stand, to his left) and cued up a film. If I wasn't going out to the movies, then he'd bring his holy flick to me. This wasn't one of my brother's golden oldies, scooped from the thirties or forties. No. This morning's show was a shift in direction, a few generational beats into the 1970s, into a time when American cinema (rich, tough, on top of the world) was flowing in technicolour blood. When the bones of the world were revealing post-war intrigues.

"How about it, Little Flower? Are you up for a little cinematic journey? Indoors?"

"Not a home movie, please."

"No, no. Just some vintage, mid-life Brando. Post-*Streetcar*, post-*Godfather*."

I was twelve years old when *Apocalypse Now* made its North American debut, in August of '79. Another hot, sticky summer. The dog days. Zee worked that summer at the grand, old University Theatre (long since demolished and now a parking lot), where the film first showed in Toronto. It was the cinematic event of the year, a film years in the making, offering its own lure and mystique, as if you were about to peer in behind a mystical curtain onto a world that was illegal and bereft. The film was restricted, off limits to youth such as myself, and even Zee was too young but had fibbed about his age in order to get the job, just to see the film he'd heard so much about. And Zee, in his Zee-fashion, with his Zee-smile, snuck me in the back door, where we stood in the low shadows of the emergency exit and watched the film, day after day, for weeks, dazzled, as if filling our minds with visions of the world at a glorious, quickened end.

And there (in the basement, late June of '95) Zee hit the remote and let the film roll, sound up, buzzing the room. I watched him in his cinematic mood, dropping into his Brando impersonation. Like Brando's Kurtz running a hand over his forehead and squeezing out every ounce of jungle sweat he could muster from his skin, his shadow picking its way across the far wall. Between his teeth, I could see him chewing on the past, a bug-thin slice, that he spat back out. I was sitting still but felt myself coming apart. There are films, you see, that show us a character's most intimate gasp. There are films we scour as if to place ourselves in history, dressing ourselves in the uniforms of the ancestors we long to touch. And there are films that ravage, that scar, that remind us of our own places of discord. Of nightmare and hot, wet wind.

I strained my eyes, knowing the film by heart. There was the opening sequence, like a lament stripped of care. Only its rawness coming through, its brutal cut. I watched (is it real? is it tangible?) a world of stunning forests and riverside villages and its citizens come under the fire of jet fighters and helicopters, bombers, the sky caving in, everything green and earthed buried beneath a heavy blanket of North American napalm. All the while accompanied (music is important in film, lures as well) by the wailing voice of Jim Morrison, pop guru of the End Times, as the screen and dank basement erupted, in sound, in vision, in my mind. There was just no way around the heat of it, the bone of it. The illusions I had to absolve between each breath.

Zee turned the sound up another notch. Harsh bombs, fires raging. Zee abandoned his Brando impression and sat in his trance, lost in his holy flick.

That's when something in me tightened, then suddenly collapsed. I could no longer stomach these images of war in my mind, the currents of celluloid that rocked through me. Too many movies had made a ghost of my soul. I couldn't hold myself back from this feeling, this double pull of emotion. This tightening and collapsing. The ancestral pain in my eyes and no hint of illumination.

Sitting here now, I can tell you there is something clocked into time that is both alluring and tragic. A life of pain and change and moral worlds are challenged. Men (my grandfather, my father) go to their battles, step into gunfire, cursing and praising their God, and if lucky enough to survive, dividing the spoils no matter the cost. This, if only to justify ourselves, our place. One culture and civilization over another, one God against another God who turns out to be the same bloodied God, lifted from the same holy book. Each war taking more and more of our humanity with it. Our departing spirit.

I lifted my eyes toward the basement ceiling, a ribbon of spittle across my lower lip. Sweat. I could taste the sheen of my own salt. Then a bitterness I could not account for.

Zee finished his beer and popped open another. He pulled a stash of weed from his packsack and rolled himself a joint. The opening scene dissolved beneath the sound of helicopter blades, slashing air, time. Zee lit the joint, inhaled, then blew the excess smoke at the TV screen.

I opened the beer he had handed me and felt the bottle's dampness at my fingertips. I allowed myself an exacting sip, then another, longer pull. Why not? I was out of work. It was summer and hot. Zee was back and the world was closing in, as were the energies that were gradually, with stealth, slipping into place, the drunken locksteps that would later (as the summer progressed in heat and trembling) ravage us, purge us. Almost as if we were not even there.

I turned and gazed out the window, looking south. A slight breeze stirred the treetops. I felt my hand losing grip on the bottle of beer. I hurried another sip, out of habit, then placed the bottle on the coffee table. Zee offered me the joint; I shook my head. Why? Why not? I left my brother and his movie-of-the-day, all those wailing images, flames and forests and villages consumed by that mock battle. I stepped into the back yard, I passed the Virgin in her garden and realized I was without shoes and socks. Warm air against my skin and cool grass against the soles of my feet. A summer breeze and a sky soaked not in silence, but intent. I felt a stab of energy push through my chest, a rush, as if grace.

Every day for a week or so, it was the same routine. An endless summer alteration between a basement and a back yard, the weather blazing like a torch. Zee would roll his morning movie (*Apocalypse Now*, *The Misfits*, *Lost Weekend*) and I'd watch a moment, then ease like the wind into the back yard. Barefoot and pondering the stone wall and beyond, where branches rubbed against sky.

4

LISTEN. JUST THERE, RIGHT NOW. Whoo-whoo-whoo-whoo. That's the sound of a raven's wings, in flight over the dock. It's a sound that pulls in its contour the pulse between earth, sky and water. Follow that sound and you will, one day, find a home for yourself.

Like the day, two autumns ago, when your mother and I arrived here. As we drove up the stone road, carving bends, four ravens flew ahead, arcing just over the hood of the car, the green canoe strapped upon the rooftop. The ravens guided us for over five kilometres, squawking and diving through the pines. The maples and birch and cedars.

"A good sign," your mother whispered. "To be in the company of wings."

The blackness of their wings is like your mother's hair.

We moved here not only for wings but air and water, rock and night fires. Soils we could turn like a phrase. We came for the vitality of each season. The splendour, the ruggedness. We came on a night when the northern lights formed a canopy over the house. Intense greens and oranges, speckled reds and purples lapping at the sky. The silence and heat of our night arrival was delicious, like dessert after a four course meal. It was Thanksgiving weekend.

We unpacked by firelight. We took a sauna, then swam naked in the crisp, black waters. We dried one another off, quickly in the cool air, then made love on the dock, nuzzled inside a sleeping bag, a second skin of feathers. We imitated the leap of the night sky, the soft waves against the dock. I'll tell you a little secret: There is a time after love making when even the deepest sorrow will break out the best wine in the house.

Within a year, you became more than just talk, a hope. You began to take shape, a hooded pea inside your mother. Then you began to carve yourself against her belly, a small handful of you, the heart of you.

We trained for your birth for months, breathed in and out in the presence of a midwife. I first spoke to you through a thin but resilient wall of skin, your mother's malleable belly. I felt the years between that summer with my brother and this moment of womb life with you and your mother slip like rain from a page. I saw there cannot be fullness without emptiness, and there cannot be emptiness without a longing to be filled again. As we pour ourselves, our stories, one into the other, the universe is at work, pouring into our lives, star by star, each morning the sun or some rain. None of this prepared me for the sudden cry of you, your own particular coo. One minute there was your silence, a slight kick, then there was a stillness about you that I can only describe as the moment when possibility becomes flesh. You came burning into the world like a wild dove, all heart. Your soul visible and beating this way and that. Your moon ascending like a bubble from your lips.

You were born in the kitchen, almost popped out. Rachel was preparing peppermint tea. Morning light was streaming in from the lakeside windows. She turned to me at the kitchen table, a quiet look of *Oops* across her face. Water. I had a moment to ring the midwife. You were a few days early, a surprise. Eight hours of labour on the kitchen table and a pillow beneath your mother's head. Just our hands cupping you and your mother's pushing, as if she were flinging off her star coat to make room for you. She howled and groaned and laughed, dripping wild with you. I watched you crown, shining and red. This is why people will lay down their lives for a loved one, I thought. The morning sky opened its blue doors onto the lake. When I cut the umbilical cord, I'd never experienced such terror and love grip me. I saw the months of whispering to you through your mother's belly ripen. Those months of planting for you, word by word.

We named you Christopher, after the patron saint of travel. It's a name with the strength to carry the body, contoured by the ground where one stands. A name through which your soul might learn its own art between fullness and emptiness. Between a first cry and lasting permission.

The sky is shifting through layers of early morning reds. A delicate sky, with the feel of fresh pressed violets. Like the morning sky from the day of your birth, eight quick weeks ago, waking us at 7:04 a.m. A clear and balanced sky.

Christopher Sky Savage. Singh-Savage.

You were born in the month of May, the 15th, under the sign of Taurus. An earth sign.

Your mother and I desired a name that would have you feel safe within yourself, wherever you might find yourself traveling, one day. Whatever emerging land, whatever accompanied pillow. A name you might use to look within yourself, your story, and not fear.

A key to yourself.

5

IF YOU BELIEVE THE ANKLE bone is connected to the knee bone and the knee bone is connected to the hip bone, then you'll understand what a simple gesture it must have been, after so many years of my looking away, to finally stand and step out into the back yard and lift my eyes and not fear. As if the opportunity, the blessing had always been there, a kind of angel in the wings of my name. The truth is part philosopher, part humourist, always with a ready foot, like an old friend in a market, to trip you up. All those years living on Merton St., at the north end of the cemetery, and all I had to do was put a beer down, lift myself from a chair and step outside. Then, passing the Virgin in her garden, I'd just have to scale a stone wall, jump and slip south through the cemetery grounds, the ample foliage, then skip a small, linked fence that ran along Moore Avenue at the south end of the cemetery, cross the road, and without much thought or further adieu, find myself immersed in the ravine, green bowl of wonder and terror and appeal. All those years living on Merton St. and I was a matter of metres (small, deliberate paces) from that underworld.

Now, imagine this, you and I, standing in the ravine's dense basin, in the sheltering stillness of its damp shade, and all we'd have to do is look up through the oaks and elms and maples, and there, plucked like an island in that strange sea of trees, would be the family home, dashed and frayed on Hudson Dr., next to a footpath and a bridge that spans the ravine's dark layers.

It was a house that denied the affections of the weather. A place surrounded by hedges and gnarled oak, trunks like sentinels, knotted gargoyles, their tongues sticking out, warding off each passerby. Not one of its bricks communicated a sense of light. Only its intricate display of ivy, creeping up the sides of the structure, near and around the windows, dared gesture a glance of something wild. Step into that house and you might think that someone (an ailing priest, a retired Justice of the Peace) had just finished delivering a very long, a very painful eulogy.

Our family narrative was a dry fuse. Words were an inconvenience. Short, quick jabs. Voices were seldom raised. We wore our silences like a soldier's greatcoat. There was nothing as elegant as a conductor's wand sustaining a symphonic note when it came to the act of communication in that house. Sleepwalkers. A tired house. I grew up in the grip of this fatigue.

My parents did not wade through gentle hours of prose, nor dip into the lives from the saints and fairytales. They believed in the necessary world, time that was levelled. Stark. There was no added extravagance in our furniture, our clothing, our food and work. Everything of sustenance was served in diminished halves. Half an apple, half glass of water, half-truths. Giving the stomach not more, not less, than was required. Tentative slices, drips. Gratitude did not enter our mealtime prayers or the slight petitions we might make for those less fortunate than ourselves.

In my mother and father's kitchen table expressions, I could see that pride obscured every viable emotion. At the slightest tick of inner fury, crucial feelings were dropped. We'd walk out on ourselves, wherever the room. I learned at a young age that there had been a time of depression and two world wars, years of scarcity handed down like a family heirloom. Remember, my grandfather was living in the attic room, on high. At an early age, as if taken aside, shaken into me, I was told by my mother not to ask my father or my grandfather about those times of depression and their respective wars. Even Zee (just a boy, not yet loose of tongue and anger) warned me not to ask about those years and wars. A ground of history that was bitter. Raw. Yet the ground that somehow penetrated how we sat and ate and prayed. The stones we carried deep in our fears. I knew by the way my father cut his morning orange that every half sliver, every drop of juice, counted. Waste was a sin. Seeds were to be swallowed. I knew by the way my mother took my father's plate and cleaned it in her sink, in a small pool of steaming water and liquid soap, while wearing her blue apron and a pair of pink rubber gloves, scouring deeper and harder, not breathing in, I knew we had left behind ourselves an aspect of our potency, our flesh. I could not articulate this at the time, but I believe a child knows this in his or her marrow, knows when a path has been diverted or dammed. The first shudder. I learned to finger-walk my way around the house, a bone traveller. I brushed past shadows on walls like sad frescoes, pale mosaics leaching through the air and the house. The lean impossibility of the place.

I wouldn't have believed it then, that something of the soul and past creeping through that house, would also prepare me for you, for fatherhood. This talking out no matter the scar, near open waters and the sound of untiring waves.

Let me tell you about my first memory of water and the ravine. It began with a storm at my bedroom window, thunder and the fierce whiteness of lightning. I felt an immediate energy between the storm and my heart beat, waving me closer. I got out of bed, not feeling my feet touch the floor. The storm pulled back into the bright darkness beyond the window panes. I could see each of the panes, eight of them, coloured differently. Purple, red, orange, white, yellow, blue, green, and a second blue hue that seemed black. I collected in my mind the glimmer of each colour. I put a hand upon a single pane that was somehow warm, eerie. The orange pane. Suddenly the storm was gone. It might have been just a second, a blink, the whole gleaming experience, but there, before me, was the ravine. A wet world made brilliant by a quickened moon that broke through an opening in the storm clouds. It was early autumn. The leaves of maple and oak beyond the window were on fire. I sat up all night, watching the aftermath of the storm, blistering shapes of water rushing along branches and leaves. Trunks gleaming like sea shells. Wet lichen, soft as pollen, clinging. A dark tangle of roots floating up from the earth. Eyes of raccoons. Fox. This quiet heat seeping into my pores. A tree had cracked and fallen in the storm and now rested at a forty-five degree angle in the perch of a second tree. Thin, strong branches growing interdependent with one another.

There were other nights when I waited upon further storms. I faced the ravine, longing for its beauty to enter me, then release me. Even then I knew. There was that hardened silence in the house, at my back, creeping. My mother insisted I never open a window without her permission. Her fear was of fallen angels getting in and staking their claim on my soul, but on these slim nights of storm vigil, seized by visions of the ravine, I dared open my bedroom window a crack, hoping the heat of the ravine would replace the coolness of our learned silences, our pet-like fears. But the house was stronger in those days, more forceful than my will and age. It was too much to ask of the weather and wild to grant me release, to take a spirit-storm too seriously.

Whether these ruminations of thunder and rain, lightning and the ravine, were sent to save me or repel me, I don't know. Their mark continues to shimmer far within. I've never been able to escape their vivid pallor. Their waters, like a verse I long for.

6

MEMORIES OF MY MOTHER OFTEN elude me; a perpetual game of hide-and-seek. Her image sneaking up from behind and placing both hands around my eyes and whispering, 'Guess who?' I can still see the constant manner of her sadness, her pale aura. Her hair that is strawberry blonde and almost blinding, blurring her finer features. The thin nose, the rounded chin. Then my eyes drop and look away from her face, distracted by her pink rubber gloves and the lime green cigarette holder. She smokes two packs a day. She sits at the kitchen table, on a break from our household chores. I'm three, four, five years old. She angles her chair away from the window onto the ravine. Back straight, posture 'P' perfect. Last of the Victorians. Her smoking hand moves in a deliberate arc from lighting the cigarette to the long puff and release of smoke through her nostrils, then the slow movement of the cigarette to the ash tray on the kitchen table, tapping the butt, loosening its fiery weight. Each puff is a well-honed gesture, as if she is inhaling the world, then slowly, like a faded queen, blowing it all back out into the kitchen air. There is a spirit of death in that smoke, in my mother's kitchen that has been wiped clean (daily, diligently) of germs and dirt and unnecessary odours. I feel my heart snap each time she takes a dish cloth in hand or twists a cigarette into the holder. With each wipe of counter top and puff of smoke, she seems to lose herself, to disappear within. She's just thirty, thirty-one at the time of this memory, but these are our shared moments, in the days when Zee is already in grade school or making his quiet detours into the ravine. These are also the days when my father is off at work, at the bank, or on one of his frequent business trips, overseas, up to his own secret deal making.

At this tender age, I sit with my mother at the kitchen table. I have my drawing things, coloured paper and pencils and my collection of plastic army men, handed down to me from Zee. I draw stick figures and storm shapes over battlefields where my plastic battalion can scour and fight. This, while in the circling cloud cover of my mother's second hand smoke.

My mother has her litany of does and don'ts.

Say pardon, not what.

Keep your back absolutely straight when you're sitting and drawing. No, much straighter.

Don't mix your colours. See what happens when you mix your colours? They become positively dreary. Everything turns brown, like dirt. And we don't like brown, do we? No, we don't like dirt.

My mother and I have our weekly chores, bowing to the god of cleanliness. There is the laundry to do on Monday mornings, beds to be stripped, hampers to be emptied. I stand guard over the washing machine and learn the machine's heated quirks, when to add fabric softener, wait each cycle out. When transferring the wet wash to the dryer my mother insists I not drop a stick of wash. If a lone sock falls and touches the floor, we turn back to the washing machine and begin the procedure again, the cycles. Just one dirty item has the power to infect a whole load of wash. The procedure cannot be tainted. A moral imperative. I learn out of necessity to tighten my hold on the wet, clean laundry. I use larger articles (my father's white business shirts, our bed sheets) to wrap other, smaller articles when removing the wash, rolling the bundle into my arms, nothing loose. This way I can go weeks or months without dropping a sock or a pair of underwear. This way I appease my mother and her painful demands.

Tuesdays we polish the silver at the dining room table and check the pretty china for cracks. These are the few times my mother might loosen and allow music to penetrate the house. She plays the soundtrack from *The Wizard of Oz*, Sinatra or Tony Bennet. These are also the times when a slight smile might crease my mother's face and lighten her mood. We become almost ordinary in the dining room light, its oak trim, its crimson glow. My mother seldom speaks, except to suggest I ease my touch when polishing the silver and work in slow, careful circles from the inside out.

During these times, she is transported by the music, she is another woman, briefly dazzling. She removes the pink rubber gloves and I see the shape of her hands, her thumbs with their tiny hip-like curves, as she eases cloth and polish around her silver. She has a fondness for spoons, she admits. How light plays in their shape. In this spoon-light, I see my mother's eyes are green and cozy and lack in the difficulty I sometimes hear in her voice. I must admit there are times, even now, when I cherish those moments in the dining room: my mother turning a silver spoon in her hand, music lifting, morning delicate as a flower.

Wednesdays we dust. Living room, dining room, bedrooms. Then we vacuum with the Hoover. Thursdays we clean out the fireplaces, the one in the living room (the one, if my brother and I are good and neat and quiet, that Santa might use), and a second fireplace in the second floor den. Fridays we sort newspapers and magazines, tie them off with coarse brown string and stack them in the basement. Everything must be saved. On Friday afternoons, there are the bathrooms, three of them, to be scoured. My mother's mood tightens again. She has me scrubbing tiles while on hands and knees, scrubbing sinks, bathtubs and toilets. I use Ajax, tiny blue and white pellets that burn at my fingertips. My mother stands in the doorway of each bathroom, watching. If I miss a key spot, she is there, a finger pointing. I imagine I am in a tile river, a prisoner working at my escape, yet caught in my mother's guard house beam. When I complete my scrubbing, my mother slips behind me and begins washing the bathroom down a second time. She goes over my effort, getting, as she says, behind the ears of each tile. She scrubs with a ferocity that unnerves me, pouring heaps of Ajax onto the floor and into the tub and toilet, creating a thick, stinking solution, stanching all domestic wounds. I still receive lucid dreams in which I'm being pulled down by the haunting sound of my mother's scrubbing, weird horror film clippings enter my sleep and scrub the insides of my skull, burning through my imagination. I don't remember my mother ever touching me, holding me. Not a tender finger through my hair or across my brow. This lack of touch, I believe, haunts me more.

Each weekday we take our break at noon. Pressured by time, there is little pleasure in our release from chores. My mother and I make tuna or egg salad sandwiches, on white bread, crusts trimmed. On cool days, autumnal days, there is mushroom soup from a can. If my work has gone well in the morning, if I haven't missed a spot or dropped a sock on the laundry room floor, my mother allows me to eat my lunch in front of the TV, while watching *The Flintstones* or *The Dick Van Dyke Show*. Scrubbing dreams are replaced by cartoon shapes or a Van Dyke prat fall. I feel a rare energy, away from my mother and our chores. I even sneak a peak out the back den window, onto the ravine, and wonder. I soak in what I can of the outside world, longing for its unknown wonders.

Still, there is the house and our work. A compulsion toward cleanliness. And there is still my grandfather in his attic room, on high. This is another place, like the ravine, where I am not allowed to enter, yet it is my duty to serve my grandfather his lunch, daily at noon. I navigate the sharp silence leading up to the third floor, my mother having prepared a silver tray with toasted cheese sandwiches, a glass of milk, and a plate of thin carrot sticks. I climb the two flights of stairs, balancing the tray in my hands. The third floor is darker than the rest of the house, a no man's land. I do not want to make a noise for fear of breaking a code of silence there. Once at the top of the stairs, I leave the tray on the floor by my grandfather's door. The door is always closed. My instructions are to knock on the door, knock gently, to let my grandfather know lunch is being served. My knock is hesitant, my ear alert for the sound of his breathing, his slow shuffle across the room. Then I turn and descend the stairs, two at a time. I look to the small windows on the stairway landing for relief, to spot a possible branch upon which I might slither out into the world, but the air is like brick up there and pushes back at me. And there is that other energy pursuing me, the sweeping silence that emanates from my grandfather's floor, clinging to my back like wet sand. I do not know then if the silence is that of depression or an exercise in faith. Because an hour later, my mother sends me back up into the attic, into the quiet of that indifferent energy, to retrieve the silver tray and dishes. The tray is in the same position in which I had left it, on the floor, outside of my grandfather's room, but the door is now open a touch, and I catch an angled glimpse of my grandfather, on his knees on the floor. He is surrounded by papers and books and photographs. I can't tell if he is busy at prayer or if he is just scouring the room for a lost article. I look to the tray and dishes and see that the food is gone. The crumbs suggest an animal presence has visited. I must admit there are times when I finger the crumbs, attracted by an innate curiosity I cannot hold back. My own quiet hunger to know my grandfather's soul, his war and history. This is what begins to take shape there, in those crumbs and ghost-shapes on my grandfather's plate. If I knew then a will to write, the gift to assert my tongue, I might have worked his story out, articulated the elements of his crumbs. Even then, I sense there is a potency to be gained through what has been devoured in that attic room.

I always return to the kitchen world of my mother, feeling foolish and strange because of this other hunger growing in me. I feel more comfortable (if comfort is the word, the feel) in the hard, practical world my mother provides in our chores and order than coming up against the invisible power of sorrow that seems to enfold my grandfather's room. That upper world that never seems to change colour.

My mother's requirement for perfection is an ethic. How I use a broom or spray Pledge over a coffee table has the same moral veracity as a priest preparing the altar, saying the Mass. This is how we build faith, my mother insists, through house work, through annihilating germs like demons. By not allowing garbage to sit around for more than a day, one is maintaining certain harmony. Even if we are cut off from the stars, hardly step outside. Now I know: faith that is blind is murder. It is erasure.

Still, I see our weekday afternoons. The muted yellows in that kitchen world. The firmness of the table top, the silence behind objects along the window sill. I see my mother's non-smoking hand, thin, clean fingers concentrated around her tea cup. I see the china's floral pattern, blue stems and petals. I see our small world all fragile and composed and tight. Always at 4 p.m. Tea time. In the movies, good ole westerns, cowboys take their required alcohol (after the high noon duel, the bar room brawl) in small, murky glasses that are filled to the rim with dark whiskey. We all know (through Hollywood lore) that the dark liquid is really black tea. My mother, though, reverses this effect. She drinks her first drink of the day, her gin martini, from a tea cup. Only a wave of vermouth to cradle its flavour.

I'm in my fourth year when my mother first instructs me in the delicate procedure of fixing her a drink. A big boy, she confides, should know how to fix a lady a drink. My mother sits at the kitchen table in that hour of clinging light and I set to my task of facilitating her first drink. I retrieve the step ladder from the kitchen closet, place the ladder next to the refrigerator, climb the steps and open the freezer door, pinch the bottle of gin, clasp it close to my chest, close the freezer door and climb back down, angling a shaky foot toward the floor. In my imagination, I'm carrying precious cargo, nitroglycerine, deadly explosives. My mind always plays at these games, these missions. If only to distract myself, amuse myself. No matter how hard I try at these little games, there is always my mother's exacting eye at my back. "Be sure of your step... watch yourself... why can't you be more careful and step down like your brother used to do? ...like a good little priest." All of my actions leading back to my mother's version of the sacred world, her moral order.

Once secure with my feet on the floor and the gin in my hands, I take the necessary high wire steps back to the kitchen table. I climb onto a chair and place the bottle on the table top. My mother nods, pulling on a cigarette. In her eyes, I see the temperature dropping. I climb down to the floor and skirt across the kitchen to a lower cupboard, open the door and find the vermouth stashed there like a secret. I take the bottle in both hands and angle back to the kitchen table. Sitting in my chair, I open both bottles and first pour the gin, half a tea cup full, to a point where my mother holds a pinky finger against the cup, marking her desired fill. I watch an eerie anticipation stammer across her face. Pouring the vermouth requires a steady hand and art. Not so much an act of pouring as a flick of my wrist, watching as the bottle tilts toward the tea cup, the liquid also tilting inside the bottle, and just as the vermouth is about to be released, I pull back, lifting the bottle, a dash, so that only a drop remains upon the rim of the bottle. Flicking my wrist a second, delicate time, the tear of alcohol drops into the tea cup, rippling in warm persuasion with the gin. Mission complete, explosives rigged.

There is one more rite of passage I must witness before my mother takes her first sip. Carefully, with skill, she steps up to the kitchen sink and looks into the mirror there, a kind of rear-view mirror onto her kitchen-world, so that nothing gets past her. She looks at herself a moment, then fixes her hair and takes a lipstick applicator from her apron pocket. She pauses, looking at herself again, then applies her red lipstick and works the colour deep into her lips, smacking them and kissing the air, as if delivering that red kiss to a gone lover. Her mood becomes occupied as if with a sideline of dreamy activity, a fleeting dance there in the mirror. I can almost see the carousel of her past, suitors in blue blazers. A sadness in her eyes of someone or other trailing away. Then, with a slow wave of her hand, she returns to the table and directs me to run into the living room and turn on the stereo and plunk down the only record that is fitting for a first drink, my mother's beloved Sinatra, her Frank. *Strangers in the night...dobedobedo...*

When I return to the kitchen-world my mother is changed again, as if her demeanor has put on a long, bright gown fashioned out of lolly pops. Girlish, like Scarlett O'Hara.

My mother's first sip smacks of justification, as if it is owed her. I watch as her slight body lifts in a small flood of relief. Over the course of an hour and three gin martinis, I watch my mother disappear, then reopen like a strange desert flower, risking the airs of a world that to her has continually disappointed, let her down. I watch her solo dreams and steps, her past take over an entire dance floor.

If lucky, my mother's tongue might loosen on these afternoons. Her language bathed in alcohol. I might hear her real voice, her subtle accent, Old England, land of her birth, breaking through. Her love of the adjective—*Positively Absolutely Heavenly*. She might whisper about white cliffs and cool beaches and London during the blitz. Using a finger to point out these childhood nooks, these secrets and hurts like dark spirits eating the air around her.

"I know we're absolutely not to speak of that time of war, but..." she says and checks over her shoulder, as if expecting the secret police to break down the kitchen door and charge us and rope us to the chairs, then gag us. Because these little tales my mother speaks of are real, are dangerous.

It's then that some of the silences that push down on the house are peeled back. Timid, disconnected fragments. It's up to me and my young imagination to piece things together, stitch stories. Because my mother uses me as a kind of bowl into which she tosses her scraps and memories. She seems to speak in code, as if to protect herself from her own mind. She leaves a story off at a vague bend, alters a sentence mid-stream. She whispers to me as if through a key hole from another room, then opens her door a touch, only to catch herself in her own secret-breaking, her own admonishment not to speak. She closes the door back on herself and covers the key hole with a finger.

One week I might hear of the English Channel and occupied lands, armies and France. Another week I hear of the German war machine and madman Hitler (a horribly real sinner a horribly real terror) and his hatred of the Jews. I hear of experiments and crooked doctors, of bodies stuffed into ovens, like garbage, stuffed into burning pits, a whole race reduced to stick people, like my drawings, my mother points out. I hear of bombs falling from her childhood sky, wreaking havoc over her London, blood in the streets, neighbourhoods demolished. I hear of air raid warnings and Flak. Children scavenging for food and clothing, trading in bullets and bones, china and jewellery, three stringed violins. Then a week later, or months, my mother might change the whole story, leave her ruins, and speak of older men. She might drop a hint about her father, a pilot, flying a Spitfire over the channel, beating those German bombers back. The times he is shot down and left to wash through the waves, returning wounded from the cold of war, only to climb right back into a Spitfire and begin his shooting missions again. I hear of Churchill heroics and radio speeches binding a country, bringing home the sounds of war. This my mother reveals between drinks and slow minutes of sipping. I absorb the chameleon nature of her mood, her face in alteration. I know I cannot interrupt. I'm acquiring vital information, a spy, swallowing cryptic orders. I am the one who has plied my mother with the alcohol, my accomplice working her tongue. I'm young but I know how to work a spell, apply my own techniques (Is it torture? Is it a break with the Geneva convention?) to get at the truth.

Over time and a little more drink, she will speak of her father in closer detail. A big man, slim and fit, with large hands. When he's gone, flying his fighting machine, my mother and her mother (Grandmother Littlewood) cover all the windows and doorways with heavy wool blankets, making sure not an ounce of electric light or candlelight will escape the house, making sure the German bombers cannot see them, the bombs not find them. There is one night, during an air raid, when my mother ("Don't tell your father this." Why not?) sneaks from her bed and slips back a blanket from a window, just a pinch, you see, just to look into that thick night sky and spy on the fat bellies of the German bombers and the quick, streaking Flak. She imagines her father, she tells me, in his Spitfire, up there, shooting the enemy down, wrists cocked and strong. Then, just as quickly as my mother has stolen this peek into the sky, her mother is there, taking her by the neck and guiding her to the bomb shelter at the rear of the house, in the yard. They huddle and wait and listen to the night raids, my mother dreaming of her father. Her sweet man, she says, the man who brings her candies or newly minted bullets that he tells her he uses to shoot down the enemy. He asks her to kiss the bullets, for luck, for her part in the war effort.

Then, months later, my mother might alter her path of remembrance while stirring another martini. She'll whisper of a different world that is brilliant because of her father, soft before the war. She recalls for me a summer, by a beach. Sun and salt air. Just the three of them, a family. She's up on her father's shoulders, being carried by the sea. Her mother in the bright July distance, beneath an umbrella, concealed from the hard sun. My mother speaks of her father's eyes, like candies, as she rides his shoulders and peers over the top of his head, dangling her own bright hair over his face. She looks into his sweet eyes, his upside down eyes, bouncing, she says, like jelly beans in a jar. Oh, if she could bounce like that again, she confides, the whole world bouncing like that, all colourful in his arms, by a sea, like that. She remembers feeling like a prize won at a fair. Her father, who made the whole world safe and sweet for her, forever soaking beneath her tongue.

Then my mother stops her talk and fades. Her face becomes sea-worn, no longer an attendant reflecting upon her journey.

"But I've told you too much, absolutely too much." Her voice sways, a little Blanche Dubois in her tone, more Vivian Leigh.

My mother's sense of the past is like a pale shell she has pulled from sand and placed upon a high mantle. A trophy vision, polished. Until the day her father, grandfather Littlewood, does not return from the sky. Here my mother's voice sinks, the beach world darkened for her. She speaks of a funeral and her little hands clutching dirt and my grandmother Littlewood instructing her daughter to throw that dirt upon a coffin, near a hole in the earth. Because, in the end, that's all we are, my grandmother Littlewood tells my mother. Dirt. That's where your father is going to be now, in that coffin, in that dirt, my mother is told. And she swallows this image, turns away. She tells me (in a voice from the other side of her tea cup martini) that this is the last time she ever touched dirt. Believe it or not, she says, but it's positively true. No more earth, no more dirt. Do you understand? she raises her voice at me. Our God is not an earth God, she says. He is a sky God. One day He will take us away from this earthly mess, my mother instructs. Take us away for good, for the better. To a far world. Outside of ourselves.

Even then, as a young boy, listening, I sense the performer in my mother's voice. The contradictions. Her want of sky and her God to rescue her, and her fear of sky and fallen angels come to get us, ravage us. I hear her voice stretch, as if to dismiss herself and history. As if those years of war and her father and his death are nothing more than a strange collision, fated, yet accidental, and not hers. I want to believe in everything she tells me, each of her pale shells, but her voice, the tone of alcohol, feels prone to a kind of fiction, a world made up. My mother lifts her accounts toward my ear like the elusive corpse in those old whodunit movies, the corpse dressed in a tux and moved from room to room by two thugs, from trunk to back of closet door, left hanging from a hook, hidden from the cops, the lead sleuth. There is always an impending mishap in my mother's tales, characters who swap clothing and personalities while riding on the edge of a getaway car. A father becoming an uncle, an uncle becoming an old family friend. Because, you see, if I had possessed then the ability to do the math, calculate the years, I would have known there couldn't have been a time before the war, with my mother young and high on her father's shoulders, bouncing on a beach by a sea. Because my mother was born in 1940 and the world was already nine months with war. And because I remember one very distinct exchange with my grandmother Littlewood, one spring's visit, when I learned the weight of my mother's fictions, her little white lies.

Grandmother Littlewood visits for two weeks each May, an old English fortnight. She is a small and quirky woman, not at all like my mother, and not much taller than a fern. Her hair is white and curly. She smells of used perfume. Her features are flush and crinkled. She wears beige stockings and black dresses and Stratford brown shoes with a slight lift. She advances through rooms and into our lives, always picking up after us and wiping things down. Busy in her own pink dish gloves and a paisley apron, two old allies. But she takes to me, courts my affection. Always stroking my hair and tweaking my cheeks. At times, she presses an English coin into the palm of my hand, for a rainy day. And she likes to show me off, swagger, but this requires her to negotiate with my mother and barter for my release.

"Let the boy see some sun."

"I'll do with him as I please."

"My goodness, have you looked at his hands, how dry they are? The smell of ammonia."

"I positively need him around the house."

"I'm sure you can afford a maid."

"This is my house."

"I'm just worried the boy will shrivel up one day and blow away, like you."

At that my mother leaves the argument and kitchen, throws up her arms, while saying,

"Take the boy for a walk then. But only for an hour. Just an hour."

Grandmother Littlewood lifts me from my household chores and takes me for walks through the neighbourhood. She escorts me up and down Hudson Dr., letting anyone present know that I am her grandson and she is my grandmother from England. Her blood and eternal hope. On these walks, I'm allowed to bring along a favourite toy, a plastic army man or a dinky toy car. Because we always find our way to the local park, Moore Park. I'm allowed to try the slides and swings and dare the open air on the teeder-todder. I'm given permission (after asking, always asking, such a polite little boy) to play in the sand box with other children. I remember times just sitting there, not moving, feeling unsure. As if my mother was nearby, behind a tree, her leg-iron hold on me. My grandmother Littlewood prods me at these times in the sand box, lifting me and shaking me free, like Pinocchio cut loose from his strings. She tells me I'm much too young to be that terrified of play, that stiff in a world for which our freedom has come at a great cost.

Now, I remember a particular day of distinction, a day in the sand box. Sun and spring. Lilacs. The toy I have included in our walk to the park is a small replica toy plane, a Spitfire. There I am in that sand world with my Spitfire balanced at my fingertips, my arm arcing, pretend flying, my mouth revving, mimicking take offs and landings and firing at an enemy sky. My grandmother Littlewood is kneeling close and framing me. She says, "Perhaps I'll take you flying with me back to England. Would you like to fly, one day, in a real plane?"

I remember nodding. Yes, yes. The sky. Away.

Then I say something, cut to an imaginary wish and truth, in a way that only children can. I say, "I want to fly a Spitfire."

"A Spitfire," my grandmother Littlewood says. "And why a Spitfire?"

"Like my granddaddy did."

"Your granddaddy?"

"My mother's father."

"You mean my husband?" I remember my grandmother Littlewood saying, twisting her cheek.

"Yes. My granddaddy. He flew Spitfires in the war and shot down Germans to save the Empire. Then he crashed one day in the channel and died and was buried in the dirt and never came back."

"Who told you that?"

"My mother."

"Did she now?"

"Yup."

My grandmother Littlewood looks at me. Her eyes, her expression, suggest a table top with collapsible legs. She puts a hand on my cheek and says, "I'm afraid you must have heard your mother wrong, my dear. Your granddaddy didn't fly a Spitfire. No. He was a mechanic. He fixed the planes and made them fast. He was gone for most of the war, working. And your granddaddy, my husband of just a few years, died in an air raid in 1942. He was young and overworked, but it was his duty. We had to make those kinds of sacrifices. Endure loss. Now," she adds, leaning close to my ear. "It was your father, I believe, who flew in bombers. Yes. He flew Lancasters over France and Germany. He was a very young man, but we didn't know him yet. And he was shot down, my dear, and taken prisoner for much of the war. Now, perhaps you heard your mother wrong. Sometimes children hear things differently and make things up to make things better, like a dream. Do you think that's what you are doing, dear, making this up to make it better?"

I don't know what to say, my fingers grounding the Spitfire into the sand.

She adds a detail concerning my mother that I've stored in my mind all these years. She says, "I'll tell you a secret, but you mustn't tell your mother I told you this, just as you mustn't mention what I told you about your father. Do you promise?"

I promise.

"Cross your wee heart, dear."

I cross my wee heart.

"Hope to die, dear."

I hope to die.

"There have been times in your mother's life when she has been like a little child too, making things up to make things better. I don't pretend to know what makes your poor mother so sad, but she's always been a wee bit hard, dear, and sometimes she exaggerates the truth. Sometimes she tells what we call little white lies. It makes living with our loses less painful. Because she was just a baby when her father died and she never knew him, but I believe not knowing him has left a terrible little hole in her life. Sometimes there is sadness in life, dear, that is stronger than happiness and we can never get our wee selves back."

Through a few more conversations with my grandmother Littlewood (in the sandbox, on our walks, sneaking behind trees), I learn a little more about my father and his experience in the war. How he did fly a Lancaster but was shot down over France, in August of '42, just like my grandmother says. Even my mother, during some of our tea time talks (drunk and loose), adds to this same tale, though she insists my father flew a Spitfire and not a bomber. And she still mixes up the story of her father and my father and interchanges their names and styles, height and weight, and even goes so far as to refer to my father as her father one time, without noticing. How that father was shot down on his first and only bombing mission and taken prisoner by the Germans. How he spent the rest of the war behind barbed wire. A POW, my mother spells out on the kitchen table, using a finger. Three humiliating letters, she says, slurring the words.

What was I to do with this information and all the energy I had invested in listening to my mother's tales, then weighing them against my grandmother Littlewood's corrections? I could no longer look at my mother's face without seeing the bruised perimeter around her countenance. The sorrow, the absence. I could never press her on the matter of her alleged fictions, the various tricky shades of her tea time openings and closings. I listened but from a distance. A disordered habit. I learned to cloak myself when in her presence, like a man guarding an affair, the bite marks of his mistress. I watched, those few years with my mother at the kitchen table, as the world left her face. As the past and her words crept further and further apart. As she hardened and even her language (her *positively, absolutely, heavenly*) left her tongue. There were times, later in the years, when she'd look at me as if at a total stranger, a spy come in from the cold. I'd pour her a drink, hoping she'd recognize me, talk, throw me a bone, but years of alcohol had left us drifting in the inexpressible. My tongue hurt from holding back, and my own silence had become eerie. Misshaped.

7

ZEE STEPPED OUT OF THE basement, left his movie-of-the-day and joined me in the back yard. He curled up on the patio and lit a cigarette. He removed his shoes and socks and rolled up his fatigues. Three beers into the morning. Throughout the neighbourhood, air conditioners were humming. That, and the stillness of the heat, the hard haze.

"Beer?"

"No thanks."

"Come on."

"I'm done."

"Done?"

"That's right."

"As in, you're quitting the golden brew?"

"I've been sitting out here, days and nights, watching the sky, the weathers, the stars, and I've been thinking."

"About?"

"Feelings, the heart, the gut."

"That'll get you in trouble."

"Haven't we always been?"

"You're hardly what I'd call a classic drunk, Little Flower. Dear Mother, sure, she could drink herself into any one of a dozen moody characters. Father, well, on sentimental occasions, just to snuff out his inner life. Me, I'll confess a predilection for the golden brew, my road toward perfecting the self and what we might call spiritual insight. But you, it's more like a gazing into a well and dipping your fingers into magic waters, what, a few times a year when you really get pissed and stumble through the nights and wake up the next morning in the cemetery, mumbling something prophetic."

"Like I said, I'm tired of it. Tired of the spell."

"My gentle prediction: you'll never conquer it."

"I'll take that as a sincere vote of confidence. Thank you very much, sir."

"It's just too much a part of our blood, that's all I'm saying."

"A long line of drunks."

"A royal birthright, Little Flower. It's how we tap into the gods, through this luscious nectar. It links us with the pseudo miseries of the world and our past."

"You're the one who says I've got to forget the past."

"A white lie."

"Another birthright."

"There's an impressive list we've inherited, little man. Many hyper-materialistic disorders from which to choose. Chronic boredom, fatigue, jadedness, psychic-deadness, Ennui, consumer vertigo, fatness... good ole fashioned alienation."

"Dark nights, darker days," I said.

"You've got it, Little Flower. But this is good soul stuff, that's the way I see it. Which brings me to another delicate point of spiritual discourse. Travel. Where will it be? Rome? Athens? Or something completely out there, like Thailand, and getting ourselves a cheap, easy lay."

"I'm out of work just now."

"I've got cash. My treat. And you've always said you'd like to see France, where our blessed grandpapa fought and lost his soul. So open your mind, cock your soul. Travel is all that's left. Everything else is a sham. Besides, tell people you're off on a journey and it's like you take on this star quality, become an instant celebrity, like a god, a cartoon character, forever young."

"Cartoon character?" I said, genuinely curious about this one.

"Cartoon characters are our modern day version of the old gods and saints. They never age. Mickey Mouse, Donald Duck, Bugs Bunny. They never lose their vigour, they never really die. And they never really grow up either. Why the hell do you think so many people run to Disney Land, Little Flower? It's our new world Jerusalem, our Vatican, our Mecca. I mean, you don't really believe in the old gray God Jehovah, do you?"

Good question.

"Now, back to the matter of your soul," Zee said and winked.

"What about it?"

"You drinking enough water, getting your eight cups a day?"

"I do what I can."

"Because you look somewhat parched for a guy who's been sitting outside for days and days. What colour is your urine?"

"My urine?"

"Doctors of the Renaissance studied urine for its visible and invisible properties, spiritual as well as physical. It was easy to see in the urine of a man or a woman the state of their body and soul. A rich looking urine, all gold and..."

"Don't tell me," I interrupted, "a sign of high art."

"No, no, you'd be surprised, little man," my brother pursued. "A rich looking urine, all our fabled gold, is really a sign of dehydration. The darker the urine, the worse it actually is in the world of soul. Yellow urine is a sign of the dry soul to the Renaissance doctor. Yellow urine under the modern day microscope is simple de-hydration. No God involved."

"What's the tale of a good piss?" I smiled.

"Clear. Absolutely pristine. To the point our urine is almost transparent. Spiritually, that's what you want. That's what the masters teach. Mr. Ghandi purified his stuff and drank it. In the Great War, a urine soaked rag placed over the mouths and nostrils saved many a good soldier from the terrible gases. But to the average North American Joe, we urinate a fine yellow piss and we think it's a sign of great wealth and appetite. But it's fool's gold, I tell you, a Confidence Man's potion, a pathetic diet of sugar coated liquid that's advertised under the guise of quenching our thirst, when all we're really doing is dulling the imagination. That's all I'm saying, little man, because you look somewhat dry and pasty, if you want the truth."

"Please don't turn this wasted moment into another one of your quasi-therapeutic sessions."

"Humour me, will you?"

"Don't I always?"

"Stitches, little man. I'm always bent double over when I'm around your psychological brew. For example, if I were to say the word *soul* to you, how would you respond? A one word response, please."

"Not this game."

"It'll be good for you, mon frère."

"Can't I just defer?"

"Not on your shining life. You opened up the heavenly vault with this little idea of yours, this giving up of the holy brew. Now it's up to you to verbalize the temperate zones of your decision and get to the guts of your choice."

"How about we head out for a burger and fries instead?"

"You know the drill, little man. I say to you *soul* and you say..."

"Weary. I say, weary. Is that good enough?"

"No. I say *soul* and you say?"

"Ah, betwixt."

"Soul?"

"Unquotable."

"Soul?"

"Barbarian consumer."

"Soul?"

"Shoeless. Lethargic. Myopic..."

"Don't get ahead of the game, little J."

"Just trying to speed up the process."

"Soul is about slowness, like slow, loving sex. Now, can we get back to the session?"

"Be my guest."

"Try this word. Death?"

"Ah, unrelenting harshness."

"God?"

"Unrelenting beauty."

"The Jewish question?"

"I'm not Jewish," I said. "So it's probably wise I don't attempt a perspective from which I know nothing about."

"Nevertheless, imagine," Zee implored. "Again, the Jewish question?"

"A good reason shame is this century's daily bread."

"Auschwitz?"

"Never been there."

"AUSCHWITZ?"

"A good reason this century should end."

"Which brings us to the meat of naming your present existential disorder. Take your holy pick, Little Francis, from the aforementioned list. You know, fatigue? Jadedness? Ennui?"

"Sorry," I said, "but are you not listing your own disorders there, Herr Doktor?"

"My apologies, indeed. Just got off track, a little reverse transference," Zee said, adjusting his posture on the patio and cracking open another beer.

8

THERE WERE LARGE SYSTEMS OF cloud cover by mid-afternoon, as if the city were under a big top. Zee and I held our tongues to the sky, but there was little relief or rain. Nothing offered by clowns or jugglers or trapeze artists. These systems were serious. Biblical. Impossible to talk through and around. Clouds pushed in, darkened, then passed over by 5 p.m. Only the humidity remained, repossessing the hour and scouring our skin.

I oftentimes saw my father in Zee's face. A sky-scraper glare. The ability to reflect one expression but mean another. Zee could escape our childhood home, journey the country, the globe, douse himself in all the booze and women he desired, but he couldn't escape having to carry the features of our father; the slope of the forehead, the jaw, the dark, almost neolithic complexion. The old man's eyebrow.

My father's mood was a double agent and worked on the house whether he was home or not. The mood curled into a chair like a fox or attached itself like a listening device beneath table tops. Hours before my father arrived home from work, the mood would precede him, slipping in under the front door like a police summons spelling out his grievances, his commands. Knowing his arrival was immanent (even on days when we were certain he was out of town, across the sea on business), I felt my back tighten, the invisible mood moving from room to room, checking out corners, under chipped paint. Just as suddenly, the mood would shape shift and my father would be the image of man having returned from work, now sitting in the living room, in his suit, enjoying a scotch and soda and reading his newspaper. The mood sliding into dusk.

Every moment with my father felt like 5:30 a.m., soldier-time. Like those last slow motion moments in the trench, shivering before going over the top. My father with a captain's whistle, signalling charge. But take a look into the mud and boot prints of other men's lives leading the way and you'd see my father there, hunkering, using his men as cover from the machine gun fire, trembling all the way into battle. Because even in moments of sheer stillness around my father's mood, it was his quiet tremble that I read. Not even five heart attacks and a sixth that would eventually do him in (I was eighteen, my first summer at the cemetery) might rid my father of the tremble. His right hand that always shook. Not as an aftermath of his war experience, but as if the war was still there, present in that hand, raging.

If I served the early years in the wing of my mother's domestic world, Zee was captive to my father's order. Zee did put in his time with my mother, at an earlier age, scrubbing bathroom floors, tubs and toilets, fixing her a tea time martini, but by the time I was ready and walking, Zee had become my father's handy man, a de facto appendage. A boy of seven spring cleaning, flushing out items from the garage, cleaning eaves troughs and storm windows, trimming hedges, vines, washing down the walkway and car, scraping and painting areas of the house that had been ravaged by winter storms. Not even injury (there were a few falls for my brother, from a ladder, two broken arms and a separated shoulder) would stop my father from putting Zee to work.

"You still have one hand, one good arm," my father said. "I've seen men with much less and still put in a full day's work."

Not even a brief visit from a social worker (there was a doctor's report, an inquiry into Zee's broken arms and the separated shoulder, all in the space of a year) would stop my father from leaning on my brother as his other, more trusting limb.

When the social worker suggested to my father that it might not be safe for such a young boy to be up on a 32' ladder cleaning the eaves, removing and replacing the storm windows, and that perhaps my father might want to consider holding the ladder for young Zee, or tying it off, my father offered his glare, that above-this-world, Mt. Olympus stare.

"I'll take that into consideration," he said, stepping back into the house and closing the door. The power of his dismissal was quick and to the bone. Even the social worker shrank away from my father's presence, unsure about what had just happened, perhaps sensing only what I always sensed: a ton of air pushing down at your shoulder blades, locking you in place.

Then there was the belt. My mother (dear Mum) would take the belt from the back of the hall closet and hand it to my father. And my father (after the social worker had left) would escort my brother to his bedroom and show it to him. The leather belt. An inch thick. Worn and venomous. When my parents wanted something done (an errand a deed a household chore) they would often leave the belt on the dining room table, coiled, a threat against us ever attempting to say no. The belt had been passed on, we were told (My god was this history? An actual story? The truth?), from our father's father's father. Imagine. The travels, the indignity, the violence. So corporeal punishment might remain a constant guest in the house, with its own ancestral seat, next to the belt.

I remember Zee emerging from his bedroom after having received the belt. His eyes swollen and red, his face closed like a fist. He fought back his tears in front of me, but shook, unable to breathe through the desolation. All I really saw in his face was that he would never know pleasure without first experiencing a form of humiliation, and for this to eventually turn on others. An inevitable transference.

"Do whatever he says," Zee warned me of our father. "It's when he starts to grin that he whips you harder."

I clung to his advice. Complied. I avoided my father's glare and moon.

Later, Zee would confess to throwing himself down from the ladder on two occasions, aiming himself arm and shoulder first at the ground, a human torpedo, when my father was turned away. These efforts at injury would only quicken my father's resolve. Bring out the belt. Only when my father suffered a first heart attack and then a second (both while overseas, both on business), did he begin to weaken, ordering Zee from his recovery bed. By this time, Zee had also found the will to escape into the ravine, at times with me in tow and a few beers he had lifted from the basement refrigerator. And by this time, I had been enlisted into my father's service, learning on my own how to prop myself from a 32' ladder while cleaning windows and eaves troughs, removing storm windows and replacing them with the seasons. My work was diligent and haunted by images of the belt.

I worked long, hard hours, through every kind of storm and temperature. I did not oppose my father or question his need to pull order out of chaos. If there was a spot on a window I'd missed, I was more than willing to go back up that ladder and scrub and scrub until the spot was dismissed. There was no time for play or a prayer for rain in my father's presence. We did not attach meaning to the stars. Absolute work was our religion. A conspiracy against the heart.

"I want you to be prepared for the worst in life," my father actually said to me a few days after heart attack number three. "Prosperity becomes complacent and turns to rot. If you are prepared for hardships in life, if you have a trade, something to do with your hands, you'll find yourself able to work through times of economic depression. Even if it means cleaning windows for a living or raking leaves. Because believe me, a time of hardship will come. You will see."

The image of my father's hands, that lone right hand with its tremble, always shocked me as a boy, saddened me. There were times during our chores when simple objects (a paint brush, a rake, a hammer) would slip from my father's right handed grip, and he'd stand there, looking down. I didn't know if it was disbelief or embarrassment that caused him to pause and look down at the fallen tool. His eyes were silent. As stern as he was, he was flesh. He'd stare at his right hand as if it was a refugee, waiting each tremble out. I'd bend and pick up the fallen item. When he took the tool back in hand, his left hand now, I'd see the glimmer of surprise in his face, as if no one had ever noticed his trembling right hand, as if he really believed this, felt this. The truth is, I picked up whatever had slipped from his grip because I feared him. Because if I pleased him, I could ward off his anger. The belt. I had no more power against his anger than a straw house in the wind. Nothing could hold back his painful view of the world, his mighty tremble.

9

EVERY OTHER SATURDAY, MY FATHER takes Zee and I by our hands and leads us to St. Clair and Yonge for a haircut at Jack's Barber Shop and then to lunch at Fran's. It's a good thirty minute walk. My father wears his three piece suit, a perfect cut. By the end of the walk, the pencil thin moustache riding my father's upper lip is glistening with perspiration, a slow flood he pats down with a white handkerchief. At Jack's Barber Shop, my father stands behind my brother and I, each of us in turn saddled in a huge, red leather barber chair, our small faces appearing like two small moons over the horizon line of the barber shop mirror. The shop smells of industrial soap and stale hair. Jack the Barber works the required buzz cut, shaving our hair as close to the scalp as possible. This, in an age when hair is being celebrated as a virtue, hippy hair wild as reeds. My father is the interior minister of our hair and watches us in the mirror. He admires the sound of the razor in Jack the Barber's hand, its mechanical pulse working into our scalps, currents of electricity seeping through our skulls, rearranging brain cells, as if whole species of thought were being eradicated. We walk back out into whatever the weather, exposed and mute, itching the back of our hard, sore scalps. Only a hint of blondish shadow to show.

Lunch at Fran's is as close to a celebration as we bring ourselves as a family, minus my mother. My father knows the waitresses by name and always greets them in a well-meaning manner, bowing his head and re-introducing his two boys each week.

"Sally, you remember Zachary, and little Jonathan," he says. "Boys, say hello."

Hello hello, yes, hello...

"And what do you think this week?" my father asks of our waitress, referring to our fresh buzz cuts.

"Shiny as the moon."

"Fit for service."

"Two perfect peaches."

If a new waitress happens upon our table, my father takes out his small day book and a pencil, licks its tip, and writes down the waitress's name, as if a future Christmas card might be in order for her. My father's mood is a quick change artist, swaying in the company of other women. Good cop, bad cop. To the outside world, he is a gentleman, courteous, but for the beat and tremble of his infamous right hand. No matter the occasion, he can't conceal it or deflect attention away from that shake. Waitresses are always careful to serve him on his left side, positioning glasses or utensils in places where that trembling hand might not jump and knock something over. As if these uniformed women, nurse-like, attentive, recognize the exile in that hand. The ghost.

Food time. Zee and I order thick cheeseburgers and french fries, and a Shirley Temple to drink.

"Straight up," Zee says, like a movie star. "With a twist. And easy on Shirley."

The non-alcoholic beverages are served with a small plastic sword and a maraschino cherry and slice of orange to spear and suckle. An explosion of sweet cherry syrup in our mouths.

My father orders a cheese and mushroom omelette, cooked in butter. He has a beer, followed by coffee with his meal. He glances over the Saturday *Globe and Mail*. Zee and I sword fight with our plastic weapons, until my father tells us to stop. At times a waitress (Oh, how naive) will give us extra cherries on a side dish that Zee and I set back into, stab and exchange our spoils, until my father will again tell us to calm down. That stern eyebrow. If we are not quiet, there will be no blueberry pie with ice cream, he admonishes us. We sit up immediately, unsure of our facial tics. Humour leaves our play. We learn early that to please my father might add a few precious seconds to our life expectancy. We leave the restaurant each Saturday with blue teeth and tongues, licking our silence.

Saturday afternoons, winter Saturdays, means the movies. It means walking back to the house on Hudson Dr. and going down into the basement and unlocking the steel door to my father's bunker/screening room. It's a room within a room, hidden behind the laundry room. A room of double lined cinder blocks and a lone overhead light, a single bulb swinging from a thick brown cord. This is my father's refuge, where he disappears at night, alone, or with my grandfather on occasion. One wall is lined with small shelves that are stocked with canned goods and dry foods and jugs of water, which my father empties and re-fills on a regular basis. In his mind (right up there front and centre) is the belief that a Third World War (perhaps more devastating, more end-of-the-world than the previous two) will occur at any time. Any time, he stresses, and the bombs will fall. This, when it's already the age of Vietnam, which, according to my father, is a war that doesn't involve the whole world, but is a necessary war nonetheless. Because those Communists must be held back, suppressed and destroyed. Otherwise, we'll be doomed, he says, we'll all be living like Commies. Or worse, Zee and I might be called to action, he says, put on the front lines of a foreign country and positioned to fend off the tanks and bombs. Then we'll know why he never talks about the war. *Never.* Saying this, I realize he's actually mentioning something about the war, his war. It stops there, of course, right there.

A second wall in my father's basement bunker is reserved for his tools, the hammers and saws and nuts and bolts that distinguish his particular brand of civilization from another. My father is proud of his tools and room, his creature comforts. He actually looks normal in this room and winds himself down like a man throwing off his skin. That is, until he lets his films roll.

What really dominates the room is my father's very own private 16mm film projector. His pet, his true pride. The projector sits on a high aluminum stand and looms like a headless saint on a pedestal. Its lens is covered in a fine leather cloth. The machine is clean as bone and smells of polish and metal. Behind the projector, lining a third wall, is my father's personal collection of reel-to-reel films. Silent films. Early talkies. Black and white beauties. The Celluloid current depicting our rampage through the early twentieth century. *Nosferatu, The General, Modern Times.* Endless Keystone Cop films. I remember Zee in a first trance, hardly exhaling when a film is showing. We sit on movie house seats, a small row, that my father had purchased at an auction. We sit, the three of us (my mother never joins us, never likes the room in the basement, a bunker without windows) in the flickering click and beam of the projector light. We pass my father's homemade popcorn (smothered in butter and salt) back and forth, munching and watching, as whatever chosen film bounces off the screen that is fastened to a fourth and final wall of cinder blocks. I can feel the heat of the projector at my back, the mechanical rap. There, beneath the city, on the edge of a ravine. It's a time when I feel momentarily safe at my father's side. A time away from his strict world, as if I might fly like a moth into the light of the screen and wing along on gray clouds of celluloid.

By mid-afternoon, I tire and feel myself descending as if through a film of myself, a dream. I fall through the space of my father's bunker room and land with my head on my father's thigh. Do I fall there on purpose, ease like a sly cat around the chair, onto his thigh, or does he unconsciously pull me there and allow me this rare, uncharted affection. I don't know, but I feel his free hand, the hand without the tremble, brush across my scalp. As if that hand is the alpha male, there to protect its kin. It's just a flutter, I know, a wordless exchange, but I have to sneak this gesture into my heart, just to remember, just as I sneak a peek into my father's face and see him for the lined, older man he is. The thin hair, graying at the temples, as if under a mat of fog. I look into my father's eyes and see his habit of also disappearing into films and other characters' journeys; I see his strange attention to the projected world, as if the story on the screen is the humour and hurt he cannot afford to show. A Charlie Chaplin scuttle, a Buster Keaton doe eyed stare; the bent of war. These images burn into my retinas and become intertwined with images of my father's face settling like silt in my imagination, as if this is the dark potency from which I now speak of him and unfold memory.

What I still see are images that belong to film footage of the Great War. My first taste. My father looks intently at this footage, quick cut clippings of men scrambling over trench tops and disappearing into mud and mist, or left hanging from barbed wire out in no man's land. The Somme, Ypres, Vimy Ridge. All these lands enter me, bombed and wiped clean of trees. The long hikes of men, uphill, into enemy gunfire. All this I witness in my father's eyes, as if he is there, in that mud, combing through his own potent silt for answers to time and soul and history. Sometimes I imagine these war films are my father's form of séance, how he works to contact his own father's original form and spirit, on film, and not just the ghost of the man in the attic. There is no denying the contortions in my father's face and eyes during these films. The slow motion jerk of soldiers and horses and gun carriages. Men marching in peculiar lines through ruins of villages, houses levelled. Men carrying coffins draped in Union Jacks. Men carrying men. A statue of the Virgin that has been hit by an explosive. She is left swaying from a high church tower, at an almost impossible angle. Men pass beneath her, assured, and tip their helmets or raise a rifle or a bandaged arm, then turn to the camera and smile from behind their toothless grins in those early years of the cinema when perhaps the self-consciousness that seems to dominate so much of modern day film had not yet evolved in the human face. Those early faces, the expressions of battle and fatigue and waiting (always the waiting), convey a sense of wonder, or innocence, as if these men truly believe they are somehow peering into a lens and delivering their images clear back across the Atlantic, through home towns, ports and prairies, straight into a loved one's eyes. My father absorbs this world, suffers its silent footage. If he speaks at all in those hours in the basement bunker, it is out-of-sync, like a character in a film whose mouth moves but his voice is held back by an error between soundtrack and the visual. Technical difficulty, a stubborn glitch.

Saturday afternoon at the movies is not complete without my father's home movie of the bombs going off. His attempt at history lessons. The only full sounds he allows in the bunker room, blasting our ears. No talk. Only the whizz bangs of WWI, whistling and exploding. The shells of WWII falling from the Lancasters, nailing a mapped world far below. Cities like pin pricks bursting into flames. Dresden. Hamburg. Jump cut to the Atom bomb. Hiroshima and the mushroom cloud. Humans turned into shadows in mid-stride. I remember tensing and covering my ears against the thunder of destruction, the film looping and re-looping, wisdom spliced. I remember my father pulling my hands away from my ears, saying,

"Listen to this, listen and learn. It's the only way you might understand the horrors the world has known."

Watching the bombs land and burst, I'm not sure what I'm supposed to learn. Perhaps how close human ingenuity and human darkness are intertwined.

When these films conclude on those Saturday afternoons, my father sits up, like a contortionist unwinding himself. He stretches his neck, then is quickly startled by the little pet (me) lying against his thigh. How has he allowed this momentary lapse in attention, this awkward affection? He lifts me away and shakes his arms, as if a small insect has crawled up his sleeve.

My father was a man who spent his days denying himself beauty. Did he not deserve such gifts, did he not recognize this grace? I don't know. He chose bitterness and restriction over joy and an open field. He crouched like a small child behind the mind-wall of himself. I will not see this until he is very old and thin and wired to bone. A 'Do Not Trespass' sign hanging round his neck. As if what had been buried beneath his chest, his warring past, had once been diseased. As if he manoeuvred through his sore heart in remission, always fearing the disease might flare and consume him. This, to me, is the truth of his unease and history, but you can't keep history down, staunch it or re-direct its course. Like compost for the soul, history appears again and again, in a garden, a work of art, a fist. It shows itself in a voice that won't stop trembling, generations later.

Here. Now.

It wasn't until years later, when sitting with my father at his hospital bedside, in the days before his own death (hoping he might summon a meagre sliver of energy and reveal his story), that a few things became clear to me: There are tragedies a man will guard with his life, silence, then guard with his death. Not even six heart attacks will give that man cause to break through and speak. Even after his death, I kept searching for my father's voice, as if tuning a dial on a short wave radio, passing over a blur of static, echoes of resistance. Is that you, Paris? Berlin! Come in father!

10

ZEE STOOD AND GAZED INTO the sky, a snap of wind in the air. He stretched his arms, his face gleaming with sweat. He took off his t-shirt and fatigues, only a pair of boxer shorts between himself and the evening sun. He breathed in, held the breath, then released it. He crossed the yard and stopped at the small garden shed by the stone wall. Reaching inside the shed, he rummaged around, moving items, then stepped back out, holding a garden hose and sprinkler. He walked across the yard. At the back of the house, he hooked up the hose to the outdoor faucet, then stepped out into the centre of the yard and set the sprinkler down on the grass. He walked back to the house and turned on the faucet.

The water gurgled and worked through the air in the hose, grew in intensity and began spitting through the sprinkler head, oozing, then arcing in clear lines over the back yard, away from my brother's body. Zee stood still, eyes closed, arms at his sides. The water pushed back and sprayed over his body, shot up from the earth and soaked him down. He stood still a good ten seconds, the sprinkler arcing toward his body and away, water cascading and forming a pool in the grass at his feet. He opened his mouth and swallowed the flying water, the lazy water.

"What's your favourite flower these days?" Zee asked, gargling through water bubbles that had formed on his lips.

"Oh, I'm partial to the lilac."

"Technically speaking, I think that's a shrub, Little Flower."

"Well, I don't mind the iris. It's always had a certain flare, a cunning light I've admired."

"Too impressionistic, old world, mon frère. And much too domestic."

"How about the Monk's Hood, or the Indian Pipe flower? Very rare, very mysterious," I said.

"Right then. Imagine this… imagine you're the Monk's Hood," Zee smiled and picked up the sprinkler, guiding the water in hand and soaking me down where I sat on the grass.

I didn't move. The heat. The hour. Water working through my hair and over my limbs. I closed my eyes and concentrated on the water like a thousand small tongues touching off each of my pores.

11

SUNDAY MEANS CHURCH. IT MEANS my mother's voice rousing the family early, followed by a quick scurry through the house, a wet comb across my scalp and dressing up in my dark blue suit, solid black tie and penny loafers. We're not to have breakfast before Mass. That means Sunday is also an empty stomach. Time is bent. It means my grandfather will emerge from his attic room, wind like an eel down the stairs, on weekly leave from his self-imposed isolation.

My bedroom is directly beneath my grandfather's room. There are nights when I hear him shift his frail weight in bed. Nights when he paces the upper floor, goes to the bathroom, wretches, coughs, breaks wind, or shuffles half way down the stairs, stops, scratches the wall, then turns back up the stairs, a migrant shadow. I remember sounds of glass breaking, pages being torn, fugitive groans. Deeper nights when he screams as if in a falling dream, and I wake, startled, as if in a falling dream of my own. Then I hear my father pound through the hall and up the stairs, to my grandfather's room. I hear their whispers, an aching exchange between the two men. Then gradual calm, their secrets closing. The walls of my bedroom are painted dark blue in tone but not bold enough to keep back the flood of sound, the night-screams that seep through my ceiling. These visitations of sound only serve to press me further into the night, as if into a place in a forest that has been exhausted, stumps chewed to pulp. I close my eyes to this world, blood pounding. This is futile, I know. The more I turn away, the more the fear of sound rattles me. A constant tug at the ceiling.

I imagine my grandfather's face as a map to the century, broken into two spheres; that half of the world that has been bombed and gutted (Europe, Asia, the Middle East) and that half that is still considered to be wilderness. Our supposed half. The first scar on my grandfather's face travels from the left temple down to the jawbone, and curves like a shallow trough. In areas the scar is still raw, its whiteness blinding. Not even vultures, I imagine, will dare fly over that scar, its valley of death. Behind the temple scar, the view is flat and arid. This is because of my grandfather's missing ear, a second trough of scar. No cut of breeze crosses here. There is a sense that if you speak too loudly into this ear, you might trigger a small bomb that is still embedded just beneath the levelled flesh, as if just beneath the surface of his emotions. One must revert back to a whisper when speaking to my grandfather, as if each word belongs to a bomb disposal unit, working with clippers and artificial lighting to defuse the tiny explosive device that has been buried in that ear ever since the conclusion of the Great War.

A second, shallow scar carries out like a creek from the corner of his left eye, drops down the cheek, veers left, then sharply joins the main temple-to-jaw-bone scar. The two scars form a delicate U-shape, a crag. One's eyes pause here, as if tiring from the journey and no longer wanting to look, but looking, caught, and having to furnish the pain, wondering what happened in this crag. What demon dropped what bomb (a whizz bang, a cluster bomb, something new and dirty just off the assembly line) that left that kind of disproportionate damage? You look at my grandfather's face and know the military is off in a desert, experimenting with lab rats and clay busts, watching pieces shatter and disassemble, predicting how their enemy might one day come to appear. Deciding the chill of the century, the warring dramas.

The second, shallow scar harbours a variety of colour—crimson flowing into rust and a grainy yellow-green, skin and blood hardened there, as if the scar has undergone years of ultraviolet activity. There is a last blue flare that works through the scar like a summer storm over a prairie flat, electric in intent.

Otherwise, my grandfather's eyes are blue and serene, and offer his only sense of gentleness and surrender. That, and the right side of his face that is soft and unscarred, like a section of landscape buffered by clear rivers.

Sunday mornings, before church, he appears at the bottom of the main staircase, shadow slow. He's dressed in a dark brown suit. It has wide lapels and hangs from his frame like a drape pulled by polar forces. Pinned to the right lapel is a small Canadian maple leaf. Later I will learn all soldiers of the Great War wore these pins on their army uniforms, distinguishing themselves from the enemy and the mud. My grandfather stands in the hallway with his arms at his sides, hands still and spare. Occasionally, as I pass beneath him on those Sunday mornings, I'll sense his hand reaching out, a finger brushing through my short hairs. He labours through his breathing, and says my name, as if to remind himself of who I am.

"Jonathan," he blinks. "Little Jonathan Francis, Little Flower."

If the weather is good, we leave the house on Hudson Dr. at 9:30 and make the fifteen minute walk to Our Lady of Perpetual Help, our neighbourhood Catholic church (Zee refers to it as OLPH = Old Lady's Piss House). On the walk, my grandfather might reach for my hand. I'll feel his tender grip, the first of an interlaced current working through my palm. At times, he'll grip me harder, while groping for his step over a leaf or stone or winter's ice. I'm never certain if he's leading me or if I'm leading him. Our walks are silent. My mother and father a few paces ahead, walking with that sense of ownership. Zee is just behind them, taking short, quick steps, kicking stones. My grandfather and I always arrive at church a minute or two behind the others, the three of them waiting, arms folded. The world on their chins.

We sit as a family at the back of the church, occupying the last pew. My mother insists Zee and I sit up straight and keep our focus on the altar and the image of the Christ crucified behind the altar, high on the back wall, nailed. I look at His chalk hands and feet, the singular crimson wound in His side. The angle of His head suggesting sleep. Thin, exposed hips. There is no impression of earth on His body, and I sometimes think that any Jesus worth His salt should have more dirt on his skin, sweat stains, hair mangled. My mother says this clean Jesus is the reason we're here, every Sunday, to remember what He did for us. How He came to save us through His blood and resurrection, how He died so young, how He left us picture book images of loaves and fish, bread and wine, a desert world far removed from our back pew. How admitting to sin brought us closer to Him.

During our silent years of attendance, I remember the strange pleasure of the Psalms and gospels, the prophets, the rigour of the Beatitudes, sweet incense wafting through the air. I remember the shuffle of feet. Zee poking me in the ribs. Dry coughs. Yawns forced back inside. My empty stomach growling. I remember my mother whispering into my ear, saying how impressive the priests are, how careful and deliberate they are. At the exchange of peace, my mother tells me to stand and shake hands within our back pew reach. I remember taking the hands of strangers, various styles of handshakes, squeezes, the fast release, the word *peace* trickling into my ears. I remember eyes looking away, quickly, as if there is little of the exchange we might take with us like fruit and sell at market. I remember my father and grandfather never kneeling during Mass, but sitting still, taut, looking straight ahead. And my mother whispering into my ear, 'it's because they're too proud to kneel, to bow'. That's why she has Zee and I kneeling at the appropriate times during the Mass, that we might learn our place in the sacred world, down low, heads bowed, hands clasped in prayer. It's also good practice for our cleaning duties at home, on hands and knees, scrubbing floors and toilets. Our sacred vocation.

At communion, our family splits up. My father and grandfather leave the back pew, step outside, and share a cigarette. They never go up to the altar and receive the thin, dry wafer that is the Christ's supposed body. "Because," my father once admits, "your grandfather and I are not really Catholics. We're Anglican. This is your mother's house." It's only later (again through secret conversations with my grandmother Littlewood, followed by some of my mother's drunken tea time slips of tongue) that I learn of the quiet deal that had been struck between my mother and father: She will get to take us to her Catholic church and raise us in her old faith, and he will get to pick our schools, in the public system, and honour what must be his old faith.

While my father and grandfather stand outside the church and share a cigarette, my mother takes Zee and I at the elbows and guides us toward the altar and the priest. This man in royal garb, with the bread and the pink smile. My mother takes communion on her tongue, the one time she makes herself vulnerable to human contact. Because priests, she impresses upon us, are spotless lambs, holy cleansing agents, the Ajax of the heavenly vaults. In the days before my brother and I reach the age of consent and first communion, my mother will ask the presiding priest to bless Zee and I. This he does, placing a thick white hand on our foreheads and drawing the sign of the cross with a stubby thumb. A quick exchange, a matter-a-fact-pulse. After the priest has made the sign of the cross, I find myself rubbing the brand on my forehead, as if all that has been bestowed is an itch. My mother then leads Zee and I to a side altar, the Virgin Mary's private grotto, where each of us light a single candle and offer up a prayer to the Virgin. I look up to her polished, non-flowering gaze. She isn't a woman who appears to me to have undergone the pangs of birth. I feel myself stepping back from her at these times of private prayer, only to feel my mother's hand tug me closer. I don't know what it is about this particular Virgin image, as if she's been washed in formaldehyde, but she frightens me more than she astonishes me.

"Pray to her always," my mother whispers to me in the Virgin's presence, changed. "She will keep you from sin. She will be there at your hour of death. She has been praying for her children for hundreds of years, lifting tiny souls to God. Never forget her."

Standing before her, I can't help but think that it's too early in my life to honour someone that old, who appears that young, that polished. I pray anyway, unsure of the prayer's arc. I pray because the fear of falling out of her favour is greater than the welcome I do not yet understand.

Over the years, I move through this strange faith in various shades and hungers. I confess something of love and importance grows in me after all. Something innate, stirring. Even at such a young age, even through the fear, I sense a power. My faith travels this way and that, as if in search of a cure or an original text I might flip through to check modern vernacular against ancient speech. There is always a part of me like the moon between phases, when it comes to tracking my faith. As a child, I'm the hermit, living in the presence of a cave painting that has just been unearthed. Curls of colour pass through me, reddened by mortality. Because I've listened to so many parables about death and dying and transformation, about sowers of seed and treasure and the raising of the dead, and there I am, wrapped in this faith's odd, mysterious placenta. It appears words from the altar move within and find in me the longing of the child. Sitting in church, listening to Mass, I see myself as the one in the family for whom a space for a story is suddenly important. I am the vessel into which they all pour themselves, remember themselves. My grandfather, you see, will soon die and his spirit will wander into my hermit's cave and like wet cloth set itself down. This I anticipate in our back pew. My faith having to expand, my moon open. My father will stop going to church altogether after my grandfather's death, regardless of the many heart attacks that warn him otherwise. My mother will insist he must work to save himself. What else is his heart demanding of him? Constantly breaking him open, or apart, so that God might set him straight. My father's spirit will enter me long before his actual death, travel down a shoulder-wide darkness, into my cave of faith. So, I take on our secrets, our private affairs. A part of me is all grown up before my time. Though it will take me years to conjure beauty in this, realize a painted meaning. Because if there is anything I've learned, anything of value I've loved and lost and must impart, it has been returned through the making of beauty. Beauty is essential for heartbreak to conceive.

That brings me back to Zee and the day his rebellious spirit entered me fully. Put on some music, lit a cigarette, and took a permanent seat in my soul.

At twelve and a half, shortly before Zee is to be confirmed, he escapes the back pew to become an altar boy. He says he wants to be where the action is, closer to the source. It's a career move that is short lived, lasting a single, cool winter and spring. Until he witnesses (as he says) that the changing of wine into blood and bread into flesh is nothing but a little hocus-pocus and slight-of-hand. He begins spoiling the ritual, spilling the wine, tripping over his robe, and inviting his eventual firing. This brings quick shame to our family, to my mother. The beginning of their end. This is also the beginning of young Zee gaining his voice, whipping his tongue into unholy shape. This is aided by his new found love of music, Hendrix, Young, and Dylan, especially. My mother, in her shame, takes Zee (I'm right behind) to see the priest. She wants the Father in charge of Zee's confirmation to explain her son's sudden irreverence, his talking back. The conversation is short but enlightening. Another tome for my soul.

"Is he clumsy around the house?" the priest asks my mother. I can't keep my eye off his wavy blonde hair and the leather sandals, his toes wiggling beneath the desk.

"There have been some falls, but that was years ago. He's absolutely agile and a wonderful athlete at school," my mother says, sounding like another woman, a shadow-self who hasn't had a drink in years. "He won a handwriting contest and a spelling bee last year. His script is very handsome."

"Is he prone to fantasy?" the priest asks, hands folded on the desk top, thumbs wiggling in tune with his toes.

"I know he plays in the ravine," my mother reveals. "I know he plays war games and returns home dirty. Of course, he's not allowed back into the house until he cleans himself off with the garden hose. That's just how it is in our house. Cleanliness is next to godliness."

"I see," the priest says, pondering. "And how are things at home, inside the house?"

"Absolutely fine," my mother says, resolved.

"Pssst... is anyone at all aware of the fact that I am sitting right here, listening," a voice says from the sidelines, a voice belonging to my brother.

The priest turns his attention to Zee.

"Well, young man, indeed you are here. And what do you have to say about this matter? Are you nervous up there, near the altar?"

"No."

"Because sometimes when we're in the presence of the sacred, our nerves can get the better of us. I know that used to happen to me."

"It's not that."

"Is it a matter of the robe? Is the robe too long for you?"

"No. It's nothing like that."

"Is there anything you can think of?"

"I'm just bored with the whole thing, that's all."

"Bored."

"Yes," Zee says. "As in, I'm not having fun."

"Fun," my mother blurts, winding her voice back into the mother I know. The angry one, the feverish one.

"Yes, fun." My brother prods the moment. "I think it should be fun up there, and it's not. It's too serious, too formal."

"Fun," the priest smiles. "I've never thought of it like that."

"Well, it should be fun," Zee says, eyeing my mother, then the priest. "It should be a part of the baptismal rite, to have fun."

I can see my mother twisting in her seat, hardening.

"I just don't want you to judge my family by my son's actions at the altar, Father," my mother says, with a tone aimed to please.

"Not to worry," the priest says. "He seems to me to be a boy well aware of the fact that he is now responsible for his own actions."

"But he hasn't been confirmed yet," my mother says. "Not really saved."

"Saved. I see, I see," the priest says and sits up.

"Is there anything you can do," my mother continues. "Tell him. Make him believe."

To which Zee says, "I don't believe in your God."

My mother turns and glares at my brother. Her expression is grim, and related to the belt.

"What did you say?"

"You heard me," says my brother.

"How could you... here," my mother says, lowering her voice.

"Listen," Zee presses, "I just don't think my baptism took hold, that's all. So why should I be confirmed?"

"How dare you talk like that in here," my mother says, losing patience. "In front of the Father like this."

"I'm tired of your belief. I'm tired of going to church. I'm tired of everything you make us do," Zee says, grinning. "And besides, I have my own belief now."

"You...what?"

I notice the priest move forward in his seat.

"Perhaps," he says quietly, "we might inquire into this new belief. Tell us about it."

My mother shoots a look at the priest, not pleased.

"Well," Zee says, looking at me, then back to my mother and the priest, willing to take his chance. "Have you heard of Bob Dylan?"

The priest smiles. "'*Lay lady lay, lay across my big brass bed*,'" he says, almost singing. "That Bob Dylan?"

"Right," Zee says, eyes bright and surprised, finding in the priest a kindred spirit. "That's who I believe in. I believe in Bob Dylan and The Band. I believe in Pink Floyd and the Dark Side of the Moon. I believe in Van the man Morrison and his Moondance."

"You're not serious," my mother says, shifting in tone to that of her kitchen world.

"Absolutely," my brother says, mocking my mother.

"And this belief, it feeds you well," the priest asks, curious but smiling.

"Right here," my brother says and pats his belly.

"You're not taking his side, are you?" My mother rips at the priest.

"At his age, important questions begin to arise and force themselves on the mind and soul. I've seen this with my nephew, and perhaps there's no harm in hearing your son out."

"This is not why I came here," says my mother. "Absolutely not why I came here. To have you encourage him like this. I'm the one who puts the offering in the basket every week, do you understand?"

"I'm sorry, I didn't mean to, well, you see," the priest slows, gathers himself. "I've witnessed boys like your son come around on their own, with time and trust."

"I don't have that kind of time and I don't need that kind of trust," my mother says, fuming.

"I see," the priest says, and pauses. "I sometimes ask myself how is it we come to the Lord. Do we come to Jesus out of guilt or shame, or out of love?"

"Are you lecturing me?" my mother cracks.

"I believe our God is a God of the living, a God of love. And there's the question of free will," the priest offers, taking another tact.

"Not in my home," my mother says and stands, straining at her ankles. "You should be ashamed of yourself. Horribly ashamed of yourself, do you hear me?"

"I'm sorry you feel that way," says the priest, bowing his head.

"Sorry?" my mother glares at the priest. "You'll be positively sorry for this, you will. You'll see."

That's it for my mother. Her anger goes straight from her feet to her face, and back. She takes my brother and me by the arms and walks us out of the priest's office, one hard step at a time. I remember the priest standing up behind his desk, bowing his head again as we leave. His wavy blonde hair, like hippy hair. Out of place. To be envied.

Just like that, my mother's angry spirit crashes through me. Her back bench Catholicism. She will continue to march her faith between our back pew, communion, and a prayer at the Virgin's altar, but never, so help her God, will she take communion from *that priest, that man*. She'll show him, get him with her devotion. At times she will actually line up for communion, in *that priest's* line, then once before him, switch us to the other line and priest. It's the only time I witness her meet her anger head on, if only with her body, an act of physical defiance.

Otherwise, we were whisked in and out of church by my mother, skirting Biblical wisdom. Over the years, I never saw her in the presence of a Bible. As if the Good Book was too bright, a far sun. Why risk touching it, let alone flesh out its heat and character? My mother's sense of religion was mixed with a certain degree of xenophobia, a private English tea party with an electrical fence thrown up around its perimeter. She did everything possible to keep any wisdom of the ancient world from entering the house.

My mother's spirit would become yellow like her kitchen, empty into my cave of faith and not dip much further than my eyes for water and relief. It would take me years to arrive at my own emptying, and to see that this emptying is as necessary to fulfill the inner life as are the colours and clouds that move in and out of our travels.

Faith must sway like a censer in all weathers.

Now, I don't pretend to know much about the invisible processes within our present climate, but this I see: Water is water, and there is in the work of evaporation and journey an art I cannot see.

12

ZEE BROUGHT A SMALL BOOM box out into the back yard. He set up the system and detachable speakers against the stone wall, assuring me he'd keep the volume low and respect the neighbours. He winked and put in a CD. Crosby, Stills and Nash began filling the back yard, pitching harmony across the grass. Listening to their voices, I imagined the moisture plucked from a perfect peach, a whole bowl full of resplendent peaches.

> Find the cost of freedom
> buried in the ground...

Zee lay back in the grass, half naked, five or six beers into a hot summer afternoon. In a yard that had become our own private Woodstock. It didn't take more than thirty seconds for him to fall asleep, which he did, lying there, facing the sky. Eyes fluttering in a dream.

> Mother Earth will swallow you,
> lay your body down...

In the heat, cicadas worked their buzz and shrill. I listened to both songs, drifting in thought, heat bubbling on my skin.

13

MY GRANDFATHER ALTERED HIS HABITS in the spring and early summer months leading up to his death. These days stand out for me like a beacon in my memory. Part wonder, part fear. I was growing closer to his silence and studied him like a collection of stamps or rocks, or those little prayer cards with the saints on them. Sometimes I saw the ghost in him leave his body, and once gone, he seemed relieved, as if for a brief second he had let the past fall from the grip of his pain.

My grandfather began leaving his bedroom door open on those days when I delivered him his lunch. Even in my first years of grade school, I stuck to this habit of coming home for lunch and serving my grandfather his meal in his room. He'd be sitting on the edge of his bed, in his blue trousers and undershirt, a hand scratching his scalp. On the floor were scraps of yellow foolscap, newspaper clippings, old photographs, and maps. Everything rumpled. There was the dusty feel of an archaeological dig in that room. This is what I found myself attracted to, as one is attracted to an urn half buried in sand. I began to look and listen for reports from other worlds and civilizations.

It happened that my grandfather (I don't know what possessed him then, what heat perhaps altered his silence) began to invite me to 'dine' with him. That's how he put it. 'Would you like to dine with me?' Very formal. Dine on warm cheese sandwiches and carrot sticks. Enter that dark room and ease into a long sought after communion with him. If I took on the same diets and likes as his, he might reveal himself to me. So quietly, we picnicked on his bedroom floor, and quietly, to my surprise, my mother allowed this to happen. I think she might have been intrigued as well by my grandfather's shift in character and the open door. More likely she was glad to have her kitchen to herself.

My grandfather cleared a small space on the floor when I arrived, each lunch hour, at 12:15. I'd run home from school, a flash, and my mother would have the silver tray ready on the kitchen table, decorated with linen doilies and small china plates, bright carrot sticks, the warm cheese sandwiches and two glasses of milk. I'd ascend the staircases, two steps at a time, not losing a breath. My grandfather, I think, would hear me coming, because as I stepped up the last stair he'd be clearing a space on the floor, moving foolscap and newspapers, brushing items away. We'd sit, encircled by his papers and maps and pens and pencils. We didn't speak much or nuzzle our place. It was enough for me to be in his presence, tapping into the silences which, though still and haunting, now radiated with a richness I could not ignore. My grandfather might ask me about school and did I like it and was I forming an idea about what I might like to be when I grew up. My answers were short but well meaning. At the time, I was entertaining the usual dreams that occupied a child's mind in our neighbourhood, that of becoming a policeman, a fireman, a doctor or a lawyer. I even mentioned something more daring, that of becoming an artist, a sculptor, because I had recently discovered that curiosity of form in grade school and also down in the ravine with Zee. I detailed for my grandfather how I'd scoop chunks of dark red clay from the earth, wet it and mould it into various abstract shapes, branch shapes, creek shapes winding through the ravine. How all my shapes flowed back into nature. My grandfather would nod while chewing his sandwich, listening. He never judged my choices of occupation, only commented if my choice was an easy one or a difficult one, one which would require hard work or not. He spoke softly, guarding his breath. His tone did not match his face, the ravages there. His voice surprised me, because of the years I had been frightened of his appearance, those scars. I always believed his voice should have been rough, like a dog's growl. And for years he did not speak at all, the early years I remember with him, but now he was speaking, if even it was about the weather. We did not enter great, sweeping vistas of narrative. I did not learn of warmer details concerning his past, where he was born, where he enlisted for the Great War. Looking into the folds of his face, I could guess at each contour and scar. Still, I longed for details, to know, and no longer to fill in the blank spots on my own. As we ate, I'd secretly look over his writings and photographs and maps. I'd spy on curls in sentences I did not recognize, ridges in paragraphs, foolscap upon which a word had fallen like a stone, ink rippling. Maps struggling through unfamiliar landscapes. There were photographs of other soldiers, graves and headstones and white crosses. Everything in the room lived in exile. I was like the boy in a children's book, stumbling my way through a world of treasure, having to read by the light of a distant moon. Wake up in the morning and everything I had imagined myself as having picked through might be gone, a dream world slipping through my fingertips. Because nothing in that attic room, in the pages of my grandfather's foolscap and maps and writings, rose easily into view.

Only once did my grandfather allow me a closer look at a particular photograph and its content. The photo was of a landscape, barren mounds of earth, blasted and gray. I remember sensing the cool wind rip through the image. My first thought when looking at the photograph was, 'No, this is not the Earth'. Not the lush feel and colour of the ravine I'm coming to know. The Earth in my grandfather's photograph was from another age. Pre-colour, pre-Genesis. The human being, man, woman, child, other myriad species, had not yet evolved. No God had pronounced them good. This was not a land that a young sculptor might lean toward and begin to mould. I looked to my grandfather, and back to the photograph, and back to my grandfather's eyes. My hand, I know, was trembling.

"Do you see?" my grandfather asked.

My eyes scanned the photograph, looking deeper, until they settled on a figure in the landscape, bent into the earth, as if hiding within a crease within the photograph. The figure belonged to a young boy in uniform. The uniform was the colour of the blasted soils that made up the foreground and background of the photograph. I tightened my focus on the boy in uniform, found his face, his concentrated look. Everything in the image, as in my grandfather's room, was blurred. The figure in the photograph was just there, a part of the mud, like a tree stump. I looked to my grandfather and caught just one of his eyes, the good eye, looking at me. I felt his presence, his sudden imprint without shadow. Then I caught his other eye, the eye nearer to the temple from which his world of scars began their ride down his cheek. Two very different eyes, looks. One was advancing, the other was in retreat, but not in the way I imagined. It was the good eye that was in retreat. The other, advancing eye wanted to speak.

"That's Vimy Ridge," my grandfather whispered. "We were destroying the world, you see. All of us there in God's mud. And for no reason at all. In the end, nothing at all."

That was my grandfather's only verbal offering about the photograph and his Great War. All that he revealed. He had spoken and it felt like a body of water opening toward the sky. He didn't need to say anything more. I had seen enough still images and moving pictures of the Great War in my father's bunker room, to know what happened at Vimy Ridge. That tremendous gain; that tremendous loss. I had seen enough images of ravaged men, bent men, to know that the uniformed figure in the photograph was my grandfather. He didn't need to confirm this, or point it out with a finger. What he really wanted me to see, I know, was that whatever had happened to his face, those acquired scars, had occurred sometime after the photograph had been taken. Because of the way he looked at me and looked back to the image, studied it, and looked to me again, as if he was somehow looking for himself in my expression, my reaction. A clue to who he was. And because the face in the photograph, though blurred and forced in age, was well shaped and almost handsome. It was the face of a boy whose story was still ahead. Just ahead. I would not learn of the details or the aftermath of that photograph and its story until later, until after my grandfather's death. Until I'd have to steal his past and photograph, pocket some of his writings and hide them in a secret place. Until I'd have to see myself as the good thief in our family. There for history, the stone tablets of memory.

> ...Mother Earth will swallow you,
> lay your body down...

During this time, I gained access to the ravine, with Zee or sometimes alone, after school or on weekends. Nothing, not a classroom or scientific fact, came close to teaching me what the ravine educed in me. The oaks and maples, gangly branches stretching across the creek, touching ground on the other side. My ritual of getting down on hands and knees in the spring muds and bearing witness to the Earth's supple shifts. I watched saplings attempt to become a part of the greater canopy that the older trees had formed overhead. Only as an older tree died off, was felled by storm and wind, would a sapling find an opening in the canopy and break through to become an equal citizen with rights in the wild. For every dead or dying elder tree, there were fifty or sixty saplings attempting to get at the light above the canopy, into that cathedral of atmosphere. This is how I saw myself, waiting upon my own body like a sapling.

The ravine was speckled with intricate pathways and hide outs, defunct logs bent over a thick-leafed forest floor. There was a lone creek that wound through the ravine and spilled into the greater Don Valley river basin, flowing south to a Great Lake. It was the first tangible water I knew and took me in without condition. Often Zee and I would hook up with other kids and swarm the ravine and get behind trees and bramble, disappearing for a barefooted afternoon of river depth glory. We acted out soldier games, hide-and-seek, we tied ropes off over branches and swung out over the creek, or just hung from limbs, like bats, and took in the sounds and scents of the seasons converging, flaring, and diminishing. I was being shaped by these earth mysteries, I knew, creek mysteries. Energies that were as much a part of me as they were outside of me. These energies did not pin me down with a morality or dogma. In these spaces, I was a boy who might just fall in love one day and step down any number of paths for desire to be fulfilled.

A rumour began to swirl through the neighbourhood at this time. Midsummer. Boys and girls were buzzing with information about a strange man down in the ravine. A wild man, a kind of hobo, prowling through the haze of undergrowth, howling, sometimes screaming. He appeared at dusk, it was said. Or was it midnight? Dawn? He had been spotted in dark, old clothing. All torn. He had been seen curled up in a ball, rocking on the ground, crying. Once he was spotted naked by the creek, bathing under a full moon. He had long, mangled hair, like heat conductors. No, no, someone else would say, he is bald and dirty. An eternal dust halo round his head. He was tall and thin, like an alien. Bug eyes. No, he was stubby and short, a hound. No eyes. He had jagged teeth; he had no teeth. He smoked a corn cob pipe. He smoked pine needles wrapped in toilet paper. Bumwadoes, the kids called the hand rolled cigarettes, and rolled their own. You could smell his body from miles away. If you get too close to him, it was said, he sensed you and scurried, five quick leaps down the creek, footprints concealed by water. Someone said half of his face was missing. The face was so scarred (just the one side, the left side) that the other, smooth side of the face looked always to be terrified of the scarred side. The look of a snarl, a bite. It was this rumour about scars that intrigued me and kept me up nights. A story of scars I was familiar with.

Weeks passed and I heard my grandfather leave his attic room late at night, while everyone was in bed. I heard the shuffle of his feet overhead, the exile putting on his slippers and easing down the stairs, stopping in the unlit hallway, then continuing down to the main floor. His breathing behind him, his labouring ghost. I got up and tiptoed to the bedroom window and peered into the back yard. I held myself there and anticipated my grandfather's appearance. The slow bones I knew. I listened for the back door to open and then saw my grandfather step out into the night. He stood below me in the summer air of the yard, the hot, humid night, his body angling toward a distance I could not make out at that hour. My grandfather shook his head, swayed, the smoke of his breath rising. Then he removed his slippers and pajamas, dropping everything at his feet. Even in the darkness the whiteness of his skin shone through, the frailty of his nakedness. There was no sense of recuperation in his flesh. I imagined him as a moon that had been blocked from view by city light, and the ability to see him for who he really was had been lost. My grandfather dipped down onto all fours and crawled into the ravine, disappearing from any trace of night light or a previous life.

Night after night, I watched from my window, witnessing my grandfather crawl into the ravine, and the hours I waited for his return, only to fall asleep with my head on the window sill. Until one night I snuck into Z's room and woke him and told him about grandfather going into the ravine, slipping away naked. That I believed grandfather must be the wild man in the ravine, the hobo everyone whispered about. Zee laughed at my thesis, said the old man was just a freak in the attic, a crazy old bird who farted sometimes, that's all. But my brother, sensing an adventure, snuck out of the house with me, if only to prove to himself that my sightings were real or imagined. When I showed him our grandfather's slippers and pajamas gathered on the ground in the back yard, on the edge of the ravine, Zee winked.

"You sure you didn't plant these here, like a crooked cop planting evidence?" he said.

Then we crept into the ravine, Zee leading the way. We were in our pajamas and stayed low to the earth, keeping an eye out for our grandfather's footprints, potential markings we might follow. A broken branch here, a smudge on rock there. We stopped at strategic points, listening. Soldier-boys, well-versed in the ravine's fragile terrain. We pressed our ears to the night earth, listened through circuits of roots and trunks. Sounds rose, resounded. Crickets. Claws. The night was suddenly incomprehensible beneath a thin layer of mist. I wanted to turn back. Zee insisted we press on. He took a handful of dirt, spat into it, and rubbed the solution over my face, then over his face. Camouflaged warriors, linked. The night sky turning silver, the mist slinking below.

We moved deeper into the ravine, side stepped dry leaves, careful not to make a sound. We angled from oak to oak, to maple, using trunks as shields. Every now and then, we received a glimpse of something moving, a flicker of skin. Grandfather? Must be. We stopped. Zee climbed an oak and wound himself round a branch, to gain a higher vantage point from which to view the ravine. I could hear the creek ripple near by, water over rock. I felt my heart bend against the earth where I lay. Zee dropped a leaf that landed on my back, a signal. I looked up, only to see him pointing a finger across the ravine. The mist peeling back.

There he was, my grandfather, at the creek's edge. His body like a Shade that had been delivered from the past to the future, in spite of the present. His skin with a hue like ash. I remained face down, all eyes, and Zee on his oak limb, looking. We were two young lions, sensing the old one had set himself out there to die. There was nothing saintly about this doing or my grandfather's posture, nothing more of his life to offer or raise. Only his disturbed flesh and an old sheathe of scars. Where once his ground might have been fertile, not even fire and water could restore. He was curled up, arms around his knees, thighs to chest, and rocking. The silence of his motion was deliberate, placed there long before language could articulate the influence of stars on earth and maps. All this, until I heard my grandfather's breathing fill the ravine, echo, and shudder. The last of his strength flickered, like a despairing cry that had never been brushed by faith. The rolling humidity of the night broke across my skin, the sweet sweat of fear. My grandfather rolled onto his back and rolled into the creek, spreading himself out like parchment in a thin layer of water. I don't know what was more disturbing to me: the night sky turning black as a raven's eye, or the sound of my grandfather's breath igniting against the wet ravine. My hands took on a fear of their own and began to dig into the earth, but fear has its own sway, like an aphrodisiac: We want to move closer to that from which we have turned away. We must look again. We must.

Over the next few weeks, each night, regardless of the weather, I crawled like my grandfather into the ravine. At times with my brother, at other times alone. Again, I was the spy in the house. The thief. The slick hand looking for a back pocket, to pluck history. I returned to my bed with my invisible jewels, my spoils. Each night a little more confident, less frightened. No longer the grandson of the exile, but entering that silver bangle of night sky and water within which my grandfather curled himself, dispossessed himself. I watched his ritual, wound closer to the creek and his nakedness. To his dreadful silence and beastly breath. I stashed these memories in my throat.

Until.

Mid-August and another mist filtered through the ravine and covered the creek. So thick I couldn't distinguish my fingers from branches, tree tops from sky. I couldn't see my grandfather or hear him where I imagined he soaked himself in the low waters. Suddenly the wet forest was sticking to me like slime, mist burned my eyes. The earth smelled like an unwashed creature. I let the fear back in and retreated up the hill behind the house, shaking from tree to tree, using bark to feel my way. I snuck into the house, scurried for my bedroom and huddled into bed. The mist, though, was at the window; wet foliage shaking, branches scraping glass. I couldn't sleep. Did not wish to dream. It must have been a few moments later when I heard my grandfather return to the house and float up the stairs. I saw him, the ghost, standing in the doorway. Then my grandfather stepped into the room and stood over my bed. The gleam of the creek on his face, a damp path working through his pajamas. He caught my eye and we looked at one another, not blinking. Is he real? Am I? I felt lost in his eyes, indistinguishable, but I had let him in. He leaned close to my ear, his mouth opening.

"You must learn to be careful about how you pick your adventures, Little Flower," he whispered. "All your tiny footprints in the leaves and mud. You must learn not to give yourself away."

He turned and left the room. All those nights following him and he knew. The mist, and he knew. I felt pulled back by the fear of him, the sorrow in him. His pain like an old star straining toward the earth, one last time, for touch, only to plunge into the sea of my imagination.

The following night there was no mist to accompany my fear, and I stayed away from going into the ravine after my grandfather, but that didn't stop him from coming into my room that night, and the next. Always wet, always looking. No matter how hard I pushed back into my bed, I could not escape my grandfather looking at me, standing in the darkness like a strange sentinel, like an unfinished stone carving, half of its body attempting to emerge from its ache of rock.

Then one night my grandfather stepped into my room and approached my bed. He put a hand out and felt for my body. He touched my face, ran his fingers through my hair. Tender. He sat next to me on the edge of the bed, a burst of sleepy darkness at the centre of his eyes. All those nights of looking at one another, studying the glare and darkness, but never spelling out the mystery of his eyes. Was that a saint I saw in him? Excavator, gravedigger? A mythical beast come to take scraps back to the underworld?

My grandfather pressed his mouth against my ear.

"I'm sorry," he whispered. "I'm sorry."

There was his silence again and my tongue in hiding. What was he apologizing for? What hurt, what old sin? He put his fingers against my lower lip, every cell in my body shuddered. His touch suddenly like a slow stab. I wanted to slip out of my skin like the Invisible Man slipping out of his gauze. I watched my grandfather's face shift through a series of hues. A mid-October leaf to the burnt umber of a marsh, to the gray dust of stone. Then the white of abandonment.

"I did things, you see. Things in war that we were told were legal, were morally correct, but really, those are just thin lines in the head we cross over but cannot cross back. I'm sorry... I'm sorry... please..."

He then lifted me into his arms and squeezed me to his chest, saying, 'Shhh', and, 'Don't tell anyone'. (Tell them what? What?) Then he pushed me back into the bed. I felt the full length of his body, wet and thin, follow and lay on top of me. His pajamas soaking. He rocked me, his arms around me, shivering. He squeezed me harder, turning me over. My face in the pillow, my breath going out of me. I felt my grandfather breathing, rubbing his slack penis against my thigh, kissing the back of my neck, then rubbing his face in my hair, shaking again, pressing again, until I realized the dampness I felt soaking through my hair belonged to his tears. My grandfather was weeping and I couldn't move from beneath his grip. I wanted to scream, I wanted to cry out, I wanted to disappear, become ether, high above the world. My grandfather suddenly rolled over and stood up from the bed. He was shaking. He must have seen me shaking too, struggling for my breath, and sobbing. Because he looked at me, his eyes soft and sad. He turned quickly and left the room, the ghost rushing at his back. *Don't tell anyone. Don't.* I couldn't pull my fingers away from my grip on the bed sheets and pillow. I wasn't out of the world. Not clean or gone or brilliant as a star.

There are mysteries, like that of pain, that enter a man and have nothing to do with sky. His pain has everything to do with earth. And a story, without a soil from which to emerge, is nothing but shards of looking glass.

The following day, at lunch, my grandfather's door was closed. I stood in the attic darkness with our picnic tray, but could not bring myself to knock on his door. I listened for his breathing, a rap of movement. There was nothing in echo in that room. Earlier, I had asked my mother to serve my grandfather his lunch, had said I wasn't feeling well and didn't have the energy to go up into the attic. And my grandfather is mad, I even risked saying, letting out a secret. He is the madman in the ravine, I said. I know it. Have the proof. Look at my body, Mother, can't you see his ghostly fingerprints all over me?

"You're being ridiculous." My mother pushed the silver tray into my hands.

I went. Shadow slow. Just as I had learned from all human gestures in our home. I stood in that attic asylum, not moving. I controlled my breathing like Houdini chained and fully submerged in a locked trunk full of water. Just a minute to live, break out, or die. I ate my lunch, then my grandfather's portion. Every crumb. I drank his cold glass of milk. Then I returned to my mother's kitchen world, her smoky yellow walls.

14

TIME IS FICKLE. AS IS death. Two fickle characters, often with the same mask to paint.

It was three days of this routine, that August, of my going up into the attic with my grandfather's lunch, of my mother sending me up there, and of my grandfather's door being closed. Three days of not knocking on his door and three days of eating both of our meals, standing in the unlit hallway, never hearing a peep from his room. The space within had already changed. Every conduit in my body knew this.

These memories, like the elusive butterfly.

I am a boy of eight.

Too young for war, yet caught in the shudder of two world wars that somehow crept through our lives and home, dropping waste materials without any intention of picking up after themselves.

I had not travelled further than the neighbourhood and ravine. Had not found a point in life where I might begin to distribute aspects of myself, tiny signposts for another traveller to glean and follow.

What can I tell you about the Friday when my grandfather was found dead? The morning was full of mauve cloud cover, colossal shapes sweeping over the neighbourhood. I remember the threat of rain, wind snarling at window panes. My father had been away on business the whole week. Zee, well Zee was Zee and avoided the house as much as he could. His ravine affairs were well under way. He had already taken on the distinction of being a guest in the house and not a family member. Some kind of special cunning, his trickster soul.

By eating my grandfather's lunch over the period of three or four days, I had given my mother the impression that he had been getting his one essential meal, the one meal he allowed himself, each day. Only on past occasions would he slip out of his bedroom, down into the kitchen, and help himself to a snack and tea. And only on occasion would he join us for dinner, at the dining room table. On Sundays, and on Fridays, for fish. Otherwise, my mother never checked up on him, nor entered the attic. She relied on me for information concerning his well-being. When his sheets might need changing, his clothing washing and ironing. When my father was away, my mother was either at the kitchen table, smoking and drinking, reading her domestic magazines, or she was in the back den, watching *Coronation Street* and her afternoon talk shows. Sometimes she allowed me to join her, to watch TV, as long as I didn't speak during the shows. At other times, she'd tell me to leave her alone, or to go and fix her another drink. There were times when I'd sneak out the back door and slither into the ravine and hang out on the limbs of oaks and willows, or dig myself into the red clay by the creek and dream of a world of natural shape, of intimate proportion, a place without scar.

My father arrived home at six. Always punctual. The front door opened, closed, the wind kept at bay. My father's mood was like a tire iron at the end of the work week. He wouldn't speak for at least an hour. No 'hello', no fine thanks, my dear and how was your day?' Already tipsy from a few happy hour drinks, he'd offer my mother a nod, fix himself a scotch and soda and disappear into the living room with his newspaper. This strange couple, I'd think, who met on a trans-Atlantic flight in 1962. My father the middle aged banker, handsome, dapper, linking accounts and profits between Toronto and London, Geneva and Asia. My mother the young and pretty (Not yet sad? Not yet tight?) flight attendant, or as they were referred to in her day, a stewardess. I had seen a photograph of her, a snapshot of her British Airways experience. The whole outfit. The curve of blouse and skirt, the suit jacket and hat, the stockings and show of leg, the sexy pumps. How my father lured her out of uniform and sky and into his lonely lap and city, he would never tell. Just another one of his secret banking deals, one more hush hush kept between his pockets and lips. And my mother, I imagined (though she once let slip), saw in my father a way out. Through his pockets, and through the trembling of his right hand. She saw what everyone saw in that hand: their own trembles and sorrows. She felt sorry for the man. This she also let slip. Because my mother was always a woman who wanted out. Flying the world, however briefly, gave her that. Leaving England (regardless of having to use the sky to achieve her goal) for a home in Moore Park, another country and accent, two children, a husband, an old man in the attic, gave her that. Finally, without having to pay her way or fly or swap continents, alcohol gave her that. Right up until the very end. Ways out, you see, they come and go, they have all sorts of manner and disguise.

Fridays in our home meant fish for dinner, an obscure Catholic ritual. A fish dinner for Christ. As if red meat, the ooze of blood and tenderness, was too close to His crucifixion. Every Friday night I'd hear the lean sizzle of white fish in the frying pan on the stove and my mother working the fish with a spatula. I remember the look on her face as if it was she who had been hooked and not the fish. We gathered at the dining room table at seven. My mother rang the hand held bell that my father had purchased in India and had brought back for her in a small gold and red box one Christmas. 'So that you don't have to raise your voice,' he had said. Ring ring for dinner and we all broke from our various hiding spots around the house and maneuvered toward the table. Zee and I took our seats, backs straight, hands folded in our laps. My mother entered from the kitchen, the hot, sizzling white fish and boiled potatoes and carrots arranged on a large, floral platter. Then my father made his entrance, suited, carrying his drink. 'Mmmm,' he always said, regimental. 'Smells good, Mother.' And always his conventional use of 'mother' when addressing her, as if she was a character in a nineteenth century novel and not his wife. More able appendage than lover or the mother of his children. He picked up his napkin and placed it on his lap, then instructed my brother and me to do the same. We followed, as if this gesture was a current within our Friday night ritual that might lead us closer to our father and into story. This hope quickly passed, of course, and my father said (just before our mealtime prayer, our petitions for those less fortunate than ourselves), repeated every Friday night:

"Didn't anyone call Grandfather?"

To which my mother said, "I suppose he didn't hear the bell."

"He never hears the bell," Zee said.

"You have to ring that instrument with authority," my father said.

"I ring it in the only manner in which I'm able. Like this," my mother said and rang the bell again, and again, louder.

"Well," my father said, looking at me. "Isn't anyone going to get him?"

It was not a question. I understood my father's look, each eyebrow's differing arc. Two stern streaks. In those days, it was common knowledge that I was my grandfather's custodian. The one in the family who saw him on a regular basis, ate lunch with him, sat in his room, stealing glances into his shade and character. And the look on my father's face, the angle of upper lip pulling away from the lower lip, always suggested the same thing: Go up there and get my father. Then his lips closed and the eyebrows followed, like two lines of ailing horizon.

And up I'd go. Again and again. I knew each step, the wired dusk into which I ascended, the air and potential loot there. This time, though, I knew things would be different when I knocked, because I hadn't seen or heard a peep from his room in over three days. Three days of consuming his sandwiches and downing his milk and making my mother in her kitchen and drunken demeanor believe that everything was just fine up there, just peachy.

It wasn't just peachy up there. Never had been, never would be. There was always something suspect about my grandfather's room, I know, like a theatrical set full of false books. Pull down any volume, flip back any cover and find nothing but the emptiness of a page to lure you. If I possessed then the vocabulary and the cunning to spell out a verse of death and anger, I might have just said to my father at the dining room table (before going up into the attic before pretending to fetch my grandfather), I might have just said: There's really no need to get grandfather. I haven't seen or heard a damned thing out of him for days. And if you want to know the truth, Father, (not to mention Zee, not to mention Mother), our grandfather, the old man in the attic, the living ghost, is dead. And he's probably been dead all this time, these past days, and any minute now we'll begin to smell him, get a good whiff of his death just like this bloody fish on this bloody plate.

And...

And I'll tell you something else, I might have added. Something else about the old man in the attic. How the other night, while you were away, Father, and while dear Mum was drunk and sleeping it off, and while big brother here was god knows where, doing god knows what, Grandfather came into my room and crawled into my bed and lay on top of me and rubbed his dead penis all over my body and squeezed the life out of me, just wrung me dry, and wept like a baby too, soaking my hair with his tears. So don't go ask me to weep for your dad, Daddy. Already done that, been there, thank you very much.

The truth is my anger was white in those days and fixed to the plots of other peoples whims. A conscript anger, made to enter foreign nations and demand their resources at gun point. At eight years of age, I have not learned to *liberate* myself from such occupation and erasure. To slip quietly across the border of myself.

And so my grandfather was dead. Died right under our noses. Or because of his position up there in the attic, in his bed (his heart giving up the ghost), he died right above our noses. Died on my watch. And at that point, that touch of discovery, of opening the door and seeing my grandfather's body and sensing that stillness and knowing it was death, his squandered history overtook me fully. All his hungers and ills and his scar of name. I can't explain this but to say it goes beyond his ghost and our blood, and beyond myth. Death has a way of seducing you the way night waters can.

Now, before I entered the room, I knocked once. I waited, as if offering a hint of courtesy, the politeness of an undertaker. 'Mr. Savage, we've come for you.' I knocked and of course, no one answered. How could he, dead and all? I knocked again and then I opened the door, my right hand just turned the knob as if with a mind of its own, and pushed, knowing no consequence. And knowing in an instant, through instinct, that my grandfather was dead. I had seen enough dead squirrels and birds and cats and dogs in the road to know how death posed. The eyes wide, the neck twisted, the mouth lost mid-breath. Gone. Yes, gone. That was the overwhelming sense, that my grandfather was simply gone. The way colour fades under glass. The body was there but the spirit had already scurried over the edge of the bed and out the window, racing for Vimy Ridge. That fallen world of maggots and worms carving out of the human corpse their own version of civilization. I stepped into the room, closer to my grandfather's body. There was nothing familiar to me all of a sudden. Only the collapsing darkness, and the yellow foolscap and maps and photographs on the floor, arranged like loose bramble. I closed my eyes to that world, then opened them, hoping I was in one of those dreams I might control, signalling who was allowed in or out, which images I might pass off like the clay I tunnelled into in the ravine, then scooped back into the creek. I opened my eyes and nothing was changed. Even the spirit I thought I had witnessed scurry away was back and sitting cross legged at my grandfather's side, staring at me. To step closer was to receive into my being this presence I had no part in conceiving. I turned away, quickly, and closed the door. Not ready for this permanent exchange with the dead. I shook off my feet, convinced that my father would detect I had been in my grandfather's room. There would be evidence attached to me. DNA samples, bits of foolscap and photographs like telling dirt stuck to my shoes, all matching the bits of foolscap and photographs on the floor. His crumbs, his mangled spirit.

That was the moment, I know. The shutting down of two lives. Jonathan Francis Savage, the grandfather, and Jonathan Francis Savage, the boy.

I tiptoed down the stairs, passing a thousand restless shadows. I wanted to make a detour into my bedroom and curl up in my bed and rock myself to sleep, then feared that my grandfather's ghost might be in my bed, waiting for me. I stopped on the landing between the second floor and main floor. Darkness. A mirror. I could hear the sound of utensils against plates. No conversation. I wanted to crash through all convention, everything I had been taught as courtesy and grace. You stand at a point in time and space that has been disarranged. Why have you been led there, to what purpose? Where there is no water, no flow.

My father appeared at the foot of the stairs. A slim shadow about him. Those eyebrows.

"What are you doing?"

Silence.

"Have you gone up there or not?"

"He's not answering."

"Did you knock?"

Slight nod.

"Did you call for him?"

I shook my head.

"Call for him," my father said.

"I can't."

Pause. A bone poking at my skin.

"What did you say?" my father said, a look on his face that suggested I find myself a good lawyer.

Now my mother was in the hallway, two shadows intersecting. Zee was right behind, chewing a mouthful of food.

"Go back to the table," my mother told my brother and pushed him back.

"But..."

"This is a waste of my time," my mother said, looking up the stairs at me. "Do as your father says, get up there and get your grandfather, or else..."

I imagined the belt.

"What are you afraid of?" my father said.

Words words. Astringent words.

"Go with him," my mother barked at my father. "This is ridiculous."

I remember my father looking at my mother, the inconvenience on his face.

"Don't look at me like that," my mother said. "Just go up there with your son and get the man before my dinner is completely ruined."

In years to come (the short, quick years), it would be my mother's voice I remember coming from behind closed bedroom doors, her red tone admonishing my father for being weak and ineffectual, for not riding her children hard enough, long enough. All these weak men and boys in her home, she'd say. Useless.

My father turned away from my mother, his face tightening. He took the first few steps up the stairs, increasing his pace. He reached me on the landing and looked down at me. His own anger was always just there, at the tip of his touch, like a small flame. He took me by the back of the arm and led me up into the attic, lifting me. The attic holding to its August heat. I felt my father's pulse work through the palm of his hand, coiled around my upper arm. I wanted to cry and smash through the last window in the attic landing, jump and shimmy down a tree.

My father didn't bother to knock at my grandfather's door. Courtesy gone. He pushed back the door and stepped into the room and pulled me in behind him, then forced me front and centre, my feet standing amongst the pale foolscap and maps, photographs and misfortune.

My father's face, his body, facing a room and a bed and a man as if in a mystery play that had lost its plot.

"Father," my father said, formal.

Nothing.

"Father," he said again, this time handing off the word like a cigarette to a perfect stranger.

A third time ("Father!") before allowing for the silence to open and alter the space.

Because he knew. He knew, like me, down to the bone and pulse along my upper arm. My father knew his father was dead. There was no mistaking the air in the room, the stain of heat, the misshape of that face, the burst blister of breath on the edge of that lower lip. My father became still. Then his hand fell from its grip at my arm. I noticed my grandfather's hand, the left hand, turned up along the bed, the fingers curled like a stone claw. It wasn't a hand that had been shaped by prayer. The fingers directed themselves into a fist, tightening as death's customs scavenged the rest of his body. This time I could not look away. For my father, this appeared to be the end of something that had already ended long ago. A life forsaken. Just punishment. For me it was a creature deity taking over my memory, an eerie carnival of spirits.

I could see, clearly, how the slim light in the room (working in from God knows where) came to a stop at my grandfather's body. As if even the light knew he was dead and gone, and now stood over him, giving the last rites. Something none of us could offer, would offer. Had I been older and confident in my skin, I might have rushed the bed and pounced with my hands onto my grandfather's chest and worked his heart back into the world. Death demands honesty. For though I feared this man and his touch, I felt he was only beginning to reveal himself, his story, and deliver our past. If only there had been more time, more picnics, my fingers running over his photographs and maps. I was sure of it. Sure he would have told me everything, spilled himself. I wanted that time back, that sense of talking cure. I would have allowed him to weep into my hair.

More time. If only...

I remember my father standing there. Fixed. At a loss. I looked at his face, expecting something. A grimace. Horror. Perhaps a tear. He just looked at the old man, more stranger than son. As if he too had been deprived of a story. As if the mystery between the two men was too great, a burden and not gift. Something you could not get your arms around, like the moon in a dream.

My father finally moved a hand, the non-trembling hand, realizing delicacy was required. He stepped toward the bed, reached and touched my grandfather's eye lids, then closed them. He moved the same hand toward my grandfather's chest that was exposed and pale. My father placed the palm of his hand flat against the chest, muttered something, and breathed out. The angle of my father's shoulders was strained, as if his body was taking a slow plunge into the past. He turned back to me and looked me in the eye. The gleam of a hawk's eye. Dangerous, quick, and containing in its glare all the strained stories my father had never told me, would never tell me, held like prey. He motioned for me to step closer and took my hand. The unexpected warmth of his touch made my eyes moist but I swallowed and pushed back the tears. At that moment, I wanted to be like my father. I wanted his hardness, his reticence. As if these were the true ingredients through which I might translate his touch into mine, and plunge with him into that untold past that no one in the house could decipher. He lifted my hand and turned it at the wrist, pulling me closer to my grandfather's body. I could not make out the colour in the room. Nor sound, nor prayer. My father pressed my hand (this hand, these fingers now holding you) into my grandfather's sunken chest. He pushed against the back of my hand and wouldn't let up. I felt the blind pressure, millions of pounds of air like stigmata pushing down on me.

"Feel that," my father said.

I couldn't speak. I couldn't find my way through that touch, saliva filling my mouth. So my grandfather was not gone, not yet. I had been tricked. My grandfather's skin was still warm, like moss. Like a place on a bed sheet where a small cat had just slept.

"He hasn't been dead long," my father whispered, no longer pressing down on the back of my hand.

But he's not dead, I thought, not...

It might have been a minute, this time with my father and my hand against my grandfather's chest. I felt the tight orbit of his life leave its path, energies with the spin of a thousand other lives. The lives of men my grandfather had known in the Great War and who had died there, unnamed; died, I would later read, in his arms, against his lips. Your mother says the past re-visits us through magnetic fields, molecular passage; the milk of her breasts. I was too frightened then to grasp what it was I was being offered in that moment of touch, what clearing I was to enter where I might whirl in my grandfather's story and learn from his last warmth and blood. True inheritance is invisible. It travels without hunger or disguise. But what did

I know of such gifts and an ability to receive them? Not in that house. The messenger of my grandfather's death moved to the back of my mind, his ghost not bothering to remove its hat and coat. What would it take for me to undress this touch and force? What discretion or wit. Would the years provide me with a clue, and how much of what I'm telling you has been stolen and what is gift?

All I remember is the heat of my grandfather's chest slowly going out. Then my hand with the beginnings of its own tremble.

Grandfather. Father. Son.

A legacy.

A pained eclipse.

15

LATE AFTERNOON ON MERTON ST. I gazed at the stone wall, the Virgin at my back. Zee carried the conversation, a downhill swerve. No brakes.

"He didn't always live with us, mon frère. The old bird in the attic. He showed up on the doorstep one day. I was five, maybe six. You were just a babe, barely crafted into the scenery. The doorbell rang and there he was. He scared the crap out of me, with that face and those scars. I screamed, actually screamed. He didn't say a thing. Just stood there, like some shy saint in this long black coat and this old fedora not quite shading his face. Mother came running and grabbed me and pulled me back from the freak at the door. She covered my mouth to stop me from screaming, then she cracked one of those pained smiles she was so famous for, that trite, dismissive grin. You know the one, little man, all those wrinkles tightening round her lips.

"Anyways, Mother looks at the old bird and I can tell she doesn't recognize him. And he's still not speaking, just looking at us, as if we're supposed to guess who he is or something. I remember Mother saying that we weren't interested in whatever it was he was selling. And then the old bird finally speaking, saying, 'It's me.'"

Zee paused to sip a beer, his mood and memory muscling through a flare of alcohol, a semi-washed out landscape.

"And that's how he came to live with us, Little Flower. Back from the front after fifty years, after having lived in some shell hole, thinking the war was still going on. For a month or so whenever he came into a room, I ran out. Those goddamned scars. And him never talking. Father set him up in the attic. Do you remember the screams and farting and his wandering around? Years and nights, Jesus. So I took him his tray of food for a while but as soon as you could waddle I got you in on the act. Did you know that? I can tell by your eyes you don't remember. For a while we'd go up there together, you crawling behind me, but then, well, you know the rest."

Nod nod, yes, I know the rest... but...

"So I don't know why you get all worked up about the old bird, Little Francis. So obsessed and sentimental. Just because he was the wounded vet, just because you share a little name and blood. I hope by now you realize you're not responsible for his death. Just because you found him like that doesn't mean you had the power to deliver death to him. That was his choice, mon frère, to live up there, to hide up there, to die up there. The war was his, not yours. Just like WWII belonged to father and not us. Wars orchestrated by the rich and at the cost of the poor. Poor kids. While the rich hunker down in their parlours and banks and mind the oil and gold. It's their responsibility, their generation's evil, little man. Not ours."

"Your holy point?"

"There's no point. That's the bloody point. That's what the old bird taught, by not saying anything, by betraying the past with his gaping silence. These men with their black holes of grief. Don't you see? Failures, the lot of them. On this blistering point, I agree with our discoloured mother. A whole generation of men screwed up. They might go on film and talk about their battles to preserve freedom and democracy, the whole bloody illusion, but they won't tell us a goddamned thing about their personal depths, the whys and hows of their souls. Oh, they might give you a tale about it being about the boys, the brothers in arms, the ancient bond of battle. Their medals. They have to make up that kind of honour and glory to make sense of it, you see, to keep them going over the top, straight into enemy gunfire like a bunch of sheep."

Zee lay back in the grass and looked to the sky through the trees.

"One time I asked father about the war," he said.

"You did?"

"Just the once. I wanted to know, like you (but were afraid to ask), about *his war, his experience.* And you know what he said, little man, all he said? He said that the war was all about the bottom line. The bloody bottom line, mon frère. This from a guy who worked in a bank all his life. But also from a guy who was a POW, who had every right to be angry and want revenge. I mean, he was probably tortured, probably starved in that camp. So I suppose even survival has its bottom line, just hanging on."

"I can't believe you got up that kind of nerve to ask him."

"Sure, why not?"

"I was always told not to ask. Hell, even you told me not to ask about the war."

"It was only that once that I got the nerve. Just before I got the hell out of the house, dropped out. Father asked me to meet him for lunch at Fran's. His last pitch at me to stay in school. What was I, fifteen or sixteen? He gave me the usual lines, you know: Stay in school or you're out of the house. Or get work, pay rent, and stay in the house. No free rides la de dah la de dah... So I said I'd stay in school. I had that part-time job at the theatre, anyways. Then I let the moment soften and I just asked him to tell me about the war and his life, anything, crap, make it up, I said. Should have seen his face, little man. The proverbial deer in the headlights. And it was Remembrance Day too. One of those beautiful ironies. He had that damned poppy pinned to his lapel. I said something like, 'Look, if you're into wearing that flower, then talk about those Jesus wars, toss us a scrap'. He said he wouldn't, couldn't. Fine, I said. Then I stood and he grabbed my arm and made me sit right back down. He gave me this look and opened just a crack. He let out a few shallow lines about the old bird in the attic and Vimy Ridge and their years in France. How the old bird was never quite right after the battle. Took a bullet behind the left ear. Had his face ripped by barbed wire and shrapnel, and his lungs were never the same after the gas attacks. That's why the old bird always laboured for his breath, remember?

"Jesus, I felt like an investigative reporter, having a tough time getting the interview out of the old man. But he told me something about the years after the Great War. The Paris years. How grandfather was hospitalized and then let go, but he didn't return to Canada. He lived in France for ten years or so, until the Great Depression. And you know what our beloved grandfather did, mon frère? He buried the dead. That's right. He worked the battlefields and rearranged the fallen. He took their remains from makeshift graves, dug during the heat of battle, and moved them to newer, fresher plots, put all of the dead together in memorial grounds all over northern France. For years after the war, that's all he did. And some of the grave diggers would get blown up while digging, hitting unexploded shells with their shovels. Sustaining further wounds, insult to injury or injury to insult. Crazy stuff. Maybe you do have more in common with the old bird than I realized. You do share a certain art and persuasion there, working your own graves and the dead."

"I found father's birth certificate after he died. He was born in Paris, did you know that?"

"That's right. Early twenties. I asked about his mother but he didn't remember much, or didn't let on that he did. Just some sentimental crap about strawberries. How his mother smelled like strawberries. Very French. The old bird met her in the hospital after getting one of his wounds. She was a nurse or volunteer or something, someone who brought a little comfort, reading to him at his bedside. The usual war time love thing. Very quaint, very Hemingway.

"So they lived in Paris while the old bird worked the battlefield graves north of the city. But she died when father was five or six. The influenza of the day, the Spanish one I think. That's when the old bird and dear Dad returned to Canada. Then the old bird went back to France in the early thirties to work on the construction of the great Vimy monument, built somewhere in the forsaken fields of all those black and white films we watched. The old guy was obsessed with that ground, apparently. That mud, Father said. So the old bird enrolled dear Dad in a private boarding school and then RMC in Kingston, just so that he could go back to France and remain close to the soils that ruined him. The psyche is a strange, dizzying place, mon frère. More moonscape than Earth scape, I think."

"But you asked Father about his war, didn't you?"

"Ah, you noticed. You see how the old man diverted me from his own story? Does that surprise you? You think he actually relented, after all of the energy he had put into not saying a bloody thing about himself his whole life. All he did was hide behind the old bird's story. Although, I'll give him some credit, he did say something about going down in a Lancaster over France and being taken prisoner, three years or so in some camp, which he wouldn't name. Said he still had flashbacks, that he could be sitting in the living room, a small branch could brush a window and suddenly everything around him would explode. That was it. Said there wasn't much about the past to be proud of, so why labour over it? Man, I took that as a bloody breakthrough. Oh, and it was easier for him to speak of other men's horrors, he said, rather than his own. Get that?"

"Sad."

"He had his chances to choose another life, Little Flower."

"Maybe he didn't think he had a choice."

"How so?"

"He was trapped, hell, we were all trapped in that house. And some people stay that way, you know, feel like they can't get out. Feel like fear is their only choice, and to live in the silences that they cannot answer to."

"Don't get all Oprah on me."

"But you dropped out anyways, took off."

"Of course."

"Didn't hold up your end of the bargain with the old man."

"Father just sat there after speaking, as if he was exhausted. He gives up a few meagre paragraphs and starts sweating, fingering that damned poppy, and orders another drink like some guy in a movie."

"And?"

"And I paid the bill. No debts between the old man and me. Just a metaphor, I know, but he knew and I knew. I wasn't coming back home or going to school or working under his roof and paying rent. Besides, Mother and I were at each other's throats and I was stoned, what, 90% of the time, and preferred that potion to their emotional toxins. Father could start cleaning his own goddamned storm windows, up on his bloody 32' ladder."

"That job was left to me, thank you very much."

"Aha."

"And that was the last time you saw him, and Mother?"

"Last time, yes."

"Didn't even show up for his funeral."

"I was in Greece, if you recall, floating on an island."

"Aren't we all?"

"Sometimes it's all we can do, little man. Then what? All we can do is laugh it off. If you can't laugh at history and a few missed opportunities in life, there's little reason to think your God will have anything to do with you, mon frère."

I stood and picked up the garden hose at my brother's feet. Squeezing the nozzle, I sent thick streams of water over his hair, down his brow, nose and lips, and gushing through his goatee. He smiled, offering up that televised glow.

16

WIND AND WATER. WATER AND wind.

With or without my conscious knowing, I was unlearning everything that had been holding me back in mood and emotion that summer; all the accumulated damage and loneliness and shame, the peculiar shame that had been passed on through generations of men and their wars. All this, like the fear of disease and not the disease itself, was bleeding out of me. What I desired was not the forgiveness or acceptance of others, but to take my heart in my own hands. Just for once, for then, for now. I wanted to know the ground and solitude of my own silence. What it might mean to become whole and still and prized.

Zee and I were shut out from attending my grandfather's funeral. It was the last week of August, school was just around the bend, and there was no way my mother was going to allow her children to see a funeral or feel the dirt of a grave at their feet. I could witness a dead body, sure. I could tremble an hour with my hand on a dead man's chest, but to see that body in a lonely coffin (my mother's phrase) and that coffin put in the earth, forever and buried, no. It wasn't to be.

My father argued that we should bury his father as a family. It would be good for the boys, he debated. To learn how trivial life is, how brutal. One minute a heart beats, the next moment there is nothing. Nada. Gone. Just the earth to prepare, or perhaps all is to be made ash. Take your holy pick.

"I've been surrounded by too much death," I remember my mother arguing back at my father, in her kitchen the night after my grandfather's death. "Too much dying. I just won't have it anymore. And they're too young to see a grave."

This was perhaps the only time I remember my mother making an effort to protect her boys. But now I know: it was her own fear she was protecting and holding onto with each gush of alcohol.

There was something else my mother didn't understand. Zee and I were already well versed in the dead and funerals and burials. Down in the ravine, there were any number of deceased red breasted robins and squirrels and small pets, creatures we had found dead in the street and had placed in shoe box coffins and had processed through the ravine, to a plot of land that we had designated as our cemetery beneath the foot bridge. As we made our processions, the shoe box coffins held at our shoulders (just as we had studied in my father's Great War movies, other men carrying coffins), we chanted in our home made Latin gurgle, Holum Dolum Molum, Put 'Em in the Holum... Ahhh hhhhmen... Then we crossed ourselves and got back to play in the ravine. Yes, we were old pros with the dead and burials and the necessity of ritual. Being shut out from my grandfather's funeral didn't make any sense to us. Besides that, there was another thing my mother didn't understand. There was a death notice in the morning paper, and Zee could read. Even I could follow a vowel's heat.

We were supposed to stay with a neighbour the morning of my grandfather's funeral, but a secret phone call to the funeral home (Humphreys on Bayview) and Zee's inquiry (lowering his voice, speaking with a British accent) into where the deceased was to be interred, we learned grandfather was to join the earth of Mt. Pleasant Cemetery, at 11 a.m. And knowing from our romps in the underworld that the cemetery was just up the block from our home and the ravine, a hop and wink over Moore Avenue, we had already learned where to go. Just as we had followed my grandfather into the ravine on his nights of mist and the creek, we would follow him to his grave.

As we strolled in our sneakers and shorts and t-shirts up the street toward the neighbour's house, we made a sharp detour down a driveway, through a back yard, and down the eastern slope of the ravine. Not requiring maps or historic documents marked for silk and pilgrims. In the ravine we were kings, warriors and thieves. Destiny was ours to shape. We angled north, ducked oaks and willows, fallen branches. We emerged at Moore, facing north, a low wind. Traffic wound past. Not a head in a car turned to look as we concealed ourselves like leaves, eyeing the road and the cemetery that was just across the street. What if Mother and Father drive past, I warned my brother. Highly unlikely, old chap, he assured me, a British leap to his tongue. An old Colonel.

We watched the traffic, studied styles of speed and casual halting at a stop sign just west of us. Zee held up an index finger and measured the wind. A little from the north-west, he whispered. Stay low and drive hard with your arms and legs, head down, he commanded. And stay at my back, one last order, in my draft. We waited out the traffic, until there was a break, and made our dash across the street. I remember my anxious speed, arms pumping, legs driving. Fear at my back. I heard the sound of a car, surprising us out of the west. We reached the other side of Moore, rushed over a gravel shoulder, up a slope toward a bush and fence that separated the road from the cemetery. Get down, Zee ordered and fell to his knees and rolled onto his side, rolling again behind a bush. I followed, stumbled and felt Zee grab my arm and pull me behind the bush, my heart thumping. The car, a tan station wagon, had slowed, then passed. A female driver, mid-thirties, blonde, two kids in the back, looked out at us. I closed my eyes, believing if I refused to see them, they wouldn't see me. That was my mistake with my grandfather, those nights with his ghostly image standing at my bedside, his body wet and thin, his pajamas soaked, his eyes panning over me like a camera, and my eyes wide open, letting him in, crushing me. Nothing could stop that feeling, that memory. Until there, behind the bush, Zee was shaking me. Keep alert, he insisted, as if intuiting my distance, the damage. And reminding me this was a game, our game, but serious as war. Our Vimy Ridge, our Passchendaele. The road was just the first hump to take and secure. Now there was the fence. Zee had come prepared. He pulled a pair of wire cutters from his back pocket and began cutting away at the lower links of fence. Keep watch, he ordered. The sun a fast pulse overhead, more heat. Zee cut a hole wide enough for two animals to wriggle through.

We crawled through the hole in the fence, slithered another hundred metres on our bellies. We stood and brushed ourselves off, posing as regulars in the cemetery. There to stroll and bird watch, to chart peculiar species of trees for which the cemetery was well known. The Oriental smooth leaf elm, the Babylonian willow, Turkish filberts. We had an hour to locate my grandfather's plot. We zigged over clean cut sections, charting our way between grave stones, scanning the names of the dead. There were graves with lanterns that had been fixed in the ground, candles blazing, wax dripping onto plastic flowers. For a while Zee and I split up; he fanned this way, while I fanned that way. We whistled as we went, using our mock bird calls like prehistoric semaphore.

After fifteen minutes or so, we had not found my grandfather's grave site. We hooked back up and angled toward the main entrance off Mt. Pleasant and hid behind a black grave stone. We'll wait for the hearse, Zee decided, then follow. It was 10:45 a.m. We guessed the procession would be small, two vehicles at most. Black and slow. It was just a moment later when a procession appeared, moving north along Mt. Pleasant from Moore Avenue. Zee and I ducked with our backs against a cool, marble grave stone, feeling the chiseled letters of its names and dates against our warm skin. Zee cranked his head around and spied on the procession as it turned right into the cemetery, near to us.

"Good work," I said, complimenting the Colonel.

"Keep your voice down, Corporal."

We were only a few metres from the road and the two cars that made up the procession. I spotted my mother and father in the back seat of the second vehicle. Their expressions of neutrality and control. No looking back. We let the procession pass and move east before we followed. Ducking once again behind grave stones, shielding ourselves with the dead. We sprinted across open measures of road, imagining these as rivers, watery spines that led toward a medieval town to be taken. The two vehicles wound down a gully behind a cemetery office, then eased up the opposite side. Zee and I took the long way around the office, keeping the building between ourselves and the procession. We huddled by the back edge of the building, watched the cars climb, then proceed left along a second flat of road. We ducked across the gully, speeding in our skin and purpose. The procession flickering through the maple trees that lined the road. The cars reached a turn, right, then left. The grave stones were high enough so that we weren't required to duck or bow as we went. The procession came to a gentle stop, two hundred metres ahead of us. We crouched, breathing in a ribbon of air. Sweating now, we curled round the section, found an adjacent lot amongst the great oaks. Closer to the grave site, we spotted a perfect tree, climbed its limbs and concealed ourselves in its rich canopy. Only a stone's throw or so separating our cover from my grandfather's place of final rest. Section 41, Lot 351. A corner plot, facing north-east. The winter winds would be harsh.

The service was short and lacked obligation, I thought. No room for mystery or gratitude. There was my mother and my father, the driver of the hearse, a second limousine driver, a funeral director and the minister, a hired holy man. I remember the funeral director wandering off and soon returning with three other men, cemetery workers, soiled with the dust of other graves. I watched as the director (lean sharp polite) slipped each worker a dollar bill as payment for their services as pallbearers. This ritual (that of pallbearer) I was already familiar with and would later continue in my years at the cemetery when there was a pauper to be buried and no formal procession, and the driver of the hearse would enlist me and a few others to carry a lone casket to its grave. These paupers who were buried three atop one another, left to the unknown. I watched as these men carried my grandfather's casket and made the short hike up a final incline to the grave. The casket was pine, a simple tanned cut. My father followed, holding a wreathe of red poppies. The minister was just ahead. My mother (dear Mum) stayed behind at the road. The funeral director touched her at the elbow and motioned with the other hand that she step forward, toward the grave. My mother shook her head and stayed put, a statue encased in stone. The coffin was placed on a pulley system over the grave. My father lay the red poppy wreathe on the coffin lid. He looked back at my mother, once. His face was pale. And my mother, well, she remained at the roadside, cleaving to the short distance between herself and the grave. Who is this woman, I thought, who can manhandle the mood of any moment, turn it over, then flick it from her fingers like a cigarette stub?

The minister stepped forward, a Bible open in his hands. When he spoke, it seemed out of habit, straightforward, a faint wisdom being stirred. *'Ashes to ashes, dust to dust,'* he recited. Those words I remember having heard one day from a priest at the altar, an Ash Wednesday. My forehead marked. I remember the weight of the words' involvement delivered from the priest's lips, the fire of interpretation entering my ears. The return to earth. But there, at the grave side ceremony, the wind quietly took over and altered meaning. The words taking off into the air around my brother and me, over treetops, scattering. I imagined ravens circling, preparing to feed.

I turned my attention back to my father, his hands behind his back, standing at the edge of the grave. There was just a slight slump of his shoulders to interpret his grief. Then there was my mother again, my eyes kept coming back to her where she stood at the side of the road. I remember focussing on her right ankle and seeing the strain of her black heels against the pavement. She was difficult to let into the heart. Even then, I felt I did not belong to her and she did not belong to us. All of us were like frauds in a drama whose plot lived in exile. I watched as my mother opened her small black purse, pulled out her lighter and a cigarette, composed herself, twisted the cigarette into her cigarette holder, then lit the butt. She drew the smoke slowly into her mouth, then slowly exhaled through her nostrils.

"Bitch," I remember your uncle whispering in our oak canopy.

Silence slammed through. Hello Mother, good-bye Mother. Rip up all familial contracts. There was nothing in my mother's smoke or posture that taught us to be her loving witness in a time of crisis or judgement. For all her drunken faith, it was like a corner tryst with an anonymous god where tenderness did not reveal a hand.

The service concluded and my father walked back to the limousine, passing my mother, not looking at her. He stood by the back door of the vehicle. The conservative gaze that had always pressed through my father's expression fell away. He looked back at the grave as if he had become one of the erased. Gone. As if he could no longer point to his heart or history in the way you could spot the villain in a silent movie. As if it was his projected faith in a Celluloid world that had been attacked and erased. The old world of silent war films in which he peered if only as a means to locate his own father's soul and self. Now the madness of that silent and dying world was no longer a case of black and white. Suddenly sound and colour entered death, there in the greenery and brown earth of the cemetery, under a hot, blue sky. A couple of birds and two children squawking in a tree.

I watched as my mother turned toward my father's changed gaze, that gone gaze. She took the few steps back to the limousine, dropped her cigarette butt on the pavement, and bent into the vehicle. She was as foreign to us as the lands in an old atlas that the Empire had declared dangerous and out-of-bounds.

A hard front moving in.

17

THERE ARE COLOURS OF SOLITUDE, like the cold black of grief, that are essential to our spiritual becoming. At times we finger these colours, and at times we turn away, unaccustomed to the richness of our own darkness. After the death of someone close, we sense a separation from ourselves, lineage broken. Bare. Though strange and foreign, this is the very land from which we must begin the ancient art of engaging and raising our souls.

My father went to work the afternoon following my grandfather's funeral.

Over the next few nights, I sat on the floor outside of my grandfather's attic room and watched as my father emptied the room of my grandfather's scraps of yellow foolscap, maps and photographs, crammed the materials into a garbage can, and later poured the heap in the back yard and burned everything with a first mix of browning leaves. During this purge, my father sat in the darkness of the attic room, a scotch and soda to soothe his mind, his eyes sliding into a private world of loss. He never paused to look over and read from his father's pages, and he never acknowledged me as a master might wink at his dog huddled at his feet. My father sat in that room, surrounded by its limp blackness. Drunk. What had he become? Who was he? These were not the questions I made out against the screen of his face? If there was a colour to go with my father's sorrow, it was Indian red. A shade containing rust, seeping iron. The eye will instinctively travel toward its immediate appeal, its blood lust, then look away. It is a colour riding closer to death and the underworld than to our thriving, our greening. A struggle to trust and love. Like my father.

This is when I pocketed our past, on a night when my father was drifting in scotch and sleep, his body slumped in an armchair in my grandfather's room. I slipped a hand across the floor, my fingers working like a dog's paw at a dig. I snatched up a photograph and some of my grandfather's writings, stuffed the yellow foolscap down my shirt and crawled backwards, down the stairs, to my bedroom. I hid my meek treasure beneath my mattress, then later (along with my first journal) stowed the contents beneath my bed where I pulled the carpet back from the wall and floor, leaving a small pocket of solitude and darkness in which my treasure might brew, might thicken.

When the attic room was emptied and my grandfather's history burned, my father bolted the door, barring us from the upper floor. There was no further attempt by my father to furnish his mood in anything other than silence. His movements slowed. And no one dared question the specter of the changed house, the depression. My mother moved her tea time drink (the fabled first drink of the day) up to 11 a.m., often wearing a bath robe and nightgown at that hour. My mother and father grew hard, revealing only the wired violence of their emotions.

One morning I stepped into the kitchen and found my mother and father locked in a monumental clutch, their bodies hung over and pale. My mother's arms were raised, her fists drawn like jewelled daggers. My father's hands were also raised and gripping my mother at her wrists, pinning her back against the wall, holding back the daggers. A tired sweat lined both their brows. They didn't see me. I watched as my father weakened first and slouched to his knees, his head buried against my mother's belly and robe, her fists suddenly free and slamming into his back. He didn't move, and received each of her blows as if in a trance. As if he was happiest when beaten. The final fist slammed into the side of my father's head and sent him to the floor. He rolled into a ball in his gray suit, breathing at a fast, dry clip. My mother rearranged herself, fixed her hair, then stepped past him, crossing the kitchen. She placed her hands on the counter top, then reached for her gin and poured herself a drink. Straight up, bypassing the vermouth. She took the drink and walked back across the kitchen, brushing past me, not seeing me. I wanted to go to my father and touch him, but

I didn't. I wished he would weep. When stillness returned to the kitchen, it arrived not with the silence after storm, but a silence before storm. A strange quirk within our household we never quite worked out.

Over the years, there would be more of these drunk dances, this brutal display of love. My father's upper back would take on a permanent ring of bruises that I would only see after his last few heart attacks. He'd be in a hospital bed, recovering, a nurse would enter his private room to change his pajamas, bathe him, and adjust his bed and pillows. He'd lean forward and I'd catch a glimpse of the bruises, a show of yellows and reds and blues along his shoulder blades. I'd watch his aging quicken, his sadness go unpalatable. There would be days when I wouldn't recognize him, the wounds turning against him, concealing him. There are ways a man will disappear on himself and leave no trace of his wanderings. Secret agent or prisoner, a haunting duality. His only oath, not to be found out. Swallow the cyanide before the possibility of interrogation.

When my father passed away (on a bed in Sunnybrook Hospital, ten years after my grandfather's death), I did not witness his ghost depart or rush for the safe haven of a Biblical promise. My father had long since denied himself that kind of faith and did not fan his heart with pages from a holy book. The clothing of his soul was permanent, like armour. He never asked for a hand to feed his hunger or for someone to remove his faded shield. And this time, when in the presence of the dying (Zee gone on his Greek Island; my mother in her kitchen, working her bottle, refusing to see her husband die), I did not place a hand on a dead man's chest. I wanted no part of my father's last warmth, that dip in climate. My anger toward him had replaced a desire to soothe him. I did not want his blood to mingle with the ink I was already using in my secret journals, filling pages with our dusk and story. I also knew I was lying to myself about this, performing a neat little trick between my mind and heart. The body teaches us through humility. It is the mind that clings to time's dirty work. I didn't have to touch my father to let him in. His sore presence, the hallow of his chest. He rose red in my imagination like a blood-tipped arrow, wounding me nonetheless. I could not erase him from the page any more than I can leave him out of this talk.

There are leaps of the heart that arrive only through further descent. Years not written, stars interrupted. Only love can change you. This I believe. My heart is a hermit's flame. Yet a lover burns there too. Because our story in the end must be a story of love. And nothing must crush this telling love, this swaddled sharing. Not the past that attempts to fool us like dream, not a pre-arrangement between fate and prey. Everything must be offered from the deep, wild now. A communion of praise.

18

THE PARTY MOVED IN AND out of the basement that summer, swirled like an eddy between my brother and I. It was a Saturday afternoon and we were on the cusp of the eve of my famous last drunk. I had returned to the basement after hours of walking. I had wanted movement and the heat, the wash of my own sweat. When I stepped into the basement, Zee was sitting on the floor in front of the TV wearing boxer shorts, T-shirt, and cowboy boots. An open bottle of Champagne at his side. He was rushing through *Apocalypse Now* for the hundredth time. I caught a glimpse of the aftermath of an early battle scene. A priest celebrating Mass in the midst of that chaos and murder. As he held the bread and blessed it, a helicopter air lifted a lamb from the slaughter, raising this small creature tied by a rope around its stomach and dangling from a flying machine. Zee muscled through the scene, passing other battles at such a blur of speed that there was little room to absorb the up river journey that the film attempted to paint.

"Here it is," Zee announced, lifting his voice across the room.

A small skirt and blouse lay on the floor next to my brother. The sound of gargling came from behind the bathroom door. The door opened and there appeared a young woman with a light blue bed sheet wrapped round her body. She had wild auburn hair, tinged with orange streaks. She entered the room as if she were the guardian of temperature.

"I used your toothbrush. Hope you don't mind."

Was she addressing me or my brother? I didn't know, but it must have been Zee, because in those days I was able to slide into a room and make a corner out of myself.

"Ah, Sophia, this is my little brother. Mon frère, Sophia," Zee said, waving me out of my corner.

"Sorry, I didn't see you," Sophia said, pulling at the bed sheet. She possessed a flare within her voice like a wick meeting flame.

Should I stay, go, sit, recoil? There I was in my space. My books, my CDs, my green canoe, my blue bed sheet...

My my my...

"Relax, little man. I'm just showing her the end of the film here, then we'll head out for some eats. Must celebrate the loss of your job and our upcoming adventures."

"I'd better get dressed," Sophia said, smiling.

"No hurry," Zee said.

Sophia walked toward me, the bed sheet rippling beneath her wavelike stride.

"Excuse me," she said, moving into the kitchen area. The bed sheet brushed against my side.

I watched this woman of orange streaks and the bed sheet approach the refrigerator, open the freezer door, reach into the ice box and pull out a pair of underwear and a bra. She turned back to me, pushing off from her toes.

"It's the heat," she offered. "It's unbearable, don't you think? So I like to keep my underwear cool. I saw it in a movie once."

"*Seven Year Itch*," Zee confirmed. "Monroe did that in the *Seven Year Itch*."

"That's the one," Sophia nodded, passing me again, moving into the living area.

"Do you want to see this or not?" Zee said, referring to the apocalyptic scene he had set up on the video.

"Can I just get dressed?" Sophia said, her voice unhurried.

"Watch this first," Zee said, reaching a hand up to Sophia and pulling her down to his side. She curled into his hold. "Come closer, little man."

"*Little man*," Sophia said to me. "Is that how I should address you as well, or is there another name that links you with your birth?"

"That would be Jonathan, or Jonathan Francis, or Little Flower," Zee said, eyeing me, but addressing Sophia.

"I think I like Francis, like the saint," Sophia said. "A man stripped to nothing and throwing off his father's wealth and possessions. Is that you?"

I idled a moment. Then froze. When was the last time someone called me by my name and celebrated it, sang it? Spoke with affection and not a threat?

"Don't look so damned frightened, little man," Zee turned to me. "She's just asking a question, pulling on your theological chain."

"I didn't mean to upset you," Sophia said.

"It's okay," I said, feeling the heat again, the distance of my name. "I just need to sit down. I'm tired from my walk."

"You'll have to excuse my little brother," Zee said. "It's not often he entertains in his monastic chamber. Now, can we get back to the movie?"

Sophia turned to me.

"I hear you lost your job," she said. "Was it really in the cemetery back there?"

Nod.

"My boy here has developed a very intimate relationship with the dead," Zee said, poking Sophia in the chin, turning her head back toward him. "An old family tradition."

"Death is always much closer to us than we'd like to admit, don't you think?" Sophia said, a whisper. "It surrounds our skin like a second veil we cannot see or touch but know is there."

"Like a guardian angel, hovering, is that it?" Zee said.

Sophia looked at my brother, closer. "No," she said, "I don't imagine death as an angel with wings."

"You're right," Zee said. "Death works with a back hoe. Strictly back hoe work."

"And what will you do now?" Sophia asked me.

"Not sure."

"We just got his passport and we're off to Paris," Zee announced. "Touch up a little ancestral scar that has been buried in France ever since the Great War."

Sophia brightened. "The first time I landed in Paris I thought, this is a city that could ravage me," she said, waving a hand. "Just ravage me."

"There you go, little man. To be ravaged, that's what you need."

"Then there's always the terror of coming home," Sophia added. "What will you do then?"

"God knows," I said.

"Let's put it this way," she continued, simplifying her tone. "What do you want to be when you grow up?"

I smiled. "I've always worked with my hands. Carpentry, house painting. I'll find something."

"So you believe in the power of touch."

Sophia shocked me with her honesty. She seemed to slip off the burdens of the world, language was no obstacle.

"And what about you, little bird," Zee turned to Sophia. "What do you want to be when you grow up?"

"Aha," Sophia lit up. "When I was young and vanity was my spouse, and friends and relatives said I was beautiful, I should be in the movies, I believed them. But in my heart there was someone different, someone quiet. I dreamt of running off and joining a community or devoting myself to God. Of going to India and being with Mother Teresa. As a child, you see, my parents took me to Mass every week. We were stern Catholics. We believed."

"Us too," Zee said, looking to me, then back to Sophia. "Except for the belief part. That we never really took to heart. Right, Little Flower?"

"What happened to the dream of running off to India?" I asked, curious.

"Well, life offers us many curves and temptations, don't you think," she smiled. "And sometimes spirit gives way to flesh."

"Body heat," Zee grinned.

"That, and I'm entertaining Buddhism now anyways," Sophia said, adjusting the bed sheet over her legs.

"You didn't tell me that," Zee said.

"You don't know everything about me, my dear."

"And how has this happened?" Zee asked, tilting his head, as if viewing a portrait at an unusual angle.

Sophia looked serious. "Studying. Going to the library and taking classes at university in comparative religions. Actually, I lean toward Zen Buddhism. I find it cleaner, clearer. You see, I find most Western teachings to be out-of-touch now, too archaic, too stiff. To be a Christian is no longer respectable. It's become too white, too right. And as a woman I just feel that Buddhism is much more tolerant of who I am and who I am not."

"Jesus," Zee said.

"Not anymore," she smiled, poking my brother in the rib cage.

"Do you have a teacher?" he asked.

"No, no," Sophia said. "I'm just reading seriously and studying koans and parables, letting ancient images and words sink into my mind and sleep and dreams. It's the humour in Zen I love. Crazy little tidbits that come and go like the wind.*'When walking, just walk; When sitting, just sit; Above all, don't wobble.'* You don't find that kind of humour in the Bible. Although Jesus did say something like, 'Why do you worry about the splinter in your brother's eye but ignore the great log in your own eye?' Now that's funny, *great log*. I mean, if a religion doesn't save you through a touch of humour, how is it supposed to be taken seriously?"

"Jesus," Zee said again, a hand slapping his forehead. "You need a master or someone for this stuff. You can't just pick up a book and remember a few sayings and say you're a Buddhist. That's like finding someone's driver's license in the gutter and announcing yourself a driver. You need a teacher, you've got to put in your holy dues, be initiated and stuff. Besides, if you were really a Buddhist, you wouldn't be here, half-naked with me."

"And why's that?" she said, calm.

"You'd renounce everything of the world. You'd live where you couldn't step on the ants. You'd have a little hut in the woods and pray for all the sinful buggers like us. You'd be so immersed in the stuff that you'd become truly universal, truly Catholic, and you wouldn't care if there were any difference between one religion or culture and the next."

"I don't, and I didn't say that," Sophia said. "I love diversity. The Chinese teach not to eat after sundown. Meanwhile, in Spain, the feast begins at sunset. I'm just saying I have more respect for the Buddhist way of life. And I saw the Dali Lama at City Hall last year and he struck me as the most spiritual person I've ever witnessed. I shook his hand and his gentleness touched me."

"I was there too," I quickly announced.

"What did you think?"

"It was moving," I said. "I wanted the kind of peace he spoke of."

"It's right here," she said, tapping her breastbone.

"I don't believe it," Zee said, rolling his eyes.

I looked at my brother and said, "This coming from a man who has long since given up on belief."

He gave me his look, that one belonging to our father, that inherited eyebrow.

"You got it, mon frère," he said. "Belief hinders the body. Look at our mother's drunken faith. Teaching us nothing but obscurity. With a faith like that, there's only shame and guilt."

"Now that's truly Catholic," Sophia smiled.

"You're serious about this stuff, I take it," he said, turning back to Sophia.

"I believe in the greater mysteries we cannot possibly see or understand with just our senses," she said.

Zee grinned. "All religion does is keep us mired in the past. Keep us submissive to someone else's story and morality and belief. That's why I believe in what we can touch and feel on our own. What's here and what's now."

"And I believe in the art of an inward life," Sophia said. "True religious experience begins with curiosity and wonder, and love. A love for creation and those invisible energies that are greater than just ourselves. People have changed their lives just by seeing a beautiful sunset. Or preparing a cup of green tea. Destruction is too easy in the modern world. Just a bullet or bomb or economic policy away. But to act religiously, to make a work of art or a child, to create a temple from the ground up, that takes years. Thousands of holy years."

"I'd never trade my flesh for something I cannot see," Zee said, defiant.

"That's tragic," she said. "You don't know what you're missing."

She looked into my brother's eyes. There was resolve in her gaze. A heart power. She raised a finger as if in a gesture of fidelity to the moment. She brushed the finger across her brow, then touched my brother's lips. I felt that place in my heart, that hermit's flame I spoke of earlier. All because of a finger against my brother's lips, a hush, and a parable she offered us that afternoon.

> *At the sound of the bell in the silent heart, I wake from my dream in this dream-world of ours. Gazing at the reflection of the moon in a clear pool, I see, beyond my form, my real form.*

There are parables that live in the voice, my son. Like an ancient river we must learn to let flow. So that love can surprise you at any curve in a story.

19

ACCORDING TO MY BROTHER, LIFE is about celebrated highs. His version of getting down and drunk. Bar hopping and crowded table tops and the smoke of discussion. Probe the world's wounds and sizzle until someone, somewhere, screams mercy.

"My treat," he was always saying. His party.

Zee piled Sophia and I into the back of a taxi. He took the front seat, leaning back to talk, and snapping a photo of us. The night was fixed. He smiled and introduced himself to the cab driver, shaking hands, and snapping the cab driver's photo. We took the cab to University and College, then walked west along College into the heart of Little Italy. The walk was slow, College St. crowded. A hazy tremble between pedestrians, traffic and the heat. Sophia strolled between Zee and myself, an arm through each of our arms. She had transformed herself, out of the bed sheet and into a flowered skirt and a thin, silk blouse. Leather sandals and toes painted royal blue. She gleamed something perpetual, something twinkling. Like a rare night spirit, tempting you along corridors known only by the light of foliage and polished stone. I kept catching glimpses of her feet, and my brother's cowboy boots, the three of us stepping out along College. A natural wobble to the hour.

Bar Italia was full, but we found luck and a table at the Diplimatico, one of my brother's favoured watering holes. A standard corner café with a southern view. On clear nights, you could gather on the patio and almost make out the stars. Sit and wear sunglasses long after dusk. Draw a target on the heart so that your server knows where to aim the wine.

Zee ordered a round of pastas. Penne vodka. Fettuccine with red sauce and seafood. A plate of bruschetta and calamari to start. Caesar salads all around, baskets full of bread and butter.

"Are you drinking?" he asked me, jabbing my rib cage with a finger.

"Nothing for me, thanks," I said.

"Come on, mon frère. One celebratory drink."

"And for me," Sophia said, squeezing my arm across the table top.

"One glass then," I said. Oh sure. "But that's it."

"That's the spirit," Zee clapped. "Little bird, what will it be for you?"

"Red, Lover Boy," Sophia said, with a flourish. "Something, let's say, from the north of Italy."

"Something Tuscan, I see," he said, looking over the wine list. "Though there's a lovely French here, from the midi Pyrenees. I once hiked the region. Trust me and trust its taste."

"French it is," Sophia agreed. "What's on a border anyways. All in the mind, right?"

"In the Pyrenees it's the stones that make the difference in the wine," Zee said, leaning on the table top, playing connoisseur. "Thick, gorgeous white stones scattered in the fields and around the base of the vines. Magic stones that retain the sun's energy all day and throughout the nights, giving warmth and warding off cold fronts and frosts. When you drink this wine, you're drinking sunlight that has travelled light years just to ride your tongue and still the heart."

"Such an existential romantic," Sophia said, taking my brother's hand in hers.

"Speaking of the existential. Anyone up for a pre-meal joint?"

I shook my head, squared my feet on the patio.

Sophia pulled Zee's hand closer to her chest, then checked over her shoulder for a convenient alley down which they might slink and light up their sacred spliff. The two excused themselves and sauntered up the block, arm and arm, then disappeared behind a church across the street. I found myself looking to the sky, its yellow-blue hue, slowly fading like a legend.

Now the table top was full of food and white plates and small wine glasses, and a wine lifted from an era when one knew who made the colour red. Zee and Sophia returned, a little high and laughing. They took their seats as if in the middle of a joke. Zee poured the wine, then offered a toast and clinked each of our glasses. I took a slow sip, letting the wine settle just below my throat. One last drink, I believed. Stepping back a moment from the tenuous beat of humanity. I listened as Sophia slipped into the philosophical.

"So, Lover Boy," she began, "Is there a spiritual world at all? And if so, is it spirit that surrounds matter or matter that cradles spirit? I mean, I know both worlds are integral to the heart, which as you know, we cannot see, but only feel at the best of times. But is this how spirit works in the world, concealed within matter as the heart is concealed in the chest? As the sun's energy is concealed in those white stones you spoke of, in France? And is all our eating and breathing and aching and fucking and celebrating just a material means toward a life of greater spiritual importance? And if so, is the love and pain I feel the love and pain of spirit or matter?"

"Mmm, the calamari is scrumptious," Zee said, winking at me. "But life is suffering, isn't that what you Buddhist's say. Good days, suffering days. And isn't there some kind of balance between the two worlds? I mean, we can't just live in the spiritual world or we'd disappear like a puff of smoke. That's why I say it's matter that matters, first and foremost."

"If it's balance you're talking about, why put one before the other?" Sophia said.

"Really, I don't care which comes first," Zee said. "In the end, I say too much religious fervour clouds our freedom. Our independence."

"Independence?" Sophia said. "You talk of those French stones and your excursions there, but have you been to see the caves?"

Zee shook his head, working on a cigarette between sips of wine and bits of calamari.

"The Dordogne caves, deep inside France. It's the place where our prehistoric ancestors first bathed in the light and darkness of matter and scratched out their tiny, terrified existence on stone walls. These are people who knew their place, shaped by the earth where they lived. When you see those caves, the art, the honour and fear there, you're seeing the earliest maps we have into the human condition."

Zee sent me another wink over the rim of his wine glass. Sophia leaned into the table top, closer.

"If you're looking for independence, see the caves," she continued. "And see how silly the idea of independence really is, and how hooked we are into one another, for better and for worse."

"Mostly worse, I'd say." My brother grinned.

"I'm serious," she said. "I used to think I was free so long as I was alone, as long as I could feed my ego and solitude. But take a look into those caves and wall paintings in the damp belly of the Earth and you'll see that when we arrive at a place of survival, of really having to survive, there's very little room for independence. Our true story is the story of our interdependence. Arms linked, hands feeding one another, beautiful acts of generosity."

Zee winked at me a third time. Comrades. The old ravine of our blood. I took a large sip of wine, draining myself of the heat.

"Can you see she has an artist's soul?" Zee said to me, then turned his gaze back to Sophia. "My little Francis here, he has an artist's soul too."

"Is that so?" Sophia said, eyeing me.

"I'd never call myself an artist," I said, turning my eyes away, feeling light headed.

Zee pressed on. "Come on, little man, don't be shy. You know the value, no, the soul there is in a piece of clay. Not to mention your perpetual canoe, your love of cedar, and your graves. Let's not forget your graves, Little Flower, digging in the dirt. Everything you do requires a touch of art."

"You're high," I said.

"Just celebrating, little man."

"To work with clay and earth, or wood, that's beautiful," Sophia said, leaning in again. "So tell me, do you believe in the Big Bang or the work of a personal Creator? Or does it all arise out of a big, glorious heap of nothing?"

"Why must there be one at the cost of the other," I said, wine on my tongue. "I've been listening to you two, matter or spirit, spirit or matter? Isn't there a marriage between the two? Isn't that the mystical core to our being? Flesh inside spirit and spirit inside flesh, just as we're here inside the cosmos, sitting on a patio, blinking like the stars…"

"Now who's high?" Zee laughed.

"No, no," Sophia said. "There's a simplicity in what he's saying, an elegant approach to wisdom. Like the breaking of bread."

"Now who's being bloody Catholic?" Zee poked Sophia. "Your Buddha would be disarmed by such talk."

"My Buddha," she smiled. "My Buddha would clap one hand."

Laughter. More wine. The humidity creeping through the night. I felt caught in this little divine game between my brother and Sophia. An exotic dance, a tease. Slowly getting drunk. I closed my eyes. My stomach was groaning as if after a fast of forty days and nights. Even though I had consumed the wine, the pasta, the calamari. There was always this emptying aspect within myself when turning from one word to another, when drunk and slurring and pretending to know so much when what little I did know was enough to blur me and make me want out.

Sophia leaned back, loosening her hair. She peered at me, curious. I couldn't avoid her gaze, in the same way I could no longer avoid the things that had been left unsaid within myself. Zee moved back in, just a hand, then a soft whisper into Sophia's ear, followed by a kiss. I knew my brother's moves. His power. A second hand on Sophia's thigh, disappearing up her skirt. Whispered promises. How much he loved her, needed here, desired her.

I turned to the night sky. Three or four stars appeared like tiny mouths, each with a delicate warning: The soul will cost you. The soul you think you possess, the energy you've kept in your back pocket all these years, the holy stuff you've allowed institution after institution to rob you of potential and dignity and esteem; that soul, that snap shot of expression, all the ridiculous means you've used to bring you to this table top, it will cost you that life.

We made our way to a dance club along College. A basement club with the feel of an unfinished dream. Everyone in the club appeared dreamy too, swaying beneath heavy strobe lighting. Faces moved in and out of focus on the dance floor. Techno-rap-pop-rock 'n roll. Dancers were decked out in army pants or jeans cut off at the knees, whole bottoms missing, asses gleaming. Guys without shirts, barefooted. Women streaming in leather tops or long black dresses that had been hauled up from the nineteenth century. Shoes like multi-layered cheesecake.

We found a table near the dance floor. The happy couple ordered a round of beers. For me, there was one more famous last drink. *Just one more glass of wine, really, and that will be it.* And then a few more glasses and one more on top of that, while we sat in the quiet of our own company, music thumping. People danced past like great necked ostriches. One guy was tap dancing in an unlit corner. A woman was standing topless in the centre of the floor, eyes closed, head back, mouth opened, as if the music was draining down her throat. Everyone was dripping with sweat and rubbing close.

"It's beautiful, don't you think? All these soaking bodies," Sophia yelled into my ear, over the music. "Like watching petals gleam after a good rain."

I could feel the music pounding, my heart pounding too. The wine and that sleepy feel of a high spilling through each of my heart beats.

"Do you two dance or what?" Sophia yelled, nudging my brother and me.

"I've been known to twist a little, disappear into the odd mosh pit," Zee grinned.

"And little Francis?"

"The gods, I'm afraid, have burdened my little brother with an intricate display of two or more left feet," Zee cut in before I could answer.

"I have the cure," she proclaimed.

She stood and eased her way onto the dance floor, taking Zee and I by the hands, guiding us by her slow shuffle. The music was also slow. There was no echo in the room but for the stir of skin.

It was Neil Young's slow, sad dirge, a live version of Helpless (from The Band's Last Waltz), that entered the room, as if dangling on the arm of an old lover. I closed my eyes and felt my hand in Sophia's hand. I heard Young's leading harmonica wave, followed by the strum of his acoustic guitar, a rhythm that seemed a touch too shy to take complete control of the song. Young opened his lyrics, his phrasing that suggested a man who had left many homes and moons but was still mindful of the way back. Within each lyric (like a gift), Joni Mitchell sang in harmony. Her warm bird voice. A sound you wanted to curl into and glide the years.

Sophia let go of our hands and danced alone. Her hips dripping beneath her skirt. I looked to my brother, his eyes wide, grinning at me. He snapped a photo, then pocketed his camera. Sophia slipped across the dance floor, feet, hips leading the way, as if her mind was free from having to guess where her body might take her. Her lips mouthing along with the lyrics.

...helpless helpless helpless...

She danced back to my brother and they twirled in each other's arms. He whispered into her ear. They kissed, then Zee pushed Sophia toward me. I watched my brother ease into the crowd, skin on skin with other dancers. Sophia put a hand out for mine. I didn't move. She took me at the waist and pulled me closer. Without thinking, I placed my hands on her hips, her hair against my cheek. Sweat. I felt flush and strange, light and away, there in the arms of my brother's summer girl, thinking of my girl, our Rachel, far way in Zambia or Rwanda. Oh God where was her last letter from? I saw Zee in the crowd, his head bobbing and rocking. At an angle, I saw my father in his movements, the man with no desire to leave a mark on life. But Zee, he was different, he wanted to leave his mark, or so he said said... Oh, I was drunk and confused, spinning and feeling this slow dance back toward some crazed semblance of self and matter. A shift, an alteration in spirit, while feeling the arousal of an old theme, my only lover, your mother. Yet there I was, dancing with Sophia, smelling her hair, the warm aloe smell of it, the moisture, the smoke. She was looking at me. I began to shake. I thought, *Zee, get back over here. You're always leaving me when I need you, always gone gone gone when it matters most...* But I was drunk, that old standard theme. Heard it a thousand times. *Sorry, honey, but I was drunk. That little kiss she gave me didn't mean a thing...* No matter how many times I shifted away, Sophia was still there, looking at me. The song tempting this slowness of thought and speech and...

"You have the feel of a sad soul," she whispered into my ear.

Her eyes. No shallowness. Impossible to look away.

"Do you pray?"

"Sometimes," I said, feeling light headed.

"Do you ask for things? For guidance? Or is it more a letting go?"

"I don't ask for things," I said, a slight slur. "Though, there is that promise, I remember, about asking and receiving, about searching and finding."

"And how has your concept of God changed over the years?"

"How do you mean?"

"Well, how do you see this God?"

"Not with a beard, not on a cloud, that's for drunken sure."

"Good to hear." Sophia smiled.

"And you, how do you see your God?"

"No God. Only the nothing of the unconscious becoming conscious. And to be like the wind, not looking back upon the self, not concerned with the self, just expanding with existence. That's what I want."

I was swaying in her arms, feeling loose, feeling warm, listening. She moved close to my mouth with hers—

"What's wrong?" she said.

"I thought you were going to kiss me."

"Kiss you."

"Yes."

"That's a little presumptuous, don't you think?"

"Sorry, I've been drinking too much," I said. "Sometimes I get paranoid when I'm drunk."

She looked at me. "Well, it would have been just a kiss. That's all. A little kiss."

"But you're with my..."

"Forget him. What do you feel?"

What do you feel? What do you feel?

"Forget him, sure, but I don't think my girlfriend of forever and ever would appreciate it."

"Isn't she away, far away?"

"How do you know that?"

Sophia waved her head back in the direction of my brother, dancing his ponderous storm.

"Did he put you up to this?"

Sophia didn't answer.

"Because he's done that before. He thinks it's inhuman of me to be with one woman. He has this habit of trying to set me up with anyone and everyone other than Rachel. He once shoved me into a closet where one of his girlfriends was waiting. Suddenly she was licking my face, kissing me wildly."

"We're just dancing, that's all. It's a beautiful night. And you can't tell me you haven't been looking at me, checking me out... desiring..."

I blushed. Yes, yes, okay... I desire you...

"There's nothing wrong with that, you know," she said, without pressure.

"But there's that other religious bit I remember, about adultery, about sinning," I said. Now I knew I was really drunk.

"I know the one," Sophia said. "About not having to actually screw to sin. It's enough just to think of *screwing* someone else other than your lover that is the real sin."

"That's the one."

"But again, it's just a kiss we're talking about."

"A kiss is everything. When you kiss, breath becomes soul."

"So, you believe that pearl in the Bible, that it's enough just to think of the sin before indulging in the act of sin."

"Right now, I'm surprised that this kind of thinking is rocking me, making me ponder. And I'm feeling too much wine to really root it out, or take that kind of risk, kissing you, to find out if I feel terrible afterwards or not. I think I should…"

"It's okay, it's okay," Sophia said. "You're a devoted soul, I see that. One who believes we all have that one lover whose ribbons remain round our hearts long after we've first met."

"Yes."

"And how long have you been wearing her ribbons?"

"Since 1980. September. A last warm day before autumn."

"Indian summer."

"Yes."

"You were young."

"Yes."

"What a night, or is it a good morning?" Zee sang as we left the club at 2 a.m., after hours of dancing and talking and drinking.

"Tell me a love story," Sophia had asked me, the two of us back at the table after our dance and more wine. I was drunk, but I told her a love story. I dropped a line or two about your mother and me and our years of pulling close, then back. Our marathon dance, our birch bark letters. Her love of far away places and my own unease about testing those distances. Because there was something of my own shade and ancestry that kept me still, an observer of other peoples travels and intrigues. My grandfather and my father, you see, had met their foreign soils, their wars, had returned home and were never the same. My mother had left her home soil for something foreign, something changed, stayed, but did not change herself after years of addiction. So to journey while keeping still became my path, those years, while your mother travelled and worked. Until she might flit back in, scoop me up, our arms finding their wild. She could instruct me with a glance, open waters and sky. We believed not in the luck of having found one another, but the intrinsic design of stars, the recognition. And this is what I shared with Sophia that night, eased myself and my story. I had found a place of conversation without hunger or fear stalking me. Until my brother reappeared, jumped in from the dance floor, loose and drunk and perspiring.

Out in the street, Sophia was quiet. I was quiet. Zee convinced us to walk along College and up Palmerston, beneath its beautiful canopy. Zee strode between us, arms around our shoulders. Beer buddies, feeling loquacious.

"When I die, God help me, burn me and sprinkle my ashes over these streets," he said to me.

"I thought you wanted to be thrown over Hollywood's star glittered avenues," I said, wobbling in his hold.

"Not tonight. Tonight I'm re-writing my will," Zee smiled. "And you, mon frère, still want a pine box, a hole in the country, beneath some pine."

"Beneath anything greening, yes," I said.

"And how about you, little bird?"

"Ashes," Sophia said. "A hilltop in northern Ontario, the wind, the four directions, and just let me go."

"And who will escort you there?"

"My last lover, I hope. Or perhaps, if lucky, my very first lover," Sophia said and reached around Zee's back and pinched my arm.

"I'm sure my little man here would be honoured to carry out that request," Zee said, pulling us close. "He's the only one I know holy enough to pull off that kind of stunt. A saint because of his work with the dead."

"I'm no saint," I laughed, trying at being sober. "You're the one closer to becoming a saint, by virtue of your being closer to a life of sin."

"I get it, mon frère. Jesus talk, dear old Mum's talk. Because I'm the saint of lust. Isn't that how she used to put it?"

"Not quite as eloquent," I said.

"Well, if anything, I'm the saint of renunciation."

"So you admit to a certain Catholic strain in your blood, after all," I said, teasing.

"No, no. I've renounced everything. Life is life and death is just a little more trash to take out to the curb," Zee said, pulling at my neck with his arm around me. "And lust, my brother, is something you know very little about. Because you've never really reached that point of losing your old life and becoming your true animal self. I mean, have you ever lusted at all, for anyone other than your bloody Rachel?"

I looked at Sophia. Was she bugged? Had Zee been listening in on us through a clever device that he had attached to one of the buttons of her pretty white blouse? Had I misread the trust I felt toward her? Oh the illusions, the paranoia when drunk.

"Now, right now, I'm lusting for silence," I said, smiling a fake smile, diverting myself from the situation through tone and cadence. "A divine silence."

"Oh, you'll never get me with your God."

"Who's trying?"

"You. You're the patron saint of bloody trying."

"No. I must be the patron saint of all fools, listening to this."

"You. You're the saint of precious innocence. A spotless and willing lamb. You're almost as naive as the two old buggers in the house and their bloody wars and never considering the consequences of their histories, on them or on us."

"So now the past has consequence, does it?" I said, tiring.

Zee stopped and took his arm away from my shoulder and stood square before me. He glared at me as if with four or five eyes.

"Listen to me, little man. I'm only saying this because I love you, but for some goddamned reason you're gripped by these skeletons, your own little attic full of holy relics. Every step you talk, you rattle. And I've got to tell you, these relics—Father, dear Mum, the old bird in the attic—they're holding you back from the living and keeping you stuck in their spell, called the past. And you know what else, little man?"

"What? What now?" I said, raising my voice.

"These people, they didn't really love you," Zee poured on. "No love in them, little man. They were evil, that's all. Especially dear Mum. Evil. Don't you see that?"

"So now they're evil, are they?" I said, stepping back. "Interesting that you don't believe in God but you recognize evil."

"Listen, when a man takes a belt to your ass and you catch a glimpse of him grinning as he hits you, that ain't love shining through."

"If you say so."

"And a woman in the back ground, handing the old man the belt for him to do her dirty work, what do you think that is? Love?"

"I don't know, you tell me."

"All I want is for you to dig yourself free of them, that's all. Just break through, please. Because you've become like a ghost too. I could walk right through you."

"You don't know me like you think you do," I said, feeling flush again.

"I know you, mon frère. I know you better than you think," Zee said, stepping closer. I lost sight of Sophia. "I'm not taking you to France for you to see how beautiful and wise history has been to our family. I'm taking you so that you might see first-hand how pathetic it is that we would even lay down our lives for such a lie in the first place. The fight for history is first and foremost a sham. A fickle boundary here and there. This side belongs to you and this side belongs to me, until our intentions change and oil or gold is found on your side and we decide to bomb again. I don't want you to go there to deepen your story and sorrow and your bloody faith. I want you to annihilate it, so that you can get on with the real holy work of lusting and fucking and becoming a useful tool in this world."

"You're drunk," I said, standing back, feeling my hands tighten.

Zee glared. "What are you going to do, hit me?"

"You don't know what you're talking about. Skeletons and ghosts."

"And you do?"

"You were never there," I yelled. The heat, the wine bleeding through me.

"Where?"

Sophia stepped back into my view, toward me, a hand out.

"It's okay," she said. Soft. Her eyes. "Be gentle with yourself."

"There," I yelled again, not taking in Sophia's voice. "In that house. You were always gone, taking off, leaving me alone with them. You did everything you could to avoid the bloody humanity of the place, the goddamned emptiness."

"And why would I want to stay in that kind of crap?" Zee cranked up his tone and stepped at me again, all chest. "Don't you get it? You have to ask yourself why you never chose to leave sooner? Why you let them crush you, use you?"

"Shut up shut up... you don't know everything... you just don't know what really happened in that house..."

I turned and walked up the street, hard, feeling dizzy and soaking through with sweat. I could hear the low dialogue of a late night mystery movie coming from a house, a door open against the humidity. I strained to disappear, my anger turning on me like one of those ghostly skeletons my brother had spoken of, insisted I had become. Words are dangerous in the mouths of the drunk. Like switchblades, drunks and addicts will cut everything out of you, every organ and pulse and hope, just for a high. They will grind you down until even your silence (complicit and charged and hardened) turns against you. If only I could weep, I thought, wash everything of the night and argument away. I could hear Zee then, and Sophia, running up behind me. Streetlights spinning on the road at my feet. It took me a few steps to realize I had broken into a drunken run, surrounded then by late night traffic, wheels. Zee caught up and grabbed me by the back of the arms, pulling me to the curb.

"Damn it, boy, didn't you see that car?'

Car? What car? Until I noticed I was standing in the first lane along Bloor St. A foreignness there, no stars pressing down.

Zee yanked me up to the sidewalk. Sophia was at his side, a hand also taking me by the hand. Touch.

I pulled away.

"You can't take me that seriously," I heard my brother open, trying to hold me again at the arms.

"Don't touch me, don't bloody well..."

"What I say, it's not meant to hurt you," he said, suddenly sober, fraternal. "This truth or how I might hurl a word, it's just meant to stir you, make you think."

"And what gives you that right?" I stammered. "What gives any drunk any rights any fucking..."

I caught myself, feeling the dizziness again, the lack of breath after my run and sweat. I slumped with my hands on my knees and shook. Too much heated exchange for a young man whose anger was like a desert stripped of skin and sand.

"It's okay, breathe," I heard Sophia say into my ear as I slumped to the pavement, curling up. "Sometimes we need these little challenges to show us another way."

Sometimes.

A late night cab ride home. The three of us in the back seat. A silence neither polite nor impolite. Zee was sitting between Sophia and myself. He was stroking the back of her hair, her head against his shoulder. She was sleeping. I wanted to turn my back on the whole night, our story, our ghosts. To hell with them, I thought. To hell.

"What's that Cohen song?" Zee said, whispering to me, as if nothing had happened. Another neat little trick belonging to the drunk. *Nothing has happened.*

"Which song?" I don't know why but I took the bait. Always taking the bait, if it meant appeasement. This was my historical role in a household of living drunks: the peacemaker.

"You know the one, little man. That one about his lover's hair," Zee said, his hand still lost in Sophia's hair. "How does it go... *I'll love you in the morning, your kisses deep and warm, your hair upon the pillow like a sleepy golden storm...* Or is it, *stone?*"

"Can't remember."

But I knew. It was *storm*.

"Her hair makes me think of that song, that's all," Zee said.

"Good for you," I said.

"What, are you still angry?"

"What was your first clue?"

"At what?"

"I'm tired, I don't want to talk," I said.

"Fine. Don't."

Sophia twitched as my brother's hand ran through her hair, the wind moving through the open window. The cab pulled through the neighbourhood, the night slowing. I heard Sophia's breath rising. Zee leaned away from me and kissed Sophia on the forehead. He lifted her legs over his, she groaned. Zee's other hand was in shadow, sliding beneath her blouse. I closed my eyes. We were characters caught up in the two or three metres falling apart around us, forced to grab at a lifetime of relational bonds within the context of a single night.

At every drunken turn, there was the despair of memory, anxious waste. A part of me (I could only speak in parts) wanted not to look any further, feel anymore. A part of my body wanted to join the extinct, or become removed like those useless parts, the wisdom teeth or the little toes that were no longer required for mastication or balance. I wanted to give into the anti-energy that was eating me up. I wanted to smash through old fictions, and annihilate the past.

Zee.

I pulled myself from the cab and walked toward the basement world. I passed the Virgin in her garden. Her sober eyes looking down. Such belief and patience, I thought. Her child-bearing hips, painted blue. But how could I believe in her belly and the Son of Man growing in her womb without her ever having been screwed? What kind of story was that?

Zee and Sophia entered the basement. I swayed drunk at the door, then turned and ran through the back yard, jumping the stone wall and landing in the cemetery. I lay down in a sunken grave, swallowed on the faintness I felt. I watched the night sky through the oaks, constellations dispersing against an infinite blackness. I heard the wind shuffle through the leaves, then slowly drop off, like nothing, across the earth.

20

WE'VE BEEN LIVING BY THE lake for two years. Two beautiful autumns, two wild winters, a few muddy springs, moving now into our third summer. Green shoots flicker over the waking earth. There's yellow pollen in the air, gently falling and clustering on the lake. When the ice goes out, mid-April, and the lake opens again, chunks of driftwood that have been caught up in ice floes and shorelines are released. As the current surges, driftwood is carried and sometimes nestles here against the dock, because of the dock's positioning, a natural alcove. Sometimes I get into the canoe and dip my way along the shore, searching for other driftwood. I unhook unique pieces from snags and rocks. Over the months, I've been collecting pieces and hauling totem shapes of wood up the hill, behind the house. Using braided grass and vines and malleable twigs, I've been making us a driftwood sculpture, a tree polished by water and my hands, rising out of the rocky earth. All these shapes I've gathered, if only to encourage a reunion with wood.

Your mother is a woman who holds operatic discourse with zucchini plants, tomatoes, trout lilies and spider wort. Philosophical debates about sun and shade. She praises colour, love's humidity, moves within their suck. Her fingers pluck at the soil as if a cello, a string quintet. Yo Yo Ma loosening good old Bach. Her passion for the earth is visceral. There is a distinct link between earth health and her practice in medicine. She moves through the garden with a select twig in her hair, always a smudge of dirt on her cheek. For her the earth is familial, a tactile ancestor. Like my driftwood sculptures, full with the power of poetry.

Tell me a love story, Sophia had asked me that summer night.

And I did.

Autumn, 1980. A time I hold like an intimate smile.

I'm thirteen and my mother has gone back to her childhood London to take care of my grandmother Littlewood, who is dying from liver cancer. The old woman doesn't have much time. The decision for my mother to go is quick and her departure a blur, with little time to negotiate its transition. The household she is in firm control of falls from her grip. My mother thinks she'll be gone a week or two, but a late summer and early autumn extend well beyond Thanksgiving of that year, and beyond Remembrance Day. The old woman just won't let go. And my mother's departure (I must admit celebrated, I must admit a relief) allows for other, subtler nuances to step in in her place. As if the sun had eased a few degrees north, deciding to stay the season a while longer.

During this time, my father comes and goes, a week here and there between London and other European capitals of commerce, and home. He returns with scant news of my mother and Grandmother Littlewood, saying only that the old woman is tough. The cancer is spreading, but she is a fierce competitor. Her pink dish gloves are off. Only when my mother returns home shortly before Christmas of that year, not saying a thing about her mother, and never returning to England, do I guess that Grandmother Littlewood is dead.

That season I wander the ravine more and more, on my own or in the small company of a class field trip. I move deeper into the ravine's pockets and wander the Don Valley river basin. I study the river's course, chart marshlands and lush greenery. Bird life. I sit for hours with binoculars and bird books and eventually learn to identify the quick silhouette of a wing or the hidden pulse of a chirp. The colour of a warbler's throat enters me like code. An art teacher has encouraged the class to write and draw. He presents each of us with a small pocket journal to begin a closer life with our thoughts and feelings and ideas. At first I am shy before the page and feel I must seek the permission of an authority (my mother, my father, a priest) before I dare write or draw of my life or a bird's. I'm not yet at a point of revelation and closeness with myself, but I do recognize in the blue lines of my first journal a potential path. Something about being given a journal while in the presence of water. I take to my journal like water and do not want to abandon the intrigue I find in words, the release. I imagine my stepping into a secret cave and, with ink, leaving on the page the markings of an inner world I'm unable to offer through the power of voice. I sense (even then, just thirteen) that there is a mutual appetite between myself and a word. I see my grandfather on the page, just as I had seen him on the floor in his attic room, scribbling away. My writing hand acting as if with an almost ancestral thrust, as if it is his ghost in me writing things out. Where his hand has left off, my hand is only beginning to dig through that world of yellow foolscap and old echo. I have not (physically, bodily) been in his Great War, but through him I have been there, yes, I have lived and died there. History begins to visit me and thicken within. I hunger for its continued message, knowing there is also something prescient to the hunger too, a haunting rumination of things to come. Like the day your mother will toss a blueberry into my life and love will enter the page.

It's during this time (Mother gone, Father coming and going; Zee also gone, drifting somewhere in the world) that I'm left in the warm and capable hands of Mrs. Pinto. A neighbour has recommended her to my father and she is hired on a weekly basis. She arrives each morning at eight, stays the day, tends to the household chores, our needs, until my father arrives home at six. When my father is away on business, or visiting my mother in London, Mrs. Pinto stays the night, or the week, nestled on a pull out couch in the upstairs den.

Mrs. Pinto sweeps into the house like a covert spiritual agent, slipping under my parent's radar. She's forty-four, she admits, and widowed. She's come from Fiji to Canada, she says, to live with her brother and sister-in-law, the professor and Mrs. Singh, so that she might meditate through her grief, and because (more importantly, she says) it's time she learn about snow angels, how to lie back in a bed of snow and let her arms and legs go. It is essential, Mrs. Pinto shares, to risk ourselves to what we don't know. Otherwise, our hearts might never catch up to our souls and stories.

With her, Mrs. Pinto brings her native Fiji, her worldly spices and waters. Her banana curry and mango chutney. She brings her palm leaf hands and a love of tickling, a surprise finger parting my hair before I leave for school. At first I step back from this touch, feel tentative as her hand reaches for me, her fingers like ribbons of night water. Yet my thirst for touch becomes apparent. She teaches me about the hands, how our palms carry in their bowl-form the scents and libations that have been gathered from a world of bloom and travel. In our hands, there are the two prayers of holding on and letting go. The crux of all spiritual teaching. The hardest prayer being the final prayer, she says, the prayer of letting go.

She is the first woman whose mood and motive does not erase me. There is nothing in her presence suggesting heaviness, drunkenness. She is a large woman and I see in her cozy curves the shape of a landscape I am drawn to. Every muscle, every ache reaches for her. By her touch, the house is suddenly turned inside out and filled with an atmosphere of jubilee. Colour leaps from walls that have otherwise been obscured by yellowing layers of cigarette smoke. Mrs. Pinto opens all of the windows, no matter the temperature, thirty minutes a day. The wind and air to crash around and rock us like a ship at sea. I love this rebellious sense of weather, this rocking clash. If my mother were to pay a sneak visit, my God, she'd have Mrs. Pinto gagged and racked. My father, when home, doesn't seem to mind this swift new wind and warmth in the house. At times, he pauses in the hallway and takes in the new smells of cooking and atmosphere. I can almost see in his face the past cleared of its obstacles, his anger forgotten. We're almost a unit then, the two of us, a family, in the charged air of Mrs. Pinto's kitchen.

She calls me 'Sweet Leaf.' 'Dear Bear.' She calls me 'Peg Leg Wiggly Bum' because of how I walk. My own, skinny sway. Skinny legs, skinny bum. Every morning she greets me with a kiss on each cheek. She's a woman who speaks of angelic presence, a spiritual topography, the lineage of saints. Prayer is nothing more than a keen awareness of the voice of God in your heart, she says, swirling like wine in a clay jug. We must listen, she teaches, listen for the stir in our heart before we raise our libation into word. Mrs. Pinto comes at me as if out of the nowhere of the lines in a favourite book. I'm surprised by her, grateful for her, and terrified too of the life opening in me. What luck, I think. Years of a growing hardness, a dullness inside the house on Hudson Dr., had challenged my senses, my intuition. Zee often said that we must have been dropped as babes from the eternal stork's beak (an accidental drop?), into the wrong yard and house. This I sometimes took literally, if only to assuage the sense of lifelessness I often felt within our walls of bone.

Each morning before I head off to school, Mrs. Pinto offers me her gems, her lessons in the spirit. I listen on the edge of my seat and follow each of her words like a pearl drop of water along a branch, glistening. There is something of a child leaping from a school bus in the way her words and accent enter the room. It's not my lineage I'm following, I know, but I see I'm being offered a rare chance, a new language that celebrates earth and aroma and long walks through the heart.

Remember, Mrs. Pinto says, you carry in your eyes the light of memory, the heat of a thousand years. What is the religion of your soul good for, your past, if it doesn't allow you to imagine a future? There are pilgrim routes all over the world, she tells me, great roads and rivers. There are stars we must trust as guides. Nothing is by accident. Yet the most arduous journey you can make, she says, is from here to here. Saying this, she bends and touches my toes and draws an imaginary path up my body, tapping my stomach, my chest, my forehead. This journey requires great humility, she says. That begins in your feet.

I give you these lessons, she confides, because they were given to me by my mother and my grandfather. And because I see a tender soil in you, she says, touching my chest again. I was unable to have children, she adds. I recognized early in my own life it is our stories we carry from place to place, like precious wine. We offer a drop here for someone's ear, a drop here for the Earth. Heaven lives in the exchange, she teaches. Heaven is a wild verb, not a flat noun. It's apt to travel, and comfortable in stillness.

Long ago, Mrs. Pinto tells me one morning, the sun eased into the South Pacific and spent the night making love with a whale. Days, more nights of love ensued, the sun moving deeper into the ocean, unseen, and making love with many more whales. For months, the world went on in darkness, the oceans groaned with pleasure. Until moons later, thousands of whales, swollen and bright, emerged from the waters, breached the Earth, and released into the world all the shapes and beings we're now familiar with. All human life, wild life, sensate life, divine life. One great rush of wonder. Blues and greens igniting. The beginning of praise.

Listening to Mrs. Pinto, I never tire. There are mornings that quick season when I pretend to be ill, on school mornings, just to stay home alone with her. She sees through this, of course, smiles, and makes us tea. She knows I want this new territory of gentleness, the elation of touch. I can feel the blood in my body, purring. I'm a neophyte, I know. I also know there is a gap at the core of my being that if not careful, I'll fall through, swallowed again by the cold fronts that still lurk in the house and fight against memory.

The truth is, at the time I am not fully prepared for my release. Do not yet have a deepened faith in a word. I'm a step along a path, as if through an old growth forest, not seeing how great is the way. I'm vulnerable to all the tricks and elements that press through creation, billions of years of pressing, and still there is the mystery of where we've come from, of where we're going. My hope is far ahead of my heart, but at least, like all the birds and saplings and pollywogs I've studied in the ravine, there is an energy in my soul, a newness. At least there is this one word altering my vocabulary. One gradual ingredient: a dash of hope.

It's a Saturday, mid-September, when Mrs. Pinto introduces her niece to the house. I'm lying on the grass in the back yard. Eyes open, listening. There is the hum of warm air and birdsong. Day stars step from one cloud-puddle to another. I've been writing in my journal, recording sounds and scents. Then I drift into a dreamy orbit. In an image, a window opens and I see the colour of someone's eyes against the colour of the sky.

A footstep in the grass.

The first blueberry lands on my chest. A tiny ping. I imagine it's a ladybug, up and fluttering. The second blueberry bounces off my hair and lands in the grass. I brush a finger across my forehead, thinking the ladybug is there. I keep my eyes closed, concentrate on the feel. She says there were others tossed my way, arcing over my head, missing me. Until a last blueberry goes plunk, straight into my open mouth. I don't gag, but feel this small, soft shape slide along my tongue. Instinctively I cradle this subject, realizing this is no ladybug. I bite into it, recognizing the fine blue taste of this berry the colour of night.

I open my eyes and there she is.

Dimpled curls. Plum black eyes. Dirty knees.

There are fifteen silver bangles along her thin left arm. Not her throwing arm and hand. A series of small musical notes are arranged around her light brown ankle, a tattoo celebrating the first few chords to All You Need Is Love. It will be a few years before I will kiss those notes, enter her watery ink, but I know I can wait, will wait. I'm lying down but instantly feel my heart hit the ground at my feet. Only a sly, casual move might bend and retrieve that blessed organ.

"I hope you like bear food?" Her voice leaps. "My aunt says you do."

She's a young woman, two years older than me. I'm a boy (a boy's crush, impossible and forever) and stuck on those silver bangles and musical tattoos. If I'm to speak, it will only emerge through rumour, innuendo, or a joke scrambling for the right punch line, but falling flat, because of course, I've become mute.

"Blueberry got your tongue?"

I want to run and shake off this dream that can't be true. Because there is more comfort in the word on the page, the recorded image, than in the miracle of my voice box or the muscle of a spoken word. Even though I know there is not enough talk in my life, talk that truly thrives. I'm too used to propaganda, or no talk at all. I swallow the blueberry and digest the image of your mother there in the back yard, standing by the steps. It's this image, I'm sure, that eventually bends and picks up the heart at my feet.

"Actually, the blueberry creates a wonderful bear hug potion," your mother relates to me that morning. "Swallow enough of its juice and you might find yourself filled with an urge to hug just about everything around you."

I can see she's a good student of one Mrs. Pinto, having absorbed her aunt's manner and speech.

She holds in her hands a full quart of blueberries, last of the season's bounty. She is visiting her aunt for the weekend, in from Guelph where she lives with her parents on twenty acres of rolling landscape and a spring fed pond. All around her house there are blueberry and raspberry patches. Her summers are full of hiking and swimming and picking berries by hand. Right away, I see the adventurer in her, the kid whose cinema is outdoors.

This is my first glimpse of your mother. Our Rachel. Rachel Raine Singh. She was born in the season of monsoon. Her parents, Professor and Mrs. Singh, were making their way from Fiji to the Netherlands, with a fortnight of travel through India. 1965. Your grandmother Singh was just nineteen years old and seven and a half months full with child, her first. She desired this child to be born in the city of her own birth, Amsterdam, but a slight bump in her road and desire led to your mother's early birth while in the presence of the Ganges. Her first holy water. So that in your blood there is this other current and continent. It is no error that your mother revels in water and pursues in her daily swims those same links and deities that are now alive inside your chest. Our Rachel is happiest when working up a good sweat, gardening, then standing on the dock and willing the moisture of her body to dot her skin as if an offering before diving into the lake. All this while nuzzling a blueberry in her smile.

"Are you familiar with the great blueberry wars of 1652?"

I shake my head, still mute.

"The Algonquin mixed a touch of their blood with the juice from a blueberry and worked it into a fine ink before going off to battle. Other tribes pelted the English with blueberries, recognizing early on that the English were often put off by the ensuing stain. Quite often settlers would turn back and board the first ship back to England, just to avoid the stain."

"You're making that up," I say, the first words to your mother.

"Nope. My grandfather on my mother's side shares in what he calls a wonderful bouquet of Algonquin ink, French cousine, and English romanticism. I swear, he told me this," your mother confides. "Arrows were often tipped in a blueberry potion; an enemy's blood would turn purple upon impact with a blueberry arrow. This colour was associated with royalty and the divine would suddenly send a shiver through a retreating soldier's soul."

My mouth loosens. "I've heard the blueberry is really a pearl in disguise."

"Yes, yes. Quite often real pearls are painted blue so that they are easier to smuggle. Custom agents are often fooled and break their teeth when testing the blue pearls. It's an art and a trick to paint a blue pearl with all the dimples and shine of a well cultivated blueberry. One needs the touch of someone like Cezanne to capture the flavour and wit of the blueberry."

"I see," I say, scratching my chin. "And what about the strawberry? Are there strawberry inks and wars?"

"No, no. Strawberries are reserved for whipped cream and lovers. Even the English recognize that."

The blood on your mother's side has many twists and humours, and circumnavigates the globe. Her ancestral past is not in shadow, she tells me that day, but lifts itself like rain raises ink on a page. A biography of water. On her father's side (Professor Singh, a teacher of environmental sciences at the University of Guelph), there is the paternal flow of Fiji and the maternal flow of Greece. Your great-grandparents meeting by chance, on a cruise ship, travelling the Mediterranean, the Red Sea, the Indian Ocean. This is in 1936, '37. He is a young ship's doctor and she is the classical nurse. Their hands compelling them toward one another in a clasp of healing warmth. Back and forth on these waters. Six months of flirtation, a month or two of calm proposals, five months of intensified love. The ship's captain marrying them on their final day at sea, the beautiful Aegean soaking through their vows. Their days and years are lived in medical practice between Fiji and Athens and the island of Crete, where they honeymooned. Every night without fail, this husband and wife read the classics to one another, exchange Homer and Dante and Shakespeare by candle light or a hint of moon. Their pages never too dark before those other intimacies of the night take over. This couple who will hold hands well into their seventies. Saved by a happiness that is both root and light. They died, your mother says, within a week of one another. Two hearts not giving up, but letting go, because it seemed right that way. Two bodies, yes, but each recognizing they were only half a soul finding wholeness while in the arms of the other. Like knowing the secret of an eye that looks upon both land and sea and envisions the countenance of God.

Your mother's maternal side contains a many ringed alliance of colour and journey. There is her grandfather Wildeblood and his Algonquin ink, French flare and English charm. There's his bride with her Dutch ancestry. These two who became instant lovers at the drop of a red tulip, 1945. He has just come through the rigours of D-day and a year of battle, maneuvering up the coasts of France and Belgium and the Netherlands, only to enter Amsterdam on a morning of final liberation. As he walks up the boulevard, tired but ecstatic, clinging to the cheering crowds, the impromptu song and dance, a young woman tosses him a garland woven with red tulips and that's it. Love at first catch. He takes off his helmet and bows, while delivering the romance of a wink. Friends nudge her to follow the lead of her stems. After all, this is a beginning, the whole length of a new world. Later that night their mouths grow wild with love during the fireworks, the canals ablaze with reflections of stars and ribbons, small boats veering like happy drunks. Within a year, after the birth of their first child (a daughter, your grandmother Singh), they are settled back in Ontario, on one hundred acres of farmland outside of Guelph. They work the land and their gardens, fields of corn, and a greenhouse, which, in spring, is devoted to tulips. This is accompanied by five other children in ten years. This couple, who after each Sunday dinner escort the family into the living room, remove shoes and socks, and lie on the floor, each with a head on the stomach of another, and begin their weekly TickleFest. Tickling bare feet and underarms with a free hand, their heads bucking and contorting, laughing, until exhaustion enters the tickle-circle, and all come to a rest, listening then to a brother's or a sister's or a parent's inner calm and force. This tradition that continues to this day, to include grandchildren and cousins. You. When we gather in great rooms at reunions, our bodies twisting on living room floors all over Ontario. That we are home wherever we are. Laughing. Listening.

It's on this farmland, near Guelph, where your mother enjoys a first taste of soil and her initial experience of water from a spring fed pond. Her father paddles his dark blue canoe in distinct circles, round the black pond, while your mother, just five, swims behind. Every muscle in her body is alert, suffused with the voice of the silver haired man kneeling in a canoe, who, between strokes, tells his daughter stories. This man who educates our Rachel through the power of swim, how her body leaves a ripple in the form of a temple bell; then later, on shore, how they snake along the ground and inhale the smell of a meadow at dusk, or lie on their backs, a family dog or cat standing on their chests, licking their faces. For your grandfather Singh there is just as much to glean from an animal's tongue and lick as from the curl of an old pond. Everything offers a clue to the divine. A garden's interior becomes an intimate sanctuary. Roll back every stone, leave no god unturned.

This becomes the stuff of your mother's marinade. A tenderness of spirit she soaks us in and presents without judgement. She is never forgetful of these gifts, never hides her biography. Her mystical charm.

Even now, sitting here and looking into the lake, we can stir her past, get a glimpse into her childhood cinema. Look, there she is taking on her first cut and permanent scar after a five-foot fall from an apple tree. She lands on her hands and knees and rolls over, hitting her head on a small pebble with a singular sharpened edge that punctures the skin just beneath her black mane. She grimaces, eyes watering. Now she places a finger against the wound, removes it and tastes her own fiery blood, the stuff that is to become our celebrated flow.

Look, there she is on her original fit of wonder as she packs to slip away for a night. She packs a favourite teddy bear, a bag of cookies, a deck of playing cards. She goes barefoot. She enters a forest and makes camp by a hidden pond. Spirits are there, I'm sure, protecting her as she sleeps and dreams in the open air. There, too, the next morning, as she returns after her night away, having circled the forest, only to arrive back at the place, Home. Your mother approaches the house, wet with the summer's humidity and the secret of a swim she has taken in the pond, her first alone, unwatched by a parent or sibling. The morning sun shifts over her face, her hair is edgy; her packsack swings from an open hand. Look again, there are the bright imprints of her bare feet over the dewy grass. No one sees her approach, humming, as she steps up onto the porch and brushes through the open door, tip toes up the stairs and slides beneath her sheets. I like to imagine I am there too, somehow present, perhaps one of those spirits, secretly tucking her in. This is enough, I believe, to satisfy our souls. Fill us until our first meeting, in the flesh, years later. So that together we might unseal what has been bequeathed. Love is the trickster at first, remember. Stars whip up a frenzy in the heart.

That Saturday, mid-morning, after the blueberry has entered my mouth and my eyes open, Rachel says, "Have you ever just taken a walk and not cared what chance might offer?"

With my mother gone, and my father away, I'm free to answer.

"No. Not yet."

"Stand up and close your eyes, then spin round and round. When I say stop, open your eyes and no matter where you face, that's the direction we'll take."

Easy. I trust her voice, its wakeful intent. I stand and spin until I'm a little bit dizzy and laughing. When your mother says, Stop, I do. I open my eyes and see I'm facing south and the ravine. I didn't peek.

The ravine opens to us on foot. We stroll under a canopy of late summer leaves coupled with a few autumnal reds and yellows. Down through the woods, my eyes jump from the path to your mother's stride and hips. I spy on her spine, travel like a caravan up and down her back. I've never felt such arousal, just walking, looking. Even your mother's shadow oozes, a watery flicker over the path. Again, I know I can wait. Will wait. Love is a charmer that way. She has no idea what I'm imagining or plotting for our future. How can she? It's not entirely clear to me. I'm thirteen. She's fifteen. An older woman, you see. I'm at a stage where I spend my day dreams like a spy, slow to flesh out my deeper arousals, but for a few late nights in bed, alone, with my journal. My strange relation with the written life. I jot down lines about your mother's remembered stride and light, her heat waking me at 3 a.m. Night sweats and erections in those early years of my desire. All this before I'm able to confirm myself in her waters, offer my own tongue and heat.

That day as we walk, something is exchanged. A spirit in flower, unfolding in the shadows around us. I sense your mother charting these petal-shapes. She has an eye for the tact of a stem. The more we stroll, the closer a need for language presses through our limbs. To talk carefully, to not waste a word, while realizing each step is part of a greater narrative. Love on the lips of the young is uneasy at first. We slowly undo. We pet one another the way a song note will rock you, folk you, jazz you from out of the folds of a stale mood.

We pick our way through the ravine, follow scents of greenery, remnant wild. We step along the fossilized tracts that crease the Don Valley river basin. We wind along Rosedale Valley Road, go west. Buildings break through the distance, rise above the canopy like futuristic tree houses. At Yonge St., we amble north and cut through Ramsden Park, while snacking on french fries and gravy that we've picked up at a greasy spoon. Your mother suggests we imagine ourselves in a time of war, in enemy territory, on the run. So we dash through the neighbourhood, up thin driveways, curl through back yards, leave a sly wink for a man sitting on a patio, reading. We hop his fence, and the railway tracks behind. Dogs bark, cats disperse. In another yard, a sprinkler is set off and we pass through lean lines of water. A yard later, we dare a moment on a double swing that is hanging from a tree. We nestle into the wooden saddle and swing out until a voice calls out from an upper window we cannot see, Hey! We leap off the swing in mid-air. In a single handheld bound we're gone, fox-trot quick. Three or four yards further north, our Rachel picks up a stray football, snaps it to me, goes out for a pass. Hup hup hup. Her breath and voice so alive. Her lightness of step is feather-smooth, yet firm as stones lining a river bed.

We emerge through the neighbourhood at Balmoral, scurry across the street (one more driveway, one more fence), and land in a small cemetery that is crammed in behind the homes and office buildings at St. Clair and Yonge. There are crooked gravestones and sunken graves that date back to the 1850s, pre-Confederation. Rachel insists on tiptoe here. She places her finger upon my lips so that we might listen to the spooky feel of a day lit graveyard. I can't keep myself from spying on her mouth, the smooth redness of her lips. That loyalty to her past and telling.

She whispers. "My grandfather says we should always leave some food for the dead. If we don't, they will feed on our souls."

I've never heard this take on the dead and ghosts before, but in my heart, it makes sense and causes a shudder. Saying this, we make our way to a corner store, buy up all the apples and oranges, chocolates and wine gums we can afford, then return to the cemetery and sprinkle the graves with our bounty. We stand still and anticipate the arrival of the ghosts while holding our breaths.

Silence.

"They must be resting now," your mother whispers.

"Probably," I say. "I've heard ghosts work the night shift. And sometimes they drink too much, so they have to sleep it off during the days."

"Not the ghosts I know."

"The ghosts I know have to. Too much pain in their daily lives. And sometimes they come into your room at night and crawl into your bed and weep into your hair and rub themselves against your body."

Your mother looks at me, concerned. "Are you sure you're talking about ghosts?"

"Probably not."

Then I tell her about my grandfather's touch. His weeping, his grinding into my body. I tell her everything I'm unable to tell anyone else, loosening the secret from my body.

"No one deserves to be haunted like that, touched like that," our Rachel says.

She leans close and places her hand in my hand, squeezing gently. A first healing salve taking shape.

We leave the cemetery, stepping out backwards and facing the gravestones. Rachel swears she notices a ghost, a woman in a bathing suit, circa 1920. This ghost gathers the fruit quickly, then dives back into the grass, behind a gravestone. I'm only able to catch the tail end of her ghostly dive, a sliver of grass parting.

At Yonge and St. Clair, your mother and I pause.

"The house is that way," I say, nodding east.

"And the sun is this way," your mother says, tugging my arm.

Your mother's eyes are equally at home roaming gutters or gardens, stained glass or open sky. Nothing is better than random discovery. We walk along St. Clair, west of Yonge. It's the same block I've walked for years, with my father and Zee, when going for our bi-monthly buzz cuts, then lunch at Fran's. All those years walking there, and never have I ventured further west than Fran's. Never have I dared the spaces where your mother and I now roam. And never have I noticed what we then see, the first piece of living bronze to undress my eye.

I don't know what it is about the sculpture's shape that lures me. There isn't a specific source of light occupying its bronze. The piece is backed up against an insurance building that looms over the street, twenty or so paces removed from the racket of passing traffic, its back to the sun. The shape of the work is that of a man rocking on his ass, his upper body twisting to the right. There are two thickened thighs, the right angling close to the ground, the left pointing skyward. He's missing lower legs and feet, forearms and hands, and has no head. He's all torso, shoulders, upper arms, thighs, a powerful belly. There is a patchwork of cuts or wounds over his green and black bronze body; in the throat, through the chest, heart cavity, and a wound where the genitals should be. At some angles, the wounds appear to look right at you. Is he attempting to get up and on with his evolving work, is he laying back in resignation, in death? I don't know.

Rachel and I step closer. We circle the rocking man's silence, his darkness. Slit that bronze and blood might pour.

My eyes lock on the rocking man's belly. The bronze there curls like blackened waves, the wounds giving the impression that there is something dangerous going on inside. I feel myself being pulled down, as if by an undercurrent, sensing the spaces within my own body that have been discoloured by time.

We search for a title to the work, an artist's name, but there is nothing to tell us about the hands that helped shape its force and weather. Unnamed and incomplete. Son to no one, not even to God. Left outside an insurance building and commissioned to silence. People come and go from the building, but no one looks to see the man rocking on his ass. If you did, I thought, you'd have to give up working for the company, sell your possessions and head out on a pilgrimage.

Rachel and I sit down on the pavement, our backs against a concrete flower box. Shoulders rubbing. Your mother asks me what I see in the piece, what mystery or anger or doubt. I excuse myself from the question and take out my pocket journal and begin to scribble furiously, doodle both words and intricate etchings of a black bronze body rocking on its ass.

My hand with a new order and gift. There is something in the sculpture's belly I can't turn away from, a pulse and storm. What I see is not a need for light, after all, but a desire for rain. A good soaking and this guy might break out of his bronze pose, become a malleable substance and re-work his posture. He might exchange the hard text of his flesh for colour and the woods. Then, in my mind's eye and horror, the shape suddenly creeps into the bed of my words and pushes all hospitality aside. His touch sweet but coarse. Another ghostly embrace. How can I ponder this figure and not think of my grandfather. His lack. Argue with myself all I want, rearrange his silence, like moving a chair in a room closer to an open window, and still this man would curl closer to a civilization bombed and lost rather than to the warmth of a summer view. A voice erased, a name erased. And all day and night this man of blackened bronze is rocking on his ass. Power and defeat wound into a single, unbloodied pose. Strangely alive, and terrifying too.

"Do you think we should name him?"

"He seems nameless to me," I say.

"I think he deserves something ancient. Something holy."

"Do you think he's holy?"

"We all have a little holy in us, in one way or another."

"I can't stop thinking of a no man's land, looking at him."

"But there's something potent about him too, don't you think," your mother says, nudging me. "Can you feel the power of his hidden sex?"

The word *sex* slides into my ear, like a blush.

"I didn't mean to embarrass you. Though a little Socialist red becomes you."

"In my house that tendency is not talked about."

"Socialism or sex?"

"Both."

"In my house that's all we talk about. Bread for all, wine for all. My mother always says that when digging a garden we must make justice and joy the stronger roots. That way when injustice or sorrow come along, they won't choke us out."

"Where do you come from? Pluto?"

"Nope. Guelph. I'll show you sometime."

Rachel stands and steps toward the sculpture. She runs a finger along its thighs. If I could extend myself and join with her fingers, I might be filled with light and heat, but this requires another kind of leap of the heart. Your mother curls a finger against the sculpture's belly and draws a series of intimate circles, as if dotting a love note with hug after hug after hug. It's impossible to outwit the gods, the slide of a red arrow through the heart. How can I explain this without dipping my finger into the lake and wetting your brow and lips? We are water. Just as your mother's touch travels in the water and heat of that afternoon.

She walks back and sits down next to me, our shoulders rubbing again. I love her calmness right away, her pause before speaking a critical word. There is a stillness about her I immediately trust, like an orange, perfectly placed upon a table top. My eyes on her fullness. There is nothing to tempt me to remove her from her skin. Not yet, not there. And I must tell you how beautiful her tears are to me. The quiet tears she has returned with, after having touched the sculpture's belly. So we all have our ghosts and night-shapes that echo throughout the day.

"Do you mind if I write something down?" your mother says, looking at the journal in my hands.

I don't hesitate, if somehow it means touch. Handing your mother my journal is, for me, a first gesture in our eventual undressing. I watch as she wipes a tear from her cheek, then begins to write a short phrase beneath a quick etching I've made of the sculpture rocking on its ass. Your mother's eyes and solitude upon the page. Serene, thoughtful. Some of the moisture from her fingers brushes through the ink of her words as her hand flows across the page, leaving a feathered blue smudge.

"Sorry," she says.

She blows against her fingertips, then writes the phrase a second time. She underlines the words with a bright ink ripple. Another river. Blue.

She hands me the journal, introducing me to these words I've since carried wild in my throat. Though they are heart words.

> *One sees clearly only with the heart. What is essential is invisible to the eye.*

"It's from *The Little Prince*. Do you know it?"

I shake my head.

"It's a story about wonder and trust. Even when your eyes are hurt and the stars have lost their influence."

To this day, I can look at these words and feel the blue moisture in your mother's handwriting, the oasis of her sex. Her print curving like the breathing skin just beneath her breasts.

21

IMAGINE YOU WAKE UP ONE day, say between three and four in the morning, and the guru is no longer the guru. The holy one you've been following turns and spits in your face. A death rattle in your bones. Predator or prey, persecuted or victim, unwilling witness; there is little distinction within yourself. Only that your anguish is as precise as the prick of a needle against the gum line.

    I wrestled beneath the sheets, turtle-like, the morning after my famous last drunk. The door closed. I heard Zee on the phone early on, speaking French. I heard Sophia in the bathroom, showering and brushing her teeth. I wanted to reach out and join her in her scrubbing and brushing. I wanted to pull her away from my brother, but I passed everything off as a disturbance in a dream. The previous night, it never happened. The walk along College, the meal, the wine, the heat and Sophia's dance; the argument with Zee and the cab ride home. Never happened. Not a fingerprint in the city to give my presence away.

    I pulled myself out of bed by noon. I expected to find Zee and Sophia curled up on the living room floor, watching TV. I closed my eyes and sunk into a silence of armistice and surrender. I had to surrender, I knew, to something other than my anger. I had to find a way to behave without carving myself a hole of loss. Mercy, compassion, tenderness. This is what I required. A recommended dosage of love. When I opened my eyes, no one was there. No Zee, no Sophia. Just a few of my brother's clothes were draped over the green canoe, like eerie remains.

I found a note on the kitchen table. 'The tickets are in,' the note spelled out in bold, black ink. 'Paris or bust, mon frère. Making other, historic arrangements today. Staying with S. See you in a few days. C'est bon, Zee.'

Paris or bust. It was the furthest thing from my mind, but the closest. I knew I had to go and encounter my ghosts and lie in the arms of a foreign soil. I paced the basement, my hands up against the wet walls, along the underside of the green canoe. I tripped over an atlas Zee had left open on the floor. My toes flipped back the pages, searching through France. I took in the gleaming map shape of the country. I saw the word *Vimy*, a ghostly dot. France doesn't have the boot distinction of an Italy or the vast stretch lines of a Russian landscape. France has a shapeliness that suggests a slow nibbling. Her shorelines and mountainous overhangs that have been worked on by farmers and monks, armies and lovers. Pinch that soil, I thought, let it talk.

There is necessary risk when wading through the waters and journals of your life. An untapped currency to the gradual realization that the past is not dead earth. That the unhappiness of others does not have to become your own. That memory endures the seasons, and preserves in its long dark nights, the already approaching climate of change.

The reprieve was welcome. Good to be apart from Zee. I didn't speak with anyone for days. No wine, no TV. Only the humidity keeping me company. I worked on the canoe, indoors. Didn't care about the dust. I patched minor holes and refinished the cedar interior and attached new stem bands. I even began to craft a few paddles out of scraps of cherry wood. Earlier in the year, during a procession while at work, the pallbearers had mishandled a coffin and I watched it fall from their collective grip. The coffin shattered on the road, pieces gleaming. There was a shudder in the air and the brilliance of cherry wood there for the picking. Not to mention a dead arm popping out from the cracked coffin. There was a scramble and the funeral put on hold, the family and mourners ushered back to their limousines. The funeral directors dashed back to their parlour for a second coffin, a replica of the first, and quickly returned to the grave side. Four of us lifted the body from the splintered coffin and transferred it to the new coffin. In their haste and embarrassment, the funeral directors departed after the burial but left behind the scraps of broken coffin, the cherry wood. There was a sheen in the pieces I was instantly attracted to, and a perfect length of wood. Just as I had been attracted to the green canoe, its belly shining, the first time your mother and I spotted it at a garage sale after a morning of love and rain.

My work those few days (re-finishing the canoe, stripping and shaping the cherry wood into paddles) was a matchmaker's work. Something to do with my own lust for water and your mother's body. A gentleness and a mortality we had learned, like lovers vowing ourselves to an end, because suddenly in our orgasms we glimpsed this end. These little deaths, the French say. Every vessel is prone to weathering. Flesh will only float you so far.

Your mother spent six months in India, working through a season of internship. She lived in a small village in the province of Madras. She tended to the locals, learned the heat and tremble of their lives. She met an elderly man, afflicted with rheumatoid arthritis. This man spent his evenings in his small home, down on his hands and knees, crafting a small mandala out of coloured sand on his living room floor. Your mother would at times watch him at his craft, amazed at the patience and intricacy of his work. The smoothness of his solitude, she said. Then one day, when it seemed the blessed circle had been completed, the man stood and unraveled himself, stepped across the living room and opened the door for the wind, in the days before the Monsoon. She watched as the wind entered the home and rearranged the coloured sand.

These are the winds that arrive to undo every trance we've used to enclose ourselves, your mother told me upon her return. Winds, she said, that carry in their pockets the already evolving seeds of change.

I hadn't come close to completing a circle of sand or my work on the green canoe, but I stepped across the basement room and opened the door onto the backyard.

Late into the nights, I lay on the living room floor and felt the slight summer breeze work across my skin. A good sweat working through my pores, the slow accumulation of moisture along my brow. I honed in on the many delicate sounds of language within my body, even when what mattered seemed so indecipherable to me. Between sweats, I felt a growing strength, as if I was shaping myself for a moment of cataclysm, and I was. I was in a wet world of imagination, an old growth forest. I saw leaves ten times my size and weight. I lifted great branches; ten reps, rest, ten more reps, rest, a final ten reps. Sit ups, push ups. Then the stillness I had to honour, the toning through meditation. I got to know my conscience, my failures, my measure of drink and its moody effects. I got to know a world of blessing, and not just the arrangement of constellations or historical consequence. Though the world within was invisible, there was form, root-mass and blackened compost. Depths not meant to be travelled by hand or foot. One travelled there by breath, by heart. By nuance and an open mind.

Night by night I assembled and disassembled. I found and lost and lost and found. You want angels, I said to my ceiling, I give you the wind. You want the end of the world, a second flood, I give you a shepherd learning to sail. You want a new creation, away from this planet, I give you a heart seeping with groundwater. I give you my breast.

I saw the Virgin at the window, her reverent posture. I imagined moonlight seeding her insides. I saw her energy fill the basement cell, like the energy of her angel, Gabriel, and his sudden visit to her bed.

After all these years, was this her story? A myth about a tryst. How she received her God, regardless of the years of certain argument and interpretation that would follow. The way we will chew on a word for generations, until there is no fault line between meaning and telling. Love lightened in me. I saw my release through story. The more I put on words, the more I put on life. And whose story shouldn't provoke new growth, I realized, and write itself out in the depths of the world?

Where there is myth, my son, there is power.

I meditated on the ghosts I had been carrying. One, I was sure, was cousin to the underworld, seared by my grandfather's war. A second ghost stood in the doorway, sleeves rolled up, an unlit cigarette dangling from its lips. A third basked in the warm glow of the green canoe. This ghost belonged to the storyteller I had always struggled to let in through the other ghost blocking the door. A last ghost was missing, lost like a soldier's limb to war, but I could still feel the presence of the missing limb, a phantom leg wiggling its toes. This ghost belonged to the assailant of time. If the world were to end, this ghost knew, just burn out, who would be there to say what happened. To remember.

Years have altered and the images of my family have only grown deeper, no matter how hard I've attempted to erase their influence from my stories. Just the smell of my skin is enough to bring them back. I can still sense the press of the ravine in my pores, days burrowing into its green pockets. I can feel my brother's hand, leading me there. Our mud play, our rolling battles. I can smell my mother's cigarette smoke, her perpetual scent of gin. Her fear that is stronger than her faith. I can taste my father's last violence, his ability to disappear at the moment my heart wants to play. I can sense my grandfather's body wet and thin in the moonlit ravine, then stepping into my bedroom and laying on top of me. His pained eyes, his weeping shame. In that house that had been divided by shame. I can see the journals I've only hinted at, the chapters I've yet to name or place. My desire for colour and word. The language I've used like a hawk in the forest of my grief.

22

THE HIDING SPOT WAS BENEATH my bed. The place where I had pulled the carpet back from the wall, leaving a small pocket between the carpet and floor. My mother (on a cleaning binge) found the undersized journal stashed inside the carpet pocket. When I walked in on her she was sitting on my bed that she had been pulled back from the wall, half of my room undone, contents overturned to make room for her vacuuming action. The journal was on her lap, propped open somewhere in the middle. Her eyes failed to meet my eyes, her mouth abandoning what I most needed—a word, her protection, her understanding. I was fifteen. At a point of flesh and the outdoors. I was secretly in love with your mother and dreaming of a night when my hands might flutter and undo her blouse, let fly her breasts. There were already letters between us, edging toward that desire. There were our meetings downtown, like tourists, visiting museums, the art gallery, after her train ride from Guelph. But it wasn't only our letters or my attempt at poetic discourse with our Rachel that my mother had found and spied on, folded into the back of my journal. It was my grandfather's ghost that had caught her eye and scrutiny. His writings against my writings, spelled out on yellow foolscap.

"You've quite the little imagination, I see," my mother said, raising her head, looking at me. "But I have to ask, what right do you have to write of other people's lives?"

I couldn't answer.

My father found us in the room, in the walled-stillness of dusk. My mother turned her head toward him, then looked away. Every cell in my body pulled tight. My mother lifted the journal from her lap and showed it to my father, flashing the yellow foolscap she had picked out from between the pages. My father looked at the pages, then looked back at me. He took the journal from my mother's hands and began to finger its eerie skin. He unfolded the yellow foolscap, he found the photograph of my grandfather that I had pinched from the attic room, years ago. My father glanced over the foolscap writings, looked again to the photograph, then read through my journal, skipping pages, lines, an awkward rush within his eyes.

"Where did you get these?" my father asked, holding up the yellow foolscap.

My mouth was dry.

"He had them hidden beneath the carpet under the bed," my mother let out.

"But where did you get them," my father pressed.

"Grandfather," I mumbled. "He gave them to me."

"What do you mean?"

"He gave them to me, that's all."

"When?"

"Before he died. He showed them to me. Then he gave them to me. That's a photo of him at Vimy Ridge."

"I know where it is," my father said, shaking his head. "And these writings, he gave them to you as well?"

Nod.

"Why would he give you these?"

"I don't know... just because..."

"They don't make any sense," my father commented, glancing again at the writings, then reading further into my journal. "He just gave them to you like this?"

"Yes."

"And this journal, this is yours?"

I couldn't look my father in the eyes, but said, "Yes."

"What you've written here, about your grandfather. What are you saying?"

"Nothing."

"Well, it's something. Look, right here. What are you saying here," my father said, pressing closer to me, showing me the page.

"It's something that happened, that's all," I said, guarding my tone.

"He went into the ravine like this, at night like this? Is that what you're saying? That he came into this room. What do you mean by this? He lay in bed with you. What are you saying happened? What?"

"Nothing."

"Well, it says otherwise right here, look. You say he rubbed himself against you. What do you mean by that?"

My father held the journal close to my face. I could hear my mother groan and say, "My God."

"Are you saying you made this up?" my father asked.

"No."

"Then what? What happened?" He glared.

"He just lay on top of me, like it says. He squeezed me hard. He was sad, I think. He cried, that's all. Nothing else happened."

"What do you mean, *Nothing else*?"

My father stepped closer.

"You're saying he was naked in the ravine, rolling in the creek. Then you say he came into this room and lay on top of you, and he cried. Is that it?"

"Yes."

"But why?"

"I don't know why."

"I don't believe you," my father said, raising his voice. "I never heard him leave this house. I would have heard him. Why are you making this up, writing like this?"

"I'm not."

"Don't lie to me. Don't..."

"I'M NOT."

"Well you're not telling the truth."

"Just forget it then, forget it."

"But you've written here that he was naked," my father yelled. "And he came into this room. That's what you've written. What are you saying he did?"

"NOTHING. He just left the room."

"Did he... did he... do something more to you? Is that what you're saying?"

"It's just like I wrote," I said, lifting my voice. "It was like he was another person and I was another person. He was sad, that's all. And I felt sorry for him, I felt..."

"What are you saying now? That you liked it? Is that what you're saying?"

I stepped back. "No no no..."

"Because if that's it, there's no room in this house for someone like *that*, no room."

My father stepped at me. The yellow foolscap and photograph and journal falling from his hands and slapping against the floor.

"One more time now," my father yelled and raised a hand at me. "Where did you get these?"

"I told you."

"He wouldn't give these up just like that. And he wouldn't just touch you like that, do this."

"Well, he did. If that's what you want to hear: he did touch me, he touched me with his whole limp body. He touched me and he wept into me and I took those papers. You were in his room, throwing his papers away after he died. You were drunk and sad and pathetic, and I wanted something to remember him by, that's all. You were drunk, like mother is always drunk, like this whole fucking house is always fucking drunk... fucking drunks."

There was no time for my mother to run and get the belt. My father's hands swelled, disassociating themselves from the rest of his body. When the swollen hands wrapped around my neck, I felt my body lift and spin, as if pulled by the force of a primitive wind.

"You dare speak to me like that," he yelled into my ear, pressing.

My father kept tightening his grip around my neck. My breath going out of me. I saw my mother sitting on the bed. Then he let go and I gagged and he swung an open hand around, slapping the side of my face and head. I stumbled back, crashed and hit the wall, then lashed forward, my fists swinging wildly and catching my father's shoulder, his chest, his cheek. He swung back at me. My mother was standing, just looking at us, expressionless. My father came at me again, wild, out of control, all fists. Even my father's left hand, that hand with its own history and tremble, was in on the act of hitting me and pushing me out of the room, down the stairs, through the foyer and right out the front door, slamming the door behind me, gone. All I could sense was the night air before me, then the ground collapsing at my feet, breaking into disorder. I choked on my own breathing. Tears forced themselves down my face.

I ran. I ran hard. I ran pounding at pavement, at grass, at my skin. I ran to break its membrane to break the pain to break my soul. I ran to abandon touch and blood and anything to do with the connective tissue that had been designed by stars however long ago.

I spent the night in the ravine, close to the creek. Everything the world above did not desire shoved into the world below. I lay on my back, half afloat, half sinking. A plastic garbage bag floated by, leaching contents. I became hard to the beauty of anything bright or living. I forced myself into the autumnal world of the dead. Life there was not measured by accomplishment, but diminishment. Ants, grubs, slugs, I was no different.

It was the darkness inside the ravine I could not avoid. The familial terror spreading from gut to throat and back. Images of my father's fists, my grandfather's midnight breathing, my ears pounding and bloodied. For all my digging and hiding, my fear and dissolving, these men seeped into my skin, occupied memory. A tempest plot. Not a bent finger, the slight brush of a hand, could remove their ancient debris and mud from my mind. I resigned myself. I gnawed on my tongue until the memories became a croak. Emaciated, I eventually got by on nothing.

The night sky turned black, then green. A storm in the distance, the rumblings of far off thunder. Then quiet. Only a soft rain washing through the earth and creek and leaves. I dug myself further into the mud, I dug into clay for shelter, but desired only to dissolve. The rain passed. I lay still, panting, the slow dampness of night locking my limbs. What's that? Night ravens flying low, looking me in the eyes, waiting their turn. There would be no formal burial for my body, no priest to make the sign of a cross. *Fuck that rite.* Too many crosses had been turned on their sides and shaped into swords. Leave me be. The dead to bury the dead. A thousand years later and perhaps I'd be unearthed, thawed and put on display. Mud Boy. Pressed by the world to justify my humanity, to explain, and to fall into step. Always the rational world of inquisition coming up against the unknown. Like my father, I would remain unrecognizable, an alien to my own soul. And like my grandfather, unable to verbalize the blank spots within a body and a history with which I wanted no part.

I pulled myself from the ravine at day break. I slumped back home, stripped down to underwear and hosed myself down in the back yard. Cold water over cold, dirty skin. I stood in the sun and let the air dry me. I stepped through the back door, into the kitchen. My mother was sitting at the kitchen table, cigarette in hand. She glared at me and turned away. The house was changed, smelled of bleach. I went to my room, feeling the hardness behind my limbs. I was as far from a point of faith as the weathers would allow. A moonless place.

My father never said a word about what happened. He wouldn't look at me for months. Hush, hush. No problem, I agreed. Keep my mouth shut, an old family tradition. Don't you dare bring any more shame to this family, my mother warned me days later. Not a drop more.

Then she deferred. I noticed the increasing number of wrinkles forming around her mouth from years of smoking and boozing and deferring. She was suddenly reduced in stature to a grim outline against a back wall. A mute presence overtook her. Though she did manage one last jab at me, one morning at the kitchen table.

"You must have committed a terrible sin to make that man want you like *that*, in *that* way."

There was a twist. My mother had put my bedroom back in order, just as it had been before her decision to clean, to the place before she found my journal, opened it, and exposed it to my father. Beneath my bed, within the carpet pocket, she had replaced the journal and my grandfather's foolscap and photograph. I don't know what moved her to do this, what sorrowful recognition. Perhaps her own burden of history that had not been soothed by love. Or was it that if she and my father had taken the writings and photograph and destroyed them, burned them, might it mean that what had happened in that room really happened? The interrogation, the fists. Would burning the evidence actually lend evidence to the terror because of the remaining ash? Were my mother and father like the haphazard thieves who suddenly realized they had burgled the wrong room and house, and so re-entered that house and room and replaced each stolen item just where it had been? Each jewel in its rightful safe, each word along its allotted line. Then, wiping down their fingerprints and slipping out a back window, they escaped that blunder, that history. Because, you see, nothing had happened.

23

RACHEL TELLS ME THAT WHEN feeding you she can feel your mouth suckle upon her nipples in direct rhythm with her heartbeat. A natural metronome, she says. A first exchange of song released through human touch.

This is why I hold you close to my chest, your ear alive to a world within. My blood heart. This father's milk.

24

I'VE ALWAYS FOUND SOMETHING TRAGIC about old black and white photographs, something closer to the bone of the soul and not its flame. The fading of these photographs speaks to me of the amorality of time. Annihilation like a slow drip leaving memory. Yet we look and look again. A need to know. We rub fingers over these photographs as if to touch the stain left by history, the waterlines that mark us like those on rock along a shoreline.

Let's take a closer look at your great-grandfather's photograph. An aged black and white shot of a young man in a baggy, rumpled turn-of-the-century military uniform. The kind of heavy woolen uniform and tin hat that doesn't enhance a man's posture or make him look at home. The photograph contains a musty bronze-gold afterglow, almost sepia, as if to highlight the aura of the young man and catch, as if by chance, what is invisible within his stance and character.

The young man in the photograph is standing in mud and water up to his shins. He's leaning a little to the left, his head and helmet and Ross rifle butt a silhouette against the gray-black morning sky. How I can tell it's morning? I don't know. There's little light present. The sky is cramped. There are dark patches of churned earth at the young man's feet, and a mist like a ghostly browser curling across the photograph. The young man's uniform is indistinguishable from the muds and mists and smoke filled airs. He looks like a stick insect, blending in with the colours of earth and liquid mud. Though in this case he is blending in with the anti-colours that surround his body, as if he is attempting to become colourless, and trying with all of his strength to remain that way, until fate or a dream might work out his escape from the photograph.

Looking at the photograph, seeing my grandfather's antiquated stance, I think of the Aboriginal belief about the glamour of the camera, how souls are stolen with each snapshot. Is this why we turn back to old photographs, looking for a clue to our original theft? A phantom imprint.

The face in the photograph is like a knot. The eyes are over-wound. Bled. There are few facial lines that have been made by laughter, nothing to indicate a coming script of wisdom. In this absence of colour there is the sorrow that has been handed down through the fathers, the shame I've taken on, not knowing how or why or when it was created. Which God sliced it, what weather blazed its path. In my grandfather's young face, there isn't a language or environment yet potent enough to give dimension to his experience of war. No talking cure. Nothing to reassemble the loss or to reintegrate a young man back into society. In war, everything is touched by mortality and struggles against the verbal world.

So boys like your great-grandfather crouch in their muds, fighting to distinguish their bones from the earth. Upon these bone-heaps the Western world quivers, one eye looking away. The other eye cannot resist the terror: this eye knows terror is most effective when the victim is made to imagine their outcome. Keep them guessing, fearing. The true battle is in the mind, I've learned. A tension between what is real and permanent, between what is illusion and waste. There's another trick of the mind one must slowly learn: To turn waste into art. The deeper need of the soul into gift.

Now, let's brush our hands across your great-grandfather's yellow foolscap. Touch his words, the sleeping giant of emotion.

His writings are not addressed to anyone, and do not begin Dear Sir or My Darling Love or Mother Dearest. The foolscap is frayed, edges hardened. Some pages have tea stains. My grandfather's handwriting is quick and looped, written by a man with an eye to a door that the authorities might break in at any moment, grab his pen and censer his words. I imagine him sprawled on the floor, secretly settling into the automatic rhythm of his hand and pen, leaving his scrawl on whatever surface might welcome him. Rock, leaf, a hardwood floor. So urgent is the need. I see his passages of mist and dying and the tale of a sniper's bullet. These words my grandfather attempts to raise like a priest who, in a time of war, dares lift the holy cup and bread. One last sacred thrust from his hands.

My fingers will also apply their holy work, and raise my grandfather's words for you.

11.xi.29

The man with the camera was crouching on the lip of a shell hole. His boots were sinking into the dark pools of rain water, wet snow and blood. He was a big man but kept his balance well. He had the face of an apple, I thought, too bloody clean and red for a war like this. He kept telling me to hold still and that it takes a while for the camera to focus and catch me as I am. And remember, he kept saying, it's Easter time, so there's something to smile about. Is he Fritz, I thought? He could be Fritz, but his English was too good and I couldn't tell who was who anymore because of the mud. We're all of us mud, I thought, the dead and the alive, English or German, all of us mud and blood and cold. Our uniforms were all the same colour, but that damned apple face, clean and smiling at me and somehow delicious to look at. Try and smile, he kept telling, look into the lens and hold still. Just a minute now, he said. He must be one us then, I thought, one of our mud-men, but why is he holding me up and stopping me in action and taking my photograph? Happy Easter, he said again. Was he joking? Did he think that would make a difference, that the bloody resurrection was at hand and meant something there in the mud? What kind of Lord or God or King or Messiah or priest or dog would rise from this mud, I thought? The dead weren't rising there. They were sinking. The earth was devouring us like pigs.

So, he said, where are you from?

I opened my mouth but nothing came out but a cold dark breath that even I could tell smelled like something dead.

Montreal? Toronto? Somewhere out west, he said, smiling through that apple face.

My mouth opened again and again nothing came out. I could feel my feet sinking in the mud. Shells were screaming over our heads, smoke was blocking out the sky, and a few men moved in the distance and disappeared into the smoke and mist.

That was something this morning, don't you think, the man with the apple face said. I hear the Hun took it in the arse over on that hill, 145 isn't?

Hill 145, I thought. But I couldn't make any sense of the question because of the morning shelling and the ringing in my ears and the feeling that we were all sinking.

Can you tell me why you are out here alone, he then asked.

Alone? I said, my mouth finally taking shape. Woods, I then said, I'm to locate these woods and report back.

Woods, he said. You're out here to locate some woods?

Yes, I said.

Well, take a good look around, he laughed. Do you see anything that resembles wood?

He was right. There was nothing left standing after the morning shelling, after years of shelling.

This is a joke, I said. We should move.

Just another second, please, and we'll be done, he said. He shielded himself with his left hand and steadied the camera against his chest with his right hand. Then he slowly stood up from his crouched position in the mud.

This is too beautiful to pass up, he then said, and we're doing bloody well up ahead, I hear. We've broken through the lines and we're pushing back the Hun. It's only on Hill 145 where we're catching any hell.

That's just over there, I said. Jesus, come on, let's move.

Hold still, just a second more, yes, he said, here we go, yes, and smile now...and click click...

I held still and watched the man with the apple face arch back, his head and neck turning upright, his eyes out of his face, and slowly, like a broken limb, he fell back into the mud, the camera around his neck, in his hands, against his chest. A mist passed over. The man with the apple face disappeared into the mud but I could hear him on the lip of a shell hole, gasping for air.

Snipers, I thought, bloody snipers. They're the living hell of this war.

I fell to my knees quickly, then went face first into the mud. I felt my tongue deep in my throat and my ears were ringing again with the sound of gunfire and the whizz bangs exploding overhead. The whole ridge was burning. I couldn't feel my heart beat. Happy bloody Easter, I kept thinking. I could hear the man with that apple face, wheezing and coughing. I crawled toward the sound. I kept my ass low, afraid that even my ass would be a sniper's target. Suddenly the earth gave again and disappeared as if a great mouth had opened and took us all into its infernal hold. The morning was on fire. Another bomb, a mine exploded, and again the muds and shell holes were rearranged. I could still hear the man with the apple face somewhere nearby. He was coughing and wheezing, harder and harder. Another whizz bang fell and blasted us another hole. I looked up across the rearranged crater and I could see a pair of legs and those boots draped over the side of the hole. I heard another shot, a sniper's bullet rip past my ear.

Get your bearings, I thought, *stay low and become like the mud.*

My hands separated. One dug in and pulled my body through the shell hole; the other gripped my Ross. I had to ready myself, get set to pick off that sniper. One against the other. That was my other talent in this war. He had to be somewhere on the other side of the shell hole, beneath the mist. If he can see me, I can see him. I had been trained to spot the smallest detail concerning an enemy sniper's position, like finding a woodpecker's position in a thick forest, on a trunk, behind leaves. The man with the apple face was still wheezing. I could see a lump of folded gray bodies, three or four on the opposite side of the shell hole. The bodies were stacked like wood. He must be there, I thought, my Fritz. He liked to use our dead boys as a shield. He thought we'd never take a shot at one of our own, even if our own were dead. Why waste a good bullet? And what if one of those bodies was still alive and there was Fritz using him as a living shield? That was the difficult part, the hard thing to know. To shoot or not? I twisted into the shell hole against a piece of shrapnel and a rock that had been thrown up from the explosion. I lay on my stomach and looked to the stacked bodies that were up there on that lip of the blasted trench. I examined the shapes from head to toe. Nothing was moving. I could still hear the man with the apple face wheezing somewhere in the mud, probably coughing up blood by then. That's when another shot ripped over my head and hit the shell hole at my back, spraying the liquid mud.

That's it, Fritz, I thought, *that was your chance. Now you've given yourself away.*

Through the stacked bodies, I could see the barrel of his gun. A metal glint. I steadied myself in the mud and took aim. holding my breath. *Happy Easter, Fritz.* I pulled the trigger and felt the force of the bullet rip through the air and pierce whoever it was lying there behind that stack of bodies. A moment passed and then I saw Fritz topple out from behind the bodies, onto his side, exposed on the trench lip. I shot him again, using skill and persuasion. How many men had I shot and killed? I didn't know, but there he was, Fritz, sliding down the side of the shell hole, the mud sucking him in. That's when I noticed his rifle topple out of his hands. That bloody sniper's rifle, that bloody Ross. Why was he firing at me? He was just a kid. A goddamned kid, like me, from Toronto or the Prairies or out there with the Black Watch. Goddamn him. Why was he targeting me? One of his own. What have I done?

Then I heard that bloody wheezing at my back, getting louder. I turned and crawled up the side of the shell hole toward those two legs that were dangling over the lip. My ears were ringing and stinging with something hot and furious. I felt behind my ear, felt this strange indentation, this wetness of blood and mud, but I kept pulling myself up the muddy lip. Forget that that hole and blood, forget that goddamned kid from Toronto or the Prairies or wherever. He's dead, I thought. Just another you've shot and killed, but one of your own. Forget that for now, forget that forever.

 I reached the lip of the shell hole and climbed the next lip, listening for that wheezing beneath the drone of the whizz bangs and gunfire and the far sound of men charging and screaming and crying out from trenches all along the ridge. I reached the man's legs but realized his wheezing was still some distance away. I was right there, holding him at the knees, pulling myself closer to his breath. Goddamn it, I thought, where is the rest of his body? That damned whizz bang must have torn him in two. I searched through the mud, relying on my sniper's eyes, my killer's eye. Just as I had spotted the glint of that bloody Ross, that kid's gun, that woodpecker's mark the way my father had taught me in the forests of Ontario, I spotted the glint of that camera lens. I saw the man's hands folded around the camera against his chest, as if he was clutching onto his only recorded moment in life. His head was back in the mud, in a hole full of brown water and blackened blood. His mouth and nose were just above the surface of the stinking water. He was wheezing. His body was ripped in two, a perfect cut. How the hell do you sew a man back together like that? I swear his legs were still twitching and dangling over the lip. I crawled closer. I reached and pulled that apple face out of the mud. I held his head in my hands. His eyes were full of blood. Somehow they looked at me and got in behind my eyes. Other men's dying eyes did that to you. No matter how hard you fought them off and thought you were different and impenetrable, those eyes got inside of you. Then the wheezing in his throat shortened and the blood in his mouth sunk into his lungs. His tongue worked hard against the back of his throat. He was trying to say something when there was nothing more to say. And there was that bloody camera around his neck and that image inside the camera, connecting me to the man with the apple face who was then dying in my hands, unknown to me in my heart, against my mouth. Because then I was feeling the blood from the hole behind my ear drip down my neck. I felt faint, I felt the gas in my young lungs expand. I was just another ghost in this war of ghosts. I leaned over and kissed that dying face, that bloody apple face, that goddamned face. I don't know why I kissed him, nor what strange promise or pain I attempted to touch. I was only thinking that this war is the absolute failure of the human heart. Thinking: I'm nineteen years old and this is my first kiss. I could feel my heart pounding harder, the blood streaming down my face, mingling with that kiss. All I kept hearing in my head were those words from the

Bible, those pulpit teachings: 'Wherever your treasure is, there will your heart be too.' Like a joke I would never get.

I have to pinch myself whenever I read over these writings, or when I gaze into the photograph at my grandfather's muddied image, remembering it was the man with the camera around his neck, the man with the apple face, blown in two, who captured this image. The bronze hue of our chimera ancestry.

War is the absolute failure of the human heart...

On the back of the photograph, there is one last thought that has been scribbled into place, inked years later.

> –the lies within words like honour, glory, blood, pride, mud, civilization, religion, victory, peace, industry and Jesus. That I would have to go to war, go back and finish what my father had failed to finish, and to fail myself. Where is the dignity in that?–

These words are dated long after the battle for Vimy Ridge, and long after Hitler's invasion of Europe, his occupation. I studied the words again after my father's death, after heart attack number six. The feeling in the house after my father's death was that of a dead end. My mother was drinking more, blacking out or locking herself into her bedroom, not even a TV to send out a sound or two of conversation, the illusion of intimacy. I retreated to my bedroom as well, or back into the ravine, alone. Sometimes I'd slip into father's bunker room and watch a film. On Saturdays, I'd head off to Guelph by train to see your mother. I'd share with her these writings, and my grandfather's photograph, as if I was dipping my hand into a well that needed stirring. I was aware of that suddenly, needed that place, my hand in water whether there was water there or not. I read to her the last words that had been penned onto the back of the photograph. I held the writings up to the day moon and her version of an Ontario forest. Until I saw what had always been clear and obvious but had not wanted to admit, fully. That those last scribbles on the back of the photograph, debunking blood and pride, Jesus and industry, belonged to my father's hand, and not to my grandfather's ink. I recognized the stern penmanship, the anger that had never been shaped into spoken word. There was never a hint of treaty between my father's lips and the world. No kiss. No joke to get.

I have lived with these words, which like skin desire only touch. I have lived knowing that my father wrote these words sometime between the hours after we had fought and my night spent in the ravine. Because the ink was fresh and came off on my fingertips the morning I returned home and found my room put back together, the journal and photograph placed once again in its carpet pocket beneath the bed. Sometimes the words appear to me as a foreign subtitle and I struggle to find my own measure of interpretation. If lucky, I find the birthmark within each word and put my anger aside. Like a poet, I trace every frenzied curve of letter, of detail. I roam this body of words as I roamed the ravine, comparing notes and colour. Even language is sacred ground.

25

THANK GOD, MY FIRST KISS held no trace of sorrow or war (Or did it?). Your mother and I were sitting on the beach at Ward's island, overlooking the Great Lake. We had met at Union Station, in the rotunda, after her train ride from Guelph. She wore a white halter top, blue jean shorts and pink runners. On the ferry ride to the island, she removed the runners and strolled the deck barefoot. I'm sure I fell in love with her, once again, feet first and from the ground up. The wind was hot, out of the south. It was June 18th. We hadn't seen each other in a few months. Various obstacles and engagements had kept us apart, but our letters were seeping with a new desire to touch. Suddenly we were signing our names to our letters with love.

And there we were, sitting on the beach, a picnic between us. Beet salad, green beans, an assortment of cheeses and breads. Rachel had also sneaked a small bottle of red wine across the harbour. The wine was a gift from her father, an unlabelled bottle that he had brought back from France for his daughter's eighteenth birthday. We toasted the sky and lake, sipping from one glass.

There was a casual shyness between us at first. We moved to make the leap between what we had expressed in our letters and that moment of wine and the lake. I could sense the various invisible caravans we had enlisted to smuggle our words up through the world's weathers and across borders. It was just an hour between Toronto and Guelph, by mail and train, but when writing your mother I knew I was rehearsing for far greater distances, lands beyond my reach. I accepted that and loved that idea of romance. How a word could hold us like a breath, for months, or years. How we'd learn to savour each other's handwriting, every hum and script. *Did you really mean? Did you really say?* There on the beach, your mother's eyes possessed an immediacy I could only dream of. She sensed this, coaxed me gently, recognizing the inexperienced pet in me. There was just enough space between her words and my ears, between the sound of the lake and our lips, for me to arrive at my own desire. She was the older woman, you see. Sure in her happiness, her alertness. I still held to an old sliver of fear, any number of human beings turning on me. Though in my heart I was learning to distinguish. *Them is them, she is she.* And *she* (beautiful Rain, wonderful Monsoon) already knew she was meant for a life of medicine. She believed in that art and cajoled it at her fingertips. She knew early she'd travel and study abroad and work in other lands regardless of borders or politics. Very early on, I grew to respect that. I was fortunate, somewhere in my soul, to see that. Though I had come from a home where emptiness was served with each meal, in your mother's presence my longing came from a place of fuller intent. How I managed that luck or meaning, I can only guess. A deeper knowing, a wonder. Or was it that everyone in your mother's family (her parents, both sets of grandparents, her brothers and sisters) believed in love at first sight? Had I then entered that delicious spell, spotting the pleasures and deities that had been cultivated in the faces of all lovers and saints down through the ages?

In this pleasure and faith, I leaned towards your mother's hair (May I? 'Why yes, of course') and pinched a dark curl between my lips. A tease, you see, while calling upon the greatest energy my heart could harness.

"What about here," your mother said, licking her bottom lip.

"Could be dangerous."

"I'll meet you half way."

There were gulls dipping over the lake, a soft world of wings and water. Through the sound of both I could feel my body quiver, almost electric. My alertness to the situation shocked me, how the heat of your mother's eyes moved me. There was no need to second guess, because we knew, at that moment, that our longing was perfect. There was the simplicity of the two of us just sitting there, nestling, as your mother's mouth welcomed me. There was an exchange of soul in our kiss, I'm sure. Estranged bits of ancestry lapping against our tongues. Kissing your mother, I felt whole, I felt prized. A new self shining through.

"You know what this means?"

"Yes."

"You've read *The Little Prince* by now?"

"In French and English, twice. Recently I picked up a Russian translation at a rare books store."

"And are you responsible for your rose?"

"Yes."

"Me too."

How easily spirit translates into matter, and matter into spirit, without a worry for what lies between.

And to be assured by such a tender mouth.

26

AN OSPREY CIRCLING, EYE TO eye with the lake. A silver trout nosing the surface.

My mother didn't (wouldn't) attend my father's funeral. In her words, she was through with graves. I tried to reason with her, persuade her (it might have been our first *real* conversation), but as usual she was drunk and preferred to walk out of the kitchen while I was in the middle of a sentence.

"Mother, please, listen to me," I said. I was sitting at the kitchen table.

"And why should I listen to you?"

"He's your husband and you might regret not going to his funeral, not seeing him buried, not..."

"What do you know about death and regret? You're just a boy."

"I know a little bit, mother."

"Well, you haven't been through what I've been through, have you?"

"No, I haven't. But..."

"This man, he was nothing to me in the end. Nothing."

"You don't mean that."

"He was weak. And my God, he was boring. You don't know how bored I've been all these years."

My mother looked old to me then, standing in the middle of the kitchen. Only bones balancing the drink in her hand.

"But you've stayed with him all these years."

"Of course I did. Divorce is a sin, you should know that."

"You believe that, even if it's makes you unhappy."

"Listen to you, the little man."

"I'm serious."

"Well, I was never in love with him, if you really want to know the truth of it," my mother glared at me, stopping me cold. "I felt sorry for him, that's all. And look where that has landed me."

"You felt sorry for him because he was a prisoner in the war," I asked, taking the risk.

"Partially, yes," she said, looking into her drink, then back to me. "But how did you know that?"

"You told me, a long time ago."

"Did I?" She took a slow sip of her drink.

"So it's true? He was a prisoner?" I asked.

"What does it matter now? And why are you asking this," she said, fingering her glass. "He's dead. He's gone. And he's been gone for years. If you really want to know, he didn't tell me about being a prisoner until after we were married. Can you imagine that?"

"Would that have made a difference?"

My mother wouldn't answer. She just looked at me, a dead eyed stare, and finished her drink. She stepped back to the kitchen counter, facing the sink and mirror, her back to me. She poured herself another drink, all the while looking at me in the mirror, then said, "Men and their secrets. Their silly little secrets. Like you and your secrets, your journal and keeping what happened with that man from us."

I felt silenced, but looked at my mother and risked another truth.

"I didn't know how to talk about it," I said. "I didn't really believe it happened. Nothing seemed real. I could only write about it."

"Well, I don't understand why you kept it to yourself, but you have to live with that," she said, turning and pointing a finger at me.

"Like I said, I didn't know how to talk about it."

"That's not good enough," she said, swirling the drink in her glass. "And how you could let that happen, I just don't understand."

"Listen," I said, changing my tact. "I just think you should come with me to the funeral. Be there. I don't think I can do this alone."

"What about that girl?"

"Rachel, Mother. It doesn't hurt to say her name."

"You seem to be quite involved with her."

"Yes," I said.

"Be careful," she said, "because things in life don't always work out the way we want."

"But," I said, risking one last truth. "I don't see the world the way you do, mother."

"Now that's naive," she said.

And she was gone from the kitchen. I never risked another conversation of depth and order with my mother. I defied her, keeping her hurt world far apart from the new world of moisture and soil I was stepping into with our Rachel. This, to save myself, and to hold to a place of texture.

Zee was not there for my father's funeral either. At the time of my father's death, I had no idea where he was. He hadn't written or sent a photograph of himself and his travels in months. Only Rachel was there to accompany me. At the cemetery, and later in my arms. It was only then, up close and personal with our family plot, that the emptiness that permeated the house on Hudson Dr. became clear to me, completely. It had been many years since my grandfather's death and my father had never bothered to add our family name to the gravestone. Nor a date of birth or death to indicate the presence of any body who might be buried there. And there was no epitaph to add metaphor to the life of the dead. It was up to me. The new *man* in the house, the new little man with the old man's soul.

At first, I had thought of using my grandfather's own words for our epitaph. *War is the absolute failure of the human heart.* I thought this to be a perfect finish, the truthful recognition. Perhaps even a last stab at my anger. It was being with your mother, listening one night to the beat of her heart through her breasts, that the only possible words became apparent to me. And because, as your mother helped me to see, it was right that I should honour the man, both men, regardless of their sorrows and incompleteness, and regardless of my own dispersions, my own soul splitting.

And so our name upon a gravestone. *Savage.* And our epitaph:

Wherever your treasure is, there will be your heart too.

Our beautiful, frightening font.

27

LOOK, THERE'S YOUR MOTHER BEHIND that white pine, sneaking a peek at us. Nothing is more exotic to me than her face. The intrigues and wonders, the humours and tears. Your mother is a woman who has eased around the world, comfortable in her skin. Comfortable in the world's skin too. She's worked through so many post-war landscapes it's a wonder she's not permanently exhausted (Though there were nights when she'd telephone, just to talk and weep long distance.). She's touched the wounded in Iraq, in Somalia, in Rwanda. She has eased the gap between living and dying. She has watched spirits pick up the journey from where their bodies have let go. *Such a gift,* she wrote to me that summer, *to witness this passing. Though I've come to see we're all refugees in one way or another, at times alienated from home and soul, sanctuary and emotion. Each life has its talent and its burden. But if one's work does not originate from a sense of gratitude, what is one doing?* In your mother's face, as in her words, there is this gratitude, this tireless joy. Even as she witnessed the deaths of parents and their new borns from wounds and diseases that were too old to heal, your mother couldn't help but realize that their love making and conceptions had continued even in a time of war. What did that mean? That the human capacity to create and endure was greater than our capacity to destroy? She was not sure. She's a woman for whom a question is a right. She found, in all that dying, her own deeper desire to return to the world of our arms, to reunite always with our lips. Lying in our beds (white sheets, white pillows) and attending to our loving poses, like John and Yoko in their bed sitting days, but only after the two of us had come through our own seasons of ghosts. Whether these ghosts were happy or not, bestowed gratitude or not.

Our letters that summer grew from bi-weekly to once a week to daily. Always including an intricate series of x's and o's nearest the places on the envelopes where our lips had touched, had licked.

> *Ms. Rachel Raine. What can I say? You're surrounded by so much dying, I'm shocked you're able to hold on and say your prayers. You're the bravest person I know. Your gratitude comes from a world in tension with itself, though somehow there is release. Whereas the tensions I have known have been less clear. Not quite tangible. I've touched the dead, yes. My grandfather, my parents. Their hearts going out. But I did not feel any joy in their passing, any fullness. Only the mad ghosts I've been carrying all these years. And here I am, having spent the last few months in their presence, re-visiting haunts and echoes. It hasn't been easy. I miss you, I love you. I suppose I thought if I let these ghosts make a home in me, then they might find ease in my welcome. As if I could save them. The peacemaker in me. That was naive, I know. Now these hungry ghosts are digging a hole through me, and I've never felt so uncertain about myself. I wish there was something artful I might attach to this experience, a place within its geography I might touch. I've been living in a kind of arrested grief all these years. Even while in the wing of your love for me, your trust. It's not that I want to shake off the past like a dog out of water and forget. No. The unease I've been feeling has had to do with the essential work about learning what is me and what is not me. It is no longer about enduring anger and old maps called sorrow, as I wrote earlier in the spring of our letters. Change requires long periods of fasting. It is not a deprivation of burden. Just a new access to beauty.*

Last night the moon visited this basement room. I slept in its spoon shape, aching for you. My nose in your hair, the circle of your tongue in my ear. Arousals made flesh.

Your loving J

28

WORLDS CLOSE. WORLDS OPEN.

The winds, the winds, the winds. The tried white winds of January, the dust red winds of summer. Winds that have swept through my hair without the effect of alteration. Slow, dry winds. Winds lacking salt. A wind that had me standing toe to toe with it, my arms raised, as a handful of my school papers blew down a street. The wind I recall from that summer in '95 pushed in at my chest like an angry child, then went for my eyes and scratched away. Until all I could do was weep. There are ways a man will look within himself, not realizing it is his agony that has him by the hand, showing him a way through.

29

A SLOW STROLL THROUGH PARIS. A five minute exchange between my feet and the road. That's all it took to see that the city had a different deal with the Earth. I stepped up from the Metro at St. Michel and realized that whatever was meant to happen in the intoxicating scheme of things would happen there.

It's a city that taps into the Earth's crust with the sole purpose to serve the human appetite with everything essential for our emotional and spiritual becoming. Each corner bleeds the unique. It's a city that celebrates life as an eternal experiment between matter and spirit, kiss and tell. For all its light and heat and flow, the sheer pungent noise of its wealth and skin and traffic, there is a sense you must die there and be honoured. Be remembered. Or else.

First impressions. Trickster impressions.

Paris became the spontaneous. Though Zee wanted maps and descriptive passages and corner cafes. He wanted the red light in every woman's navel. He wanted to photograph everything, place us like cut outs in front of famous objects and capture our images. There for history, a picture-book in time.

At first, I wanted less and less to do with the literal testaments within the city. I wanted my feet to be my teachers; to stand at a place of cobblestone or park my ass on a chair and let my toes sink. In Paris there are more chairs scattered throughout parks and gardens, cafes and boulevards, than there are people. Having a place to sit and ponder is a revolutionary right.

I saw myself as a strange type of caterpillar. Something almost emerging, almost beautiful. Two seconds in the city and I was a cultural invalid. Yet I wanted that humility. I had arrived, yes, because of a gift from my brother, a plane ticket and the luck of blood. I had arrived because of some yellow foolscap and a photograph of my grandfather, and a desire to connect these stolen gifts with their rightful place. Walking through the city, I sensed a decay that was alive. The verse of a river and the heat, and the rush of humanity.

Zee took me by the elbow and lead me through his old haunts. Paris was his. We angled through Left Bank streets that blended the newly intimate with the antique. Apartment windows were closed down with painted shutters to keep back the sun. Flower boxes spilled their greenery, their lavender. The city dreamt beneath us, gushed. Zee and I had reached a quiet, unspoken place of consideration, unaware for the time being of the coming quagmires that would mark us forever. We were so used to one another, we hardly noticed the other. Though a wink or how you hung your hat might set off a tremor of unfinished argument. And there was the heat again, a hands down, slow moving current. If you didn't drink your eight cups of water a day, you'd shrivel up and be taken for just another beggar, another errant soul with a hand out.

Paris is Paris. It's a city with a big-city twist, no matter its fluid intentions. I wasn't about to get swept away by its perfume and romance. Beggars are beggars; strangers are strangers. An hour in the streets and an old woman asked me for money, her eyes like two pits held under foot. Zee tried to hold me back from helping her out. Beggars are a different breed here, he told me. Once you've given them something, anything, they'll stick to you the whole bloody day, follow you like a pack of dogs. But I'm a guest here, I thought. A little bit high on new wonder. I even possessed a trickle of French blood in my veins. I had been invited to this feast by way of the past. Paris. For all I knew, this woman with the gypsy-like hair and toothless grin was a distant cousin. So I gave her a few francs, if only to defy Zee and honour my ancestry. And, of course, she was at our backs, panting behind us. Zee gave me that look of outrage, like my father's. That stern eyebrow. He quickly wound us through a few back streets and alleys, through the front doors of cafes and out the back, just to get away from the old soul on our trail.

We strolled (hands behind our backs, like a couple of old souls too) along Rue de Bussy and Rue de Seine, then back along Rue Gregoire de Tours. This would be my haunt. Open markets, restaurants, cafes. Fruit peelings occupied gutter systems like fallen acrobats. Tides slipped off the backs of fresh fish. Sandwiches basked in open air, stuffed with tuna, lettuce, egg and tomato. Great slabs of beef mooed in windows. Pigeons hopped into storefronts, took a seat, then were tossed out a minute later. Dogs dogs dogs. A bone here and there. Lovers, arms interlaced. Everyone ambled, handling fresh baguettes, a single bite missing from their soft, warm ends. Paris sizzled while strolling. No nuclear testing there. That was oceans away, down under. Why worry? Just drink and chat and read the daily papers, then chuckle at a world that was hell bent on boycotting the very fabric we all craved. Even when a store alarm blared, nobody moved for cover. It took thirty minutes for a man to disarm the alarm and repair it, but once he did the whole corner and everyone content in their chosen cafes applauded. In a culture groomed by the Opera of Revolution, to applaud was second nature. Even if it was the setting off of a bomb, or its dismantling.

Jet lag hit me the first day at about three o'clock. I fought through it until nine. Then I required sleep, no matter my desire to keep walking. Zee stayed behind at Café de Bussy, drinking. I found my way back to the hotel, Henri IV, which was situated on Île de la Cité, smack in the middle of the city on a small island unto itself. The hotel felt empty but you could sense the life just beneath the surface, animating like a bee hive. You could hear guests in their rooms, whispering through paper thin walls, love groans at dusk. Tape recorders ruminating with classical music. You could hear toilets flush and the rush of water down pipelines just behind the wall at the head of your bed. The hotel was being re-wired for the first time in a century. The hallways and the only stairway were covered in coloured electrical wires and bits of saw dust and plastic clippings. A whole day might pass and you'd be lucky to see anyone working on the place. The hotel smelled like a five hundred year old manuscript. Open it and an odour thick with an inky pollen might rub off on your hand. There was no avoiding its inner history, the thousands upon thousands of lives seizing its beds and sleep.

In a dream, I am standing in an empty room, shaving my body down, every hair. Then a man steps into the room and stares at me, catching me in the act. I don't care that I am naked and bright with sweat. I turn toward the man and bend down, one knee coiled against the floor, the other cocked like a runner in the starting blocks. Every muscle gleaming. The man steps into the centre of the room, his body like a silhouette behind a silver screen. He is suddenly prepared and naked and shaved down too. 'I will have to work with my rage,' I think. We stare at one another, evaluating strengths and weaknesses. Shoulders, arms, collarbones, neckline, elbows, wrists, fists. How could anything so fragile contain such power.

The man winks and we charge, our bodies slamming into one another. I feel my blood, sweat coursing through my skin. Our feet dig in, plant themselves, then slide back to a 45 degree angle so that we are somehow propping up one another. Both of us determined, on fire, feverish as storm. All my life I've been waiting for this, I think. Something or someone I can victimize. A battle I can use to release myself from having anything to do with being human or animal or god. Pounce and devour. My teeth bite into the side of my opponent's shoulder, just as his teeth bite into mine. We'll eat right through the other. He's bigger than me, I realize, but look! His feet are beginning to slide back across the cheap vinyl floor. I'll push him right out the bloody window. History fills my veins like a death march. Hundreds of years of violent loneliness, of brutality and barbarous acts that have been sanctioned by parents and priests and politicians. Fuck this sorrow I've been feeling all of my life. All this rages through the dream like water. Until it happens. My opponent's body begins to straighten. The 45 degree angle that has sustained us in place is breaking down. I have him where I want him. Nearer the open window, the sounding night. His hands begin to slide down my arms; there is too much sweat and not a hair on me for him to grab. I wedge my shoulder against his chest, my hands gripping his upper arms and digging into his skin, my ear hard against his chest. I hear the quick thump of his heart, a strained beat, followed by a wild stillness. For a moment, I believe he has passed out from exhaustion. I'm afraid to look him in the eyes. I hold my ear against his chest, waiting for his heart to beat, as if I am waiting for movement behind a womb wall. Wondering, fearful. Is the child inside dead or alive? Years of isolation pours through my body. I begin to shake like someone possessed. I press my ear closer, I close my eyes and count: One, Two, Three... And again: One, Two, Three...

Until, miraculously, comes the kick inside, the blood-flow, my opponent's heat-pulse that yearns for contact. I let go and fall back onto the floor, my heart rapping against my chest. I look up at my opponent's face and see my own. In the dream, I begin to weep. I weep until the weeping slips through my sleep, waking me.

I sat on the edge of the bed all night. Darkness, the window open, no outer breeze offering relief from the heat. Naked, I stared at Zee on his bed, stretched out and fully clothed and snoring. The stench of alcohol rising from his body.

30

MY THIRD MORNING IN PARIS and I woke up sweating.

The first bomb introduced into my psyche was the whizz bang. Famous in the Great War for its whistling sound of approach, followed by the doomed thud of its explosion. I saw numerous accounts of the bomb's launch and aftermath in my father's WWI films, earth and men shattering beneath its fiery weight. To go with the thunderous soundtrack I sometimes imitated the bomb's foreshadowing whistle and thud in my head while there in my father's bunker room. Later I'd take the sound with me to bed. Sometimes when riding my bike to school the sound accompanied me and I'd expect the earth around me to give. A dreamer in a city marked with its Neighbourhood Watch signs. All of us safe and sound in Toronto.

The second bomb to imprint my psyche was the atom bomb. The big one whose intent was unimaginable, my father insisted. A bomb that could only be watched from a great distance, leaving behind its sky drop and earth thud that symbolic cloud that would forever alter how we looked at a mushroom. My head was too small to imitate or contain the sound of this bomb going off, but I could feel it tracking me, always, in sleep and while awake. Nowhere was safe. Not even my father's bunker room.

This is how my brother and I were initiated into the world's culture of bombs. As I said, we were not exactly communicating from the gut up. A tug-of-war between us, and no rope. And there was the sense (the fear the hope the history) that Zee might disappear on me just as suddenly as he had reappeared earlier that season.

We were wandering along the Seine, in the blink of Notre Dame. No hurry. Zee took a snapshot of me with the Cathedral at my back. We stepped up toward Pl. St. Michel and crossed at the lights. A young man was playing a violin on the corner before a café audience. We paused and listened to his soft notes of welcome. His partner strolled with a hat in her hand, collecting francs. I noticed garbage bins in the area had been capped. Telephone booths were taped off.

A car sped away.

Our bodies quickly gave and collapsed in a wild swirl of litter and glass. We were twisting backwards, falling through air. The world speeding up, then slowing down. We landed, flat on our backs. Zee's arm was around me. There was a subtle pain radiating along one of my legs. I saw people and things (tables, chairs, linen napkins) scattered over the street. A tornado-like blow followed close behind, dust-black and gray, but the sky was clear above me, spruce-blue. The heat continued to press down on the city. I noticed Zee looking at me, shock on his face. A sandal lying next to me, charred. Then came the cries, welling up from within the flash of debris and glass and crooked chairs.

The pain in my lower left leg burned through. Across my skin was a fine layer of dust. Sirens blared. Out of the epicenter of litter and glass, the wounded stumbled, hunched and coal-white. I looked at my leg. There were small pieces of glass sticking out of my skin, clean entry wounds everywhere. Without thinking, I plucked them from my leg. Small wounds opened and bled. I shuddered. There was such a lucid flow of blood, such a precise sense of river, that for some reason I could only allow the pain. It suddenly felt natural to have my blood loosened over a Parisian street. As if I belonged.

As if...

I looked back for my brother. He was unbloodied and walking around, a fine layer of dust on his face, over his hair and clothing. He had his camera out, fast in his hands, against his eye. He was taking his snapshots, cornering in on the terror. He wheeled round and round, strange and furious and grinning. He aimed the camera at my face. I began to shake. I covered my face with my hands that were cramped and bloodied by then. I ducked my brother's lens. Scowled. I was aware of not wanting to lose any more of my power to him. Not an ounce of colour and soul to him. The death of him in me.

I stood up from the debris and shattered glass, shaking. My leg tingling. The small puncture wounds were closing. Some closed naturally, others closed with the aid of a cloth and some spittle and water. Zee remained in looking glass mode, sniffing out the new ruins. He wanted more, he could never get enough. Ambulances and police filled the area, busy, blocking off traffic. Paramedics tended to the wounded and maimed, police questioned people, and attempted to locate the exact point where the blast had occurred. Terra Zero. Two dead. Thirty-three injured. Just a small bomb, someone said. I was asked by a police officer what I saw. *A car speeding away.* What colour? *White, I think. Perhaps silver. The sun was so bright.* A license number? *No, I'm sorry, I didn't see one.* The driver, did you see the driver, or a passenger? *A driver? Yes.* What did he look like? What colour? Black? Brown? *No, no, the driver was white, yes, white. And the passenger was a woman. A white woman.* Not black? *No, no, not black.* Are you positive? *Yes, yes, I know my colours. I know white from black, male from female, hate from love...*

Good-bye old self. Hello...

I went down again, my legs buckling beneath the aftermath of the blast and the questions. The leg wounds re-opened and bled. Notre Dame hovered close by but did not make a move to help. All Her angels and saints and no one lifting a wing or hand. If the world of the sacred wasn't going to take you out back and initiate you into the cult of their two thousand year old breadline, then the bomb makers and terrorists would take their shot at your soul. I looked into the leg wounds and my vision heightened, as if through each wound I had been given a bird's eye view into the bombing. At the nexus of the blast was the Western world's ache toward disorder, the white man's fingerprint smudged on everything war-like and criminal. The Dresden bombings, Hiroshima, Cambodia. Every trace and fuse from the whizz bangs of my grandfather's Great War to Truman's midnight decision, to the thirteen year old suicide bomber stepping into a holy land pizza parlour. News travels, history travels. I saw the moon held hostage beneath the ruins. The holy books we've burned because of their contents concerning wisdom and light and the erotics of a God's covenant between his breast and a people. I saw a long destructive line that could have only begun with a race not at home with its skin. A pale faith.

I know my colours...

Then a young man stepped out from the rubble. I saw the heat in his eyes, like the sun, rush to meet my face. A silver glint upon the violin at his feet.

Rachel. I was caught in a blast today. A Paris bombing. I gave some blood. I found myself at a mid-point in a world divided by devastation and those of us who desire breath. I looked one way and saw the terror, but just over my shoulder, nothing had been altered. People were sitting in café positions, a leg crossed, cigarettes going, world papers open on table tops. I felt sick to my stomach. No longer wanted human speech. Anything pure, anything green..

So we know it is easier to kill what we can't touch or see. To raise the axe and make the blow from sky high or a car speeding away. To achieve this we must convince ourselves that nothing of the heart matters. Not morality, not conscience. Above all, the enemy is not human. We know this. After all, we are the creatures of reason, the animals of belief. And we know that it is no longer only those with power and privilege who can afford these distinctions, this practice in the noble lie. Aha! It's all of us now. All responsible. The Pedestrian, the Terrorist, the World Leader, the Grunt, those with faith and those without. Is it not enough to breathe the air and drink the water to become conscious of how radical is our connection to one another? Any spiritual shift worth its bones knows that whatever evil or love we perceive to be in the world is a seed we first cultivate within ourselves. But how much pain (as a species, a people, a heart) are we willing to allow ourselves until we choose to love?

It was beautiful to see a young man step up from the rubble, his t-shirt ripped, singed. He looked familiar, his body trembling. Our eyes touched. But it was when his partner picked up his violin and placed it at his chin, handed him his bow and encouraged him to play right there by the rubble, offer his dirge, that I saw the raw flow that is pure gift. No matter the evil (if that's what we must call it) that attempts to divert us, dam us, and pump us dry.

If there is no God, then why does beauty make me weep for him?

The next time you come home (soon, I hope, very soon), I will come home too.

31

"HISTORY IS EXPENDABLE," ZEE WAS saying.

We were sitting in a café, back in the area of the bombing. Night and hot. I was still struggling against the verbal world. The paramedic who cleaned and bandaged the wounds on my leg had tried to engage me in conversation. All I could offer was that I was a tourist, on my way to Vimy Ridge. My grandfather had fought there, I said. The paramedic looked me in the eyes. Everyone in France, he said, has lost someone to the wars. Bombs, bullets, tanks, France has seen it all, he said. Then he looked over the destruction in the area and back to my eyes. He wrapped his hands around the bandage on my leg, warming the wounded area. A ring with the sacred heart round his pinky. There are many ways to be baptized, he said. There is water, and there is fire.

I wanted to weep, but could not.

And here was Zee talking it up, eye-to-eye with a second bottle of red wine.

"Come on, mon frère, join me."

"No thanks."

"That resolve again, is it?"

"I want to be sober for this."

"I see."

My brother swerved into one of his heated debates, taking aim at himself and me.

"So, I was saying. History, is expendable. I mean, you witnessed it first hand, felt it, no? The broken pipe lines, the sewers overflowing, all that crap and pain after the explosion. Look at them over there, still cleaning up the mess.

"Less than ten hours ago this place was rocking, exploding. It didn't take twenty minutes for things to settle and then we all drifted back to our lives. Sure, you purged and spilled some blood, felt a slight aftershock, and were debriefed. But that's good for you, I say. It means you feel, and there's no greater agony than not feeling. Besides, you're a sensitive, sentimental type. Don't like your balance thrown off. Nevertheless. Here we are, like I say, a few hours later and back at the scene of the crime, basking, drinking, getting corked... well I am, anyways. But I ask, why are we back?"

"Do tell," I said, taking the bait.

"We're back for the same reason we take photographs and save them. Because we really don't believe in the moment, nor in what happened today. And because we demand from the photograph a proof we can turn to again and again, to say, 'Yes, that's me, I was real, I was alive, I was there'. This is how we attach ourselves to history, like you and your obsession with Grandfather's photograph. It keeps us from feeling the expendable that is all around us."

"If you insist, yes."

"If I insist, yes," Zee said, leaning in. "It's obvious there's not much in life that affirms who we are anymore. I mean, if we don't believe in God, how can God believe in us? We've outwitted ourselves on that one, Little Flower. God, too, is expendable. So what's left? Good old world violence. Because violence has always affirmed the soul. That's why we travel into danger zones, hoping upon hope to see the terrorist live, by request. Whether the bombs are dropped in the name of Western freedom, the IRA or a few holy fanatics from the Middle East, it doesn't matter. Don't you see? It's because those who terrorize have nothing to lose and feel so powerless, in lands that are theirs, but which we of the West occupy, that they do what they do: bomb. And it's because we of the West project ourselves as saviours of the world and possess in our souls this condescending conviction, that we do what we do: watch. What else can a culture groomed by the camera do, but watch? Like a bunch of drunk generals at the back lines. Sure, all sides will say they do what they do for their God. The God of Abraham and Isaac and whatnot. We needn't get into that theological sham.

The modern soul wouldn't recognize a holy text if it rubbed its ancient ink all over our bodies. Inertia, apathy, fear. These are our fine wines, little man. You may think you're different, that you belong to the fat god of love. But take a good look. We're not here to witness the clean up. We're back to see if the terrorist has the balls to march back in and blast the place a second time. We want an encore bomb."

"Do you make this stuff up as you go along, or have you really worked this through?" I said, the heat of night moving in from all sides.

"I'm just being honest about it, little man. Almost brutal, I know, but what can I say," Zee said, toasting the night sky.

"You might want to share this with the parents and lovers of those whose souls were wounded or lost today," I said.

"It may be simplistic, I know. It may lack the politics of the soul I'm really after, but what do you think? I mean, you, Little Flower. What do you *really* think?"

"I think you're full of a lovely bouquet of crap."

"Aha."

"And I think you're drunk."

"I see, I see... the elegant mind is at work."

"And I'd say you are a *drunk*."

"Your holy sober point?"

"I'd say you have a certain wisdom of the bottle that I must admit I sometimes admire," I said. "A cunning that bends against the world, yes. I'd say you're the patron saint of ridicule. You trivialize just about everything alive. You mock God and those who believe. You trivialize violence, you mock grief. You belittle the past, you belittle women, you belittle me."

"Oh, come on, you know I love you," Zee said, tipping his glass toward me.

"You say that, sure. But why don't I *really* feel that in my heart or down here in my gut?"

"Because our loving parents didn't cultivate that patch of ground within us," he said.

"I don't want to give power to that ground anymore," I said, sitting up. "So our parents were incapable of loving us freely, or loved us in a very limited and violent way, yes. But you..."

"Moi?"

"You crash around the world and the emotions of others with this hatred of the past, this contempt for belonging. You slip from body to body like a phantom. You say I have my ghosts, and I do. I'll admit that, confess that. But your phantom love is like a glass of water that an interrogator brings into a cell. An accused thief is sitting on a chair, at a lone table. The interrogator places the glass of water in the centre of the tabletop, but the thief is too tired and too thirsty to ask who the water is for. Too many circular arguments have left him numb. Both men sit at the table, silent. Until the thief locks his eyes on a small crack in the glass through which the water slowly leaks and his vision suddenly opens."

"Interesting," Zee said.

"Don't you see? The love we've learned has come at the cost of everything beautiful and painful and human. I know this, I am the thief. I've tiptoed through rooms (even my own emotional rooms, in my own skin) with an eye out for something to pocket. A piece with a past, a soul, a story. I mean, I was never taught that all I had to do was ask. Everything was conditional in our childhood world, even the future had to be stolen. Only Rachel has continually shocked me out of that world and filled me with the truth of the unconditional heart. If I didn't have that love, I'd probably be a full time drunk like you."

"Anything else?" Zee said. There was no signal of retreat or advance to his tone.

"I'd say your being an ally to the bottle since you were a young pup has robbed you of this one wisdom."

"Which is?"

"The heart. The beautiful, sober heart."

Zee sat back. For once, I was not shaking, not inside, not at my fingertips. I had released that which for years I had most desired to receive. The deepest truth.

"So, are you happy with your pronouncements, your judgements?" Zee said, working a finger against his chin.

"Right now, right here," I said. "My mind has found some rest."

"A free man in Paris."

"I wouldn't go that far."

"Then you really don't need me, do you?"

I looked at my brother closely. He had beautiful eyes. A miraculous mix of blue and green.

"No, that's not it," I said. "I do need you. But it's the sober you I need. The one you've left behind, somewhere in your anger. The same anger I've inherited, the same sorrow, the same familial hurt that has blinded us."

He widened his eyes, entered another sky.

"There's just one problem with your theory, this little intervention of yours," he said, tapping a finger against the table top.

"And what's that?"

"I don't have a drinking problem, if that's what you're trying to say."

"I see."

"You don't believe me?"

There was no sarcasm in his tone. Only a quiver behind his words, cold as April rain.

"All these years I've encouraged you to be honest about yourself, but I didn't expect this," he said, looking me straight in the eye, then away. "Such morality."

"I don't know about that," I said. "I see it as choosing health, that's all."

"Do you."

"I'm sorry," I said. "In the end it's really not for me to say who or what you are or are not."

"Don't apologize. You're always apologizing, for Christ's sake. Ever since you were a kid, apologizing everywhere like some twelfth century monk whipping himself."

"I didn't mean to piss you off."

"Sure you did." He looked back at me.

"I just think you might want to try to take a break from it, from the drinking."

"It's not something I'm worried about. Understand?"

"A long line of family drunks, right?"

"A royal birthright."

"The House of Hangover."

"That's right," Zee said, his expression softening. He sat up in his chair. "Is that all you need to say?"

"Yes."

"Then it might be time to hit the clubs, mon frère."

"Listen, I don't want you to think I don't appreciate... that I'm not grateful for..."

"Forget about it, little man. You spoke your peace. Really, I understand where you're coming from, better than you think. I grew up in the same bloody house."

"That's just it. There's so much to work out. Talk through."

"You think," he said, smiling.

"Listen, there is something else I want to share with you."

"So you're not finished."

"This is different."

"And what is it, Little Flower?"

"I need to tell you something about Grandfather," I said.

"What about the old bird?"

"He... he came into my room one night, after we followed him down into the ravine those nights... remember, just before he died."

Zee nodded. "What do you mean, he came into your room?"

"He came in," I said, feeling clear. "He came in and he looked at me and he was soaking wet with the creek, soaking through his pajamas, and then he leaned down and touched my forehead and then he took me in his arms and pushed me back into the bed and he lay on top of me and rubbed himself against me and then he cried and cried and cried, into my hair... and, well, it felt wrong, it felt abusive..."

"Jesus, Little Flower... why didn't you tell me this years ago?"

"I'm telling you now."

Zee was quiet. "Are you saying he... he really abused you, got all up and ugly with you?"

"No, no," I said. "He just touched me, rubbed himself against me, and then wept. Then he just got up and left the room, like a ghost. Like nothing happened."

Zee was quiet, looking away from me, then back. He said, "Are you sure that's abuse?"

"Well, it didn't feel like heroic love, I can tell you that much."

Zee was quiet again. He sipped his wine and looked at the people milling around the cafe. No words between us for a few minutes. Something about his shoulders, his energy drunk and strangely down, his eyes watering.

"What is it?" I asked.

"Nothing," he said.

"You seem, I don't know, down," I said.

"Me? Down? Nooooo," he said.

But I sensed something, a familiarity in mood, the language of the body. I took a chance with him and said, "Did he come into your room too?"

Zee just stared at me, breathed in, and exhaled. No longer sipping his wine. Just holding the glass and running a finger tip around the rim.

"Yes, he came into my room too."

"I'm sorry," I said.

"And you think that's abuse, do you?" Zee asked.

"I believe so," I said. "He interfered with us. Stole a moment from us."

Zee put his drink down on the table.

"Can I ask you when he came into your room?"

"Earlier," Zee said.

"The same summer?"

"No. Earlier. I was younger. Maybe the same age as you were."

"Man, I'm sorry to hear that. Did he weep into you?"

"No. He just lay on top of me. He squeezed the crap out of me and shook like a baby."

"That's enough," I said. "That's abusive enough."

"Well, it's ancient history," Zee interrupted. "You know, dead earth. Gone, Little Flower."

At that, Zee stood up and settled into his stance, drunk. He looked down at me and winked. I sensed the truth that had been spoken rock between us.

"This is Paris," he said. "Time to move on, little brother. You coming?"

"I think I'll sit here a while," I said. "Absorb the night. Write Rachel. Do you mind?"

"Your call, little brother. Your call." He looked at me. Smiled. "I'll see you back at the hotel."

"The hotel, yes," I said. Adding, "What about Vimy?"

"Day after tomorrow. And the joy of your scars will be complete."

Zee stepped away. I watched him move down the block, winding through a crowd. I sensed by the angle of his back that there would never be children in his life. He hated the truth a child might bring. Oftentimes we are helpless in the wake of revelation. My brother moved like the weary fugitive, on the run from himself. The toughest escape.

Is our skin so endowed with the soul's cursive energy that it is impossible to say where one life ends and another enfolds the heart? Is this communion, why we are named after the saints? Must the body work out every angle of lonely pursuit before the spirit world is free to show itself? Before a God might tongue a burning bush. Whether at a table top in Paris or riding the glory shape of someone's arms.

32

SOLITUDE IS A GREEN CANOE. This I discovered in Paris: that I could dip my way through the city and no longer lose myself to the sound of the human drama. I walked all night, drifting through the streets, the thin streets like streams. The air was delicious. I saw the usual attractions. Curbside dramas, pimps, strip joints. I could have parted my way up and down Yonge St. for that. But there I was, quenched in my green canvas skin. I found a café near an old church, St-Julien-le-Pauvre. I sat on the curb. Music poured from the café windows that were propped open like giant book covers. A singer stood near a black piano. She had unending red hair, her eyes were dreamy, her jazz served at room temperature. I listened, while touching the tiny wounds on my legs. Every path has its risk, every scar its song. There's not a soul now in the world untouched by terror, I thought. Once you take aim at the civilians, you've lost the song line. Justification becomes just another dirty plot.

    I sat still for a few hours, listening. Just the right arc between streetlight and starlight. Footsteps crackled over the road as if everyone had seashells attached to their shoes. The jazz singer's voice took to the night, put on something see through. I leaned back on the curb and picked up another sound of song. The intricate cut of strings, something classical, emerging from the old church. Behind the open doors, there was the kindness of Bach. I felt myself coming to peace, as if drifting in my green canoe, eyes on sky, waters calm.

I walked by the Seine. I followed its lusty current, its world of tugs and barges and floating restaurants. I paused beneath bridges and listened to the muscle of the river echo off hulls and abutments. Me in my canoe solitude. Lovers strolled, drunks strolled, until dawn creased the sky, a thin line of red. Day lit constellations that mean to bless and not to curse. God is not out to get us.

I wasn't surprised when I returned to the hotel at 8 a.m. to find my brother gone. Bags and all. Even my packsack had been packed and left in the reception area. There was no note.

"But Monsieur," the receptionist informed me. "The other man has checked you out. He said you wouldn't be needing the room. And, voila! We have already given the room away."

"Did he say where he was going?"

"No, Monsieur. No."

I shouldered my packsack and walked out to the street. Morning energy was brewing, displaced sounds of traffic, human buzz. Stay awake, I thought. Everything about my experience of the city during the past night had prepared me for this morning's phrase.

Bow. Dip my hands. Walk.

Once your mother and I rented a cabin in the woods, in the foothills of the Laurentians. She was at McGill at the time and had escaped her studies for our weekend tryst. I had escaped as well from my basement world, my first long road trip, on a train to Montreal. After a night of lying together, talking out our weeks apart, I awoke at six and found your mother gone. I panicked and checked everywhere; closets, cupboards, under the bed. Then I noticed her shoes by the front door. I stepped outside and saw her footprints in the dewy grass. I followed, barefoot as well, worried, until I found your mother by a rustling creek.

"You're shaking."

"I thought you had left," I said.

"I woke up dreaming of water."

"Are you okay?"

"I dreamt all night that my face kept disappearing and reappearing, again and again. I couldn't breathe," I said.

"I'm right here."

"I don't want to lose you."

"And I don't want to lose you."

"I'm afraid I will."

"Not going to happen."

"Sometimes I just don't know what you see in me."

"When I was a girl I used to dig every child's hole to China. You know, go out into the backyard and dig the whole day. One morning, I began my dig and suddenly stumbled upon what seemed like a great bowl of fruit and flowers. Oranges, apples, lilacs. I was shocked. It wasn't China, but what a find. I ran back to the house, shouting. *Fruit and lilac, under the earth!* My parents came out to see my find. What a cornucopia, my mother said. Like Christmas morning, my father said. When they smiled, I knew how the fruit and flowers got there."

"Your parents."

"Yes."

"And?"

"And, that's what I see in you."

"A hole to China."

"No, Lover," your mother said, poking my chest. "My cornucopia."

I let the city unfold at my feet. On pilgrimage. I followed the river again, veering with the sun's arc. I breathed the air, breathed the city. Bonjour, I nodded, unafraid of the stranger. Morning light was spreading over the city, blue sky touching leafy green tree tops. I rubbed my hand along the thick trunks of the horsechestnut tree, passed through translucent shade. A growing world I knew and trusted and did not want to alter. What had nurtured me through the years? Was it not the earth, the ravine, my hands crackling with dirt and water? Was it not lingering with clay reddened by sun, or listening to the wild riff of a songbird, the reverent chant of frogs? Was it not admiring lunar rhythms, thunderstorms circulating through air and skin? Seasons like whales migrating. A world mercurial, hatching when least expected. Was it not the many climates I've loved that had bestowed intelligence and body and the pollen exchanged between ideas and dreams, thought and word, the myriad worlds of experience? Each day like a meadow gleaming, like a beautiful mood to consider, like an invitation that was always there, always opening and inclusive within each moment. Was it not saying *yes* to all this?

Along the way, I spotted The Thinker through the front gates of a museum. A power and a presence I was familiar with pulled my body closer to Rodin's great work. My heart at rest, my feet secure. For an hour, I gazed into The Thinker's rich mood of bronze, the fallow thoughtfulness. Every muscle was alive and spoke to me of exoneration. Everything worked from the ground up, the inside out. Everything said, I'm here! I'm now! People stepped up to the work, turned and sat at the base of the sculpture and burst into pose, a hand beneath a chin, an elbow upon a knee. To the side a loved one or a close friend took their snap shot.

It took all my laughter not to judge.

I saw him one more time. The familiar red packsack with the Canadian maple leaf sewn into the lining. Zee. He was sitting in a café along St. Germain. He was reading the international newspapers, a tall glass of beer in hand. It was 11 a.m. A few other travellers sat with him. Their conversation was animated. I stood across the street, six lanes of traffic breezing between us. I'll give him a moment, I thought, the benefit of a doubt. If he looked up, that is. If he was my brother and blood he should intuit my presence, I thought, my spirit like a wing fluttering at his ear. The sun turned ochre, the wind was down. There was a break in traffic, and a supple line of vision through which our eyes, all our senses, might meet. I remained still and silent. He looked up, for just a moment, and I guessed he saw me, but his face would not give him away. Do I nod? Wink? Raise a reverential hand, a signal of forgiveness, of brotherhood and lessons in blood? I felt sorry for him, but was that love, or another stone in the heart? Was it pride that kept me from crossing over to him? Pride that whispered for him to get up and cross over to me? Did he even recognize me or was I that changed? Traffic picked up, the sun angling away. I looked at him a while longer, without plea. The peace I felt did not hunger to please. Life was too precious to worry about what or what not he might think about me. I broke the trance and my brother turned back to his papers and new friends. Our exchange left to the untold. I felt no uncertainty when I stepped away.

Art turns us inside out, my son. Like The Thinker, it seizes us by place and name. What is uncovered is our dignity. The sweet sack of emotion. Ask all the questions you desire about yourself, about the world and God and solitude. About whatever in life empties and fills your heart. Please, my son, ask. Ask, and consider the answers, the various climbs and descents. Especially the descents. Because sometimes there are no answers at all, only a little salt for the soul. There are ways in which we are freed and cannot possibly turn back. Ways freedom knows the soul without recourse, and does not have to draw on so much blood and bone to mark the path.

Atom by atom, I walked the city and I wept. Everywhere I stepped, I wept in the world. For once joy was the more substantial intoxicant.

33

I TOOK THE TRAIN TO Arras, an hour's ride north of Paris. I stayed the night. Hardly slept. By five in the morning, I was on the road, making the ten kilometre trek to Vimy Ridge. I followed a Sabbath mist and the sound of early birdsong.

The Great War has one lasting image, that of mud. Always the talk and picture of mud. God's mud. Images of slaughter follow close behind. The old world of men going over the top and stepping headlong into the new world order of machine-gun fire. The earth ripped apart. But the ridge I approached that day held little resemblance to the battle photographs and black and white films of the treeless terrain I had studied, the shock of shell holes, the sexless deaths and graves. I stepped up to this conflicting world and felt in my heart the strange disconnection between my grandfather's version of the ridge of 1917 with the impressive order and gleam of today's ridge world; the groomed landscapes, the stunning forest canopy, the modern promise of shade.

I'll have to dig to find what remembers, I thought. I'll have to take off my shoes.

The slope of the ridge was slow to feel. There were a few trenches still in place. The protective sandbags that lined the trenches were no longer sandbags but concrete replicas. The modern day trench world was dry and brown, grass stretching in places where men had disappeared without a trace. Still, for all the covering grass and shade, I couldn't evade the feeling of loss there, stepping through the crushed shell holes, the depressions of a battle world, all of which remained unreconciled with the thousands upon thousands of pounds of explosive materials that had been hauled in and launched over the ridge, seventy-eight years ago. I could not avoid the terror beneath the earth. The blind unease.

I sifted through the landscape, learned its gravity. I turned over scant archaeological remains. Fragmented bones, tin helmets, bully beef tins, shrapnel, bullet shells like whistles. Sheep roamed areas of grass and craters and forests that had been roped off; sunken areas still trembling with live mines, and outlasting the more than five thousand young men who had been consumed by the soils and muds and chalk trenches that were carved into the ridge. Every now and then, a story would emerge about a sheep tripping off a mine, followed by a quick, muted blast. One more animal casualty not included in the official stats of war.

Who decides why one generation comes together in celebration, while another arrives only at a place of grief or betrayal?

Perhaps betrayal is too severe a word, but I couldn't help but think that if my grandfather were to return to the ridge that day he'd find himself stumbling over these very questions, the lost strands of reason. Why he had to sacrifice so much of himself for history and adventure, and auction his soul for a photograph.

I thought I had come to contact an aspect of the past that had been in waiting for me. I hoped to pick up a tremor of my grandfather's spirit, an authentic voice. To receive his blessing, finally, or a warning note of wisdom. No matter how pained. I longed to peel back the earth and find his soul-print, and to match his rumpled photograph with a place of soil his own. All I found was more silence. Inevitable, raw-mouthed quiet. I entered deeper craters, fault lines, I eased like water beneath the earth, I travelled archaic subway systems, damp tunnels wide as my shoulders. I sensed the worked over presence of underground men, their spirits in limbo, huddling and praying and drinking the tired darkness. I heard their bartering with death, lives crammed into a word and their unfinished letters. I crept through that underworld and felt the inexplicable sorrow and shame of the grandfathers and the fathers. A haunting choke hold on their inner lives and secrets. All this, long before there was a talking cure to stoke the heart. The grief there being so ancient, so present, it had to be savoured, I realized, and no longer denied.

Now I wept while under the earth.

For years, I had been gripped by shame. A strange current within my grandfather's story and his need that night to cross the border of my body and weep into my hair. But it was more than just a crossing, it was a taking. I always blamed myself for this act, blamed myself for letting him in through my eyes and occupying my body. That's where it began, in our eyes. His looking at me and my eyes allowing him in. Years it took me to reconcile this. That when he first touched me that night, a tender hand through my hair, it felt good. I craved that affection in a house that had denied itself such closeness. Then that affection turned on me and his touch deadened me and I could not stop him. How could I stop him? I was just a child of eight. And how could anything that felt so tender and loving suddenly feel so wrong? That was the doorway through which shame stepped. Crept in behind these very eyes that had given him the permission to lay on top of me, steal my breath, and weep into my hair.

Much of a story moves underground, my son, dream-like in its travels. Do we dream to wake, do we wake to journey? By condemning the past, do we condemn the future? Somewhere along the path, the ancestors made love. Some shaped stories; some succumbed to silence. Some pulled God from their wounds, left us buoyant crafts, rudder and oars. Others bestowed their mysteries that only our imaginations might learn to colour and chart. For me, I can't think of anything sweeter than sitting down and asking someone to tell you about their life and for you to tell them about yours. We tell stories because the soul depends on them.

I climbed out of that underground world and found a patch of green and sat down, breathing down to the depths of my lungs. The sky was calm, the hour unburdened. I lay back and stretched my spine along the earth, felt a delicate shudder beneath the soil, like the noise of love making among creatures I could not see or capture. 'Before I formed you in the womb I knew you; before you came to birth I consecrated you.' These improbable words from the altar came back to me. Jeremiah, I thought. Another power and story. The telling earth.

I remember one of my father's 16mm films, a jittery old flicker with all the feel of a home movie, which I found in the weeks following his death. With my mother incapacitated, alone and drunk in her bedroom and refusing to have anything to do with the change that had come upon the house on Hudson Dr., it was up to me to begin the cleansing. I began with my father's bunker room, his screening room. I found the film behind the other rows of war films, stashed. Only his fingerprints to give it away, and the initials: V R '36. Intuition told me I hadn't seen this film. I cranked up my father's prized projector, sat and watched.

Picture this: Hundreds of men and their wives and children gathered in black and white on a gray, breezy ridge. The men are dressed in the dark-gray suits of the day, and wear berets. Thin moustaches line their upper lips. Some men display their hero's ribbons and medals upon their lapels; some stand without that kind of distinction. There are biplanes circling the ridge and a giant limestone monument and its carved figures that are still veiled and set high on a hill. Hill 145. The masses are huddled and a king is present. He is reading from a script. His voice is hesitant but bears nuance and the affliction of both victory and defeat. Somewhere there is the sound of bugles and bagpipes. The camera pans the crowd; men stand straight, hands folded behind backs. Eyes on the humpbacked ridge. Slowly the monument's figures are unveiled. A Union Jack is pulled back and reveals the sorrowful mother figure, who stands like a sentinel at the foreground of the monument. Her gentle pose, her mournful countenance. You can hear the wind, chill and gray, cut across the ridge as the men and their families look up to the smooth, clean work, eleven thousand tonnes of concrete and the steel reinforcements that line the limestone foundation. Two pylons and their symbolic figures of Peace, Truth, Justice and Knowledge are carved into the sides of the gray and white monument. All this eternal stone overlooking the valley beyond the ridge, as if beyond time.

As the camera pans the crowd on the hilltop, I stop the film, freeze the frame. A stillness overwhelms my father's bunker room, and a solo gray image brands me. I stare at the held image, my eyes lingering. It doesn't take long to see: A man, in his mid-thirties, I guess, is standing in the crowd. There is a boy (a teen really, just sixteen) standing next to the man. Both figures are well dressed and groomed for the day. The straight backs, the rigid stance. So rigid, my eyes tear. The older man's hair is thinning and combed back. His mouth is closed. I spot the gleam of the small maple leaf pin that is attached to his lapel. And the boy, for a second, a held flicker, looks up at the man's face. That face with its requisite scars, its disfigurement that shocks and attracts. The boy's own face is ruddy, already tired for such a young face. I know the look, have seen its inherited weather in my own reflection. But there they are, my grandfather and my father, in

1936, on a day of unveiling. Two phantom images, a double mirage. What really rocks my heart is in the next frame, when I notice the boy take the father's hand.

A family safe only on film.

Framed. Held.

How is it they seemed more authentic to me flickering on film than they ever appeared to me while in the flesh, negotiating the world through their pained and breathing skin?

Truth is illusive, my son. Like trying to find God's footprint in the sky.

Like my father and grandfather, I have looked into photographs and films of the Great War and WWII, as if in search for the root of our families pain. As if such a root might solve the mystery behind our sorrow and silence. Standing on the ridge, I saw the futility in this exercise. Seeking rational answers in a photograph is like prying into a killer's head, thinking we'll find the word *Monster* etched there, and that will explain *Why*. There is no certain why.

I wished they were there with me on Hill 145. I wished we might bend together and touch that earth. I wished I saw my father weep, like my grandfather once wept into my hair. I wished every kid with a father or a grandfather or an uncle or the old man next door who fought there were with me. I wished every kid who desired to join the military were there, to see the graves and the gravestones and the ages (18, 21, 24) of those who are buried. I wished it were a prerequisite before putting on the uniform, to tour northern France and count the dead downed by war and political calculation.

I stood in the presence of the limestone monument, close to fifty years after my grandfather and father's day on the ridge, on film. I looked at the stone woman cloaked in grief, her head down; the wisps of stone hair, the curve of breast to console. She is the Sorrowing Mother in a world that has given up too many of its youth to war. Murdered youth. I reached to brush her heart, and share in our common sorrow. No longer would I live in secrecy.

We have many teachers, my son.

I remember the cries of women, Greek women, I was told, who would come into Mt. Pleasant cemetery and kneel by the dirt of a newly dug grave. The women were dressed in black, their bodies full, their hands thick and earthy. After moments of preparation, they would begin to wail and scream, they'd tear into the dirt with their fingers, they'd crack in voice, they'd weep until their exhaustion transformed itself to a pure act of faith. To them, a grave was not a closed wing, it was an opening out, a rising. Whether you crawled in spirit through the rising, limped, or were dragged by the angels, kicking and screaming, the women's voices guided you through lamentation and accompanied you on your migration from the body into spirit. No agony was too great not to sing to the dead.

I remember the Chinese families who, twice a year, would come into the cemetery and hold great feasts with their dead. They'd put out lawn chairs and blankets and sit for hours, holding conversations with their ancestors. Before leaving, they'd put out a spread of food on the graves: fruits and sweets and tender meats placed in wax paper. The living would light candles and incense and make a gift of themselves so that their dead too would return in spirit as gift, and not haunt those still engaged in living and dreaming.

All night the candles would blaze against the gravestones, like stars come down to feast. The following morning, I'd find the food gone, peelings carefully placed to the side.

Not until I walked up the ridge did I see. The ghosts I had been carrying did not mean to haunt and ravage me. They only desired a voice, and like a dream, to be heard. It's not listening to the stories of our ghosts that leaves us hungry. It's in the listening that their stories, however hurt or mute, become ours to ink and speak. Each story with its long wick of blue. The dead and your mother and a few warm others have always provided me with a hint of this path, some flint to spark the way, but I had to lie down on the ridge to really know; leave some sweets for the dead, an orange for my grandfather, to learn this:

We die well by living well.

34

IMAGINE IT'S AUGUST OF LAST summer. Your mother and I put in at Opeongo Lake, balance the green canoe upon still, black waters. The lake is a third eye on the world of above and below. It's our second trip of the season. Algonquin is a place on the map we can enter and feel the wild, and not have to worry about the world frisking our souls.

Your mother settles into the bow. Her hair wrangles down her back like a long line of verse. My hands grip my paddle, full with anticipation. We spend time in the lower bay and attend to the strokes that are unique to our own style of taste and flow, of character and intimacy, before setting out toward the bigger waters. When paddling, you must trust the other with everything vulnerable about yourself.

We paddle a few hours north, in and out of a low wind, late through the morning. The sky lowers its mantle. One or two clouds move in, release a few drops of rain, pass over without a sound of leaving. Then back into a clearing of low blue skies, we stroke our way. A lone maple blushes early red against the green and black horizon. Shadows of great cedars waver against the lake, no longer feel secretive. We eat lunch while drifting in their shade, share a simple sandwich of pita bread, cheese and tomatoes and hot mustard, but it's the numinous world, we agree, we most feel nourished by.

We paddle through the afternoon, grateful for calm waters. We make camp on the edge of the North Arm, settle against the east shore. We swim naked and wash ourselves, our hair, between the thighs. We lie on a smooth rock and dry ourselves by the last of the sun, then later by the first tongues of the campfire. We cook a warm meal of saffron rice and vegetable curry, then sit back by the fire and skip our day's story like stones through the flames, out over the lake. The coming darkness is soothing, blue on black. We secure the campsite, hang the packsacks high on a tree limb, and make our way into the tent. A hint of moon works through the lining and touches our skin inside the after hours shelter as we move closer in our sleeping bags for warmth and love and rest. The call of the loon accompanies our sleep, the first night on the lake.

There is wisdom in sleep, and journeys in dream. A necessary pilgrimage, so that we wake knowing we have not been alone in the night. Knowing that while we sleep there are shapes peopling the inner sanctuary, spirits mingling. The God of breath. We wake charged by new meaning, having crossed one shore of consciousness for another. We wake unique and universal and coupled. We wake to see, all along, as we have been losing ourselves, giving up bearing and comfort and esteem, that the shore of leaving and return is a place that has always been innate, like a pulse within the four directions, to which I now hold you.

We rise early, eat a full breakfast of oranges and coffee and blueberry pancakes, pack, load the canoe, and paddle further into the North Arm. We make the thousand metre portage to Proulx Lake and paddle a few more hours up Crow River. Along the river's edge, frogs lean upon lily pads, blink their little dark eyes as we float by. When we reach Big Crow, a moose is there, chewing on roots in the shallow waters. A black bear lumbers up a slope. The further we paddle, the deeper into the park's belly we seem to descend. The air is not cool enough to alter our direction or purpose. We grip our cherry wood paddles like scrolls and work with the muscle of the current.

We cross Big Crow. The eastern shoreline is white with sand and birch. Behind the whiteness is the force of cedar and pine. We paddle toward a place on the map where it's rumoured old growth white pine still stands. We ease ashore, curious, and tie off the canoe, water up, and make the hour's trek into the forest. We walk beneath a wide, high canopy of lazy leaves. The path narrows and turns. We step up a steep traverse, hand and hand, twist back around over a rock path and find ourselves face-to-face with the old growth stand. It takes us by surprise. We pause and let our eyes adjust to the layered radiance of bark, 35 metres of white pine labour, trunks of passage and presence. Then we reach for the great trunks and laugh as we attempt to get our arms around these wet gods, our limbs straining to the incantations of sweat and our comical arrangement of arms, elbows, hands and legs that extend around the trunks and touch at the tips, only to slip and fall away, like bark, wild with exhaustion and the dust of old growth.

Then, rolling over, we angle our backs across the huge root-paws that break through the earth, feeling this place in the world with a hold on things. We join season old saplings that stretch from their tender roots. We push back into a bed of old leaves, move against the undergrowth of shield-rock and peat. I brush a finger across your mother's hips. She takes me in her hand, unfolds me. There is no visible moon at this hour, only a mood of water, and the sun like a dimple in the upper bowl of leaves. The air is loose, the wind is roaming like a saint. And we move deeper into this wooded world, this green age, deeper into our simmering skin and that of earth, deeper into the loving colours that give us strength, into a place where touch is safe.

There, where you are conceived.

For this, I give you my body. My warm and clumsy limbs. My kneeling heart, my wild moon mind, my sparkling seed, my strength, my soul. I give you my ancestral rain and blood, my living waters, my mouth of echo and intimate chronicle, my dreams like jazz, my mothering shudder, my fathering scar. These are the voices I journey, and tongue, and pass on. The voices that are distinct from my own. Distinct as the night you too will distinguish your voice from mine. My song that is thick and powerful and passionate as the honey sun. My supple offering, my telling breast.

Take it and sip.